HIDDEN FIRE

Rosemarie Cawkwell

First published in paperback in Great Britain in 2017
by Rosemarie Cawkwell

Copyright © 2017 Rosemarie Cawkwell

For more from Rosemarie Cawkwell, visit:
rosemariecawkwell.wordpress.com

ISBN-13: 978-1546424390
ISBN-10: 1546424393

Dedication

For my sisters, and my sisters-of-heart: you have been the stokers of the fire that keeps me going, even when it feels like the embers are dying. Thanks, ladies. Love you all.

Also, thanks to my colleagues on the MA in Creative Writing at the University of Lincoln, for your encouragement and support. You are all amazing writers.

Finally, thanks to Michelle Conner, author and artist, for the fantastic cover design.

Table of Contents

Prologue

Midsummer's Eve 1309th Year of Albon Era

Prince John paced his study, looking up expectantly every time footsteps passed the door. His brother, Michael lounged on a sofa with a glass of wine.

"Stop worrying John. Eleanor is with her, and her mother."

The older prince sat down on the sofa, gulping back the glass of wine Michael passed him.

"Lady Val isn't speaking to me." John smiled slightly. "The Earl wants to remove certain parts of my anatomy for getting his favourite granddaughter pregnant."

"Yes, well, they don't approve of all this. Father isn't too happy either."

The young men stared at the wall, bowed under the weight of disapproval from their elders and the responsibility of impending fatherhood.

"Should Eleanor be there, she's not long off due herself?"

"She'll be fine." Michael took a breath, "They both will."

A knock disturbed their halting conversation.

"Come."

"Your Highness." Lady Eleanor Grace curtsied

awkwardly, smiling slightly at her lover and his brother, "Lady Mary Val has given birth."

"Twins?" John asked hesitantly, not that there could be any doubt about Lady Mary's loyalty, but it was traditional to ask.

"Yes, Your Highness."

"Congratulations John! Sons."

John smiled, his face crinkling in happiness.

"You don't understand, Michael." Eleanor tried to interrupt.

"Of course I do, if they're twins, then they're boys."

"No, love, she's had a girl."

"Well, so I have a son and daughter."

"No! Please listen, won't you!"

"What's wrong Eleanor?" Michael looked at his lover with concern, she seemed close to tears.

"Mary gave birth to two daughters, but only one was born alive."

John slumped on to the sofa, shocked. He had expected sons. They always had twin sons first, the Fire that they carried for the kingdom ensured it.

"A daughter."

"Yes, and a fine girl she is. Green eyes and a shock of red hair already. She definitely has your nose too."

"Well, at least you don't have to marry Mary now." Michael shrugged, trying to comfort his confused brother.

"Did I do something wrong? The children should have been boys." John gazed at the half empty glass of wine on the table in front of him, his mind whirling in confusion.

"Aunt Elizabeth is older than father and uncle? Maybe it happens sometimes." Michael shrugged.

"But she never had a twin. Twins are always boys."

"You should come and meet your living daughter, and say goodbye to your dead child before the Physick takes her away."

"Of course."

They hurried across the palace to the guest quarters where Lady Mary Val and her mother were staying. The sheets were pulled up to Mary's chin as she lay sleepily in the big bed, a child asleep at her breast. The child was wrapped in a green blanket edged in fur, her hair contrasting with the material

"How are you Mary?" Prince Michael asked.

"Tired, and sore. Where's John?"

"He's by the door. Can I have a look at her?"

"Of course." Mary passed her child to the prince.

"Well little one, let's have a look at you." He scrutinised her face, searching for a resemblance to himself and John. He looked inward and saw her Fire, flickering quietly in the Core. "Yes, you are definitely one of us."

"Of course she is, Your Highness. I hope you aren't suggesting my daughter would be foolish enough to have affairs. Well, more foolish than she already has been." Lady Val said from the far side of her daughter's bed, where she was washing the other, dead, infant, preparing to wrap it in swaddling for burial in East Marsh.

"Ma'am, of course not." Michael looked at his

brother, "Come on John, you need to name her."

"Oh yes." Dragged out of his stupor, John crossed the room. He took the baby from his brother, looking from him to Mary, "What do you think? Name her after our aunt?"

"Why not?"

"The Princess Royal?"

"Yes, and Lady Val, of course. You share a name with her, don't you, ma'am?"

Lady Val nodded.

"Elizabeth she is then."

"And this one?" Lady Val indicated her charge.

"No one must know, we'll say that, like auntie, she was born first and alone. The next will be twin boys."

"My daughter is not having any more of your children unless you're planning to marry her."

"Can't do that Lizzy." A new voice entered the conversation. "I'm in negotiations with Tarjan for one of the Holmgard girls."

"Father." The twin princes turned simultaneously as their parents entered the room. Lady Val, and Eleanor curtsied, while the Physick, in the corner cleaning his hands, bowed deeply.

"Let's have a look at our granddaughter then."

Mutely, John handed his daughter to his parents, a second shock in so short a time having numbed him.

Michael looked from his brother to his parents and nodded to himself. It was going to happen eventually; they were always destined for political marriages. He looked at the Physick, crossing the room to talk to him quietly.

4

"None of this goes any further, you understand?"

"Of course you can rely totally on my discretion. And the dead infant? I can dispose of the body discretely?"

"No, I think my brother and Lady Mary may have plans for her burial."

"Of course."

Three days later Elizabeth was Named in the Great Hall. John stood before his father, the king, and claimed Elizabeth FitzAlboni as his daughter, taking her from Lady Mary and presenting her to his parents and then to the crowd of courtiers. There was a subdued applause, as courtiers watched the Curates from the side of their eyes. The High Curate and his Counsel, sitting half way down the hall, on the left-hand side, refused to applaud, or acknowledge the child presented to them. She was illegitimate, her existence proof of corruption at the heart of the kingdom.

After the Naming, Lady Mary and her mother rode into the woods surrounding the palace.

"Where are we going? The gig won't go too far into the trees."

"Don't worry mother, the driver knows the way. We have to walk a little too."

"It's too much for you, so soon after giving birth."

"I know, but it has to be done today."

In a clearing in the woods, beneath a yew tree and

beside a stream, where Mary and John had made love, for the first and only time, while the rest of the court played games to celebrate the harvest, they buried the body of the unnamed twin.

Chapter 1

Three days before Spring Equinox, 21 years later

The Great Royal Square in King's Ford, the capital of the island nation of Albon, was designed to impress. In the centre stood the little-used gallows, it's sagging platform of dark wood casting a shadow over the proceedings. Around the edges, each three miles in length, covered and colonnaded shopping precincts enticed the rand poor alike to part with their cash. The weekly markets filled the centre, and the road through was thronged with carts and carriages, pedestrians and riders. The air was filled with the clamour of negotiation and encouragement. A new sound added to the din, the thump-thump of the steam press printing the first ever daily news sheet in Albon. Outside the press shop another innovation was making itself heard: the news boy:

"Read all about it; half-crown daily, read all about it. Curates demand closure of the Ford Daily. Read all about: Ford Daily to be inspected by Censors. Read all about it in the Ford Daily. Get your daily dose of information here."

Lizzy Fitzroy looked through the front window of the coach as they passed through the Square. She tapped the glass. On the box seat in front the driver slowed his four horses and turned to answer her.

"Dawson, go to the paper seller, I want a copy."

"Yes milady." He slowed the horses to a halt and jumped down to the pavement. He was back in moments, with the paper; just in time to see a young man jump into the seat and force the horses into motion. Dawson ran after them, shouting for the thief to stop.

The carriage pulled away, swerving to avoid a cart delivering cabbages. The carriage on its left-hand wheels almost toppled but was righted by the thief, half-crushing shoppers against each other and causing shouts of indignation. The driver whipped the horses as he pushed them to greater speed in the crowded square before turning into a side street and out of the square.

"What's this about?" A large burgher stepped towards Dawson, his red face matching the sash of his office, 'market inspector', stretched over his belly, "What's the hurry about?"

"My lady's carriage has been stolen. With her in it."

"I see. Who is your lady?"

"You see, well she's." He hesitated, unsure if he should disclose her identity. If it got out that he'd lost her he'd lose his job, at the very least

"Ow, hells, why did this have to happen on my duty day." The inspector interrupted "Right, you," he pointed to a butcher's boy loitering to hear the news, "Run to the Watch house; you two," Now he pointed at a pair of startled young women doing their shopping, "Go round every stall, we need to block the ways out of the square."

The two men introduced themselves.

"Well, Burgher Wrightson, I hope this works."

"Of course, of course. Why did you stop?"

"My lady wanted the paper."

"I see. Does this lady often read the papers?"

"As much as possible." he shrugged, "How does this help stop her kidnappers?"

"Oh, I'm just curious as to why you stopped. Here comes the Watch Commander. Hells, it's the Lord Commander himself." Wrightson paled. The Lord Commander of the Watch wasn't known for his forgiving nature and more than one Burgher had lost his position when he found them too incompetent to keep order during Market Day.

"So I see." Dawson walked towards the Commander, a familiar figure to his lady's staff (even if they were themselves unknown to him) since he ate regularly at the Residency.

"My Lord Summerton, if I may have a private word with you?"

"What is it Coachman? I am rather busy trying to sort out the mess you made."

Dawson blushed, "It's important sir."

"Oh well," he beckoned the coachman over to his horse, away from the gathering crowd, "What is it?"

"The carriage that was stolen." Dawson coughed, working himself up to identifying the passenger.

"Don't fuss, we'll get it back." The Lord Commander growled, "I've had my men surround the Square. What happened? Quickly now."

Dawson blushed but repeated his story, still unable to get out the name of his passenger. Aware of the listening crowd he emphasised how quickly the burgher had organised the crowd to help. Wrightson smiled sheepishly and bowed to Lord Summerton.

"Well done Wrightson; we might catch them yet, but I want more people out on market days in future." Summerton looked about, then back at the two men. "Dawson, come along, we have work to do if we're going to get your mistress's carriage back. Wrightson, I want you to keep order in the Square, and round up any potential witnesses. Bring them to the Watch House as soon as you're ready." Lord Summerton marched away from the astonished burgher who had expected a quiet day checking the quality of cheeses and ale, but found himself part of the investigating team trying to solve a kidnapping.

Dawson jogged to keep up with the Summerton who had mounted his horse and was crossing the square, "My Lord, the coach will be miles away by now. And if they know who the passenger is..."

"And just who was your passenger?" Summerton looked down at the pink faced coachman.

"Lady Elizabeth, the King's Bastard." Dawson shared the secret at last.

The commander blanched but rode on, a little faster, "We'll catch up with them. I've sent half my men to cover the exit, and half along the Royal Road on horses to track them. Besides, I've closed the Gates. I need to tell the king. Come on."

The hue and cry had spread through the Square. The Lord Commander turned back from his intended destination, the South Gate, and rode to the palace, Dawson running along beside him reluctantly.

The day lengthened, the Square and its tributary roads were searched meticulously, but no sign of Lizzy or her carriage was found. In the Watch House, Dawson once again repeated his story and waited for news; he berated himself for ever leaving his lady, even though she had given the command to do so, he should have been quicker, he should have run faster after the Broom, he should have done something!

The messenger panted and spluttered out his message again, for the King and Lord Commander to hear. Elizabeth's Broom had been found, overturned in a ditch on the road to the Hythe.

"And my daughter?" King John leaned back in his commandeered chair, wondering where his brother was; the Duke's network of agents would surely have some information, yet Michael hadn't appeared.

"No sign, that we've found yet, at least."

"Well, Summerton, what next?"

Summerton thought for a few seconds and wandered over to the map pinned to the wall behind his desk. He traced the line of the Hythe road. "Sergeant, where precisely was the carriage found?"

"About a mile from the Hythe Bridge."

"Which way around was it?"

The sergeant thought for a few seconds, "Looked to me like it were pointed away from the Hythe, on to the West Road."

"It could be a trick."

"Aye, my lord, it could. Some of the Sprinters are out following the tracks backward now."

"Good."

King John rose from his seat at Summerton's desk to inspect the map for himself. His fingers caressed the line of the road unconsciously, as he thought about the kidnappers' route.

"Well, we know for sure now; it was my girl they were after, not just a bit of joy riding."

"Yes." Summerton nodded from his place by the chimney breast, as he leafed through reports from his men stationed around the Square.

"But you've been working on that assumption all along haven't you?" King John smiled, half-laughing.

"Of course. Her Broom isn't worth stealing, they're so common. She on the other hand is one of the wealthiest women in the country, and soon to come of age."

"Yes, and it would hurt the family if anything happened to her."

"There's one person would benefit if anything happened to Lizzy." Summerton muttered.

The king looked over at him, resignation creasing his brow, "Of course; have the High Curate visit us, would you Summerton? I think I know where they've taken her."

Summerton leaned into look more closely at the map; the West Road, which paralleled the southern coast of Albon, ran through hilly, lake land country, known for its sunny slopes and fine wines. It was also home to the estates of, at least, half the Queen's Court. The king's finger rested over Mortlake.

Chapter 2

Lizzy was rather tired of this journey now. A day had passed since she'd had Dawson stop for a paper. Why ever had she done that? She could have sent him back for one once she was ensconced in the Library with her current beau, the young Marquis of Northwood, a handsome but dull fellow, fascinated by butterflies. Every meeting had to be 'secret' because the dowager-marquise would be livid if she found out her son was courting the king's heretical daughter. Unfortunately for Walter, Lizzy was only there on her uncle's orders. Lizzy nodded in her seat, pitying poor Walter; he'd think she'd stood him up.

Since realising that she was being kidnapped – a hooded man had climbed into the carriage and held a knife on her while another had taken the reins – Lizzy had been raced out of the city, pulled from the carriage, which was driven off towards the Hythe, pulled on to a horse, blind folded and with her hands tied 'round the pommel, forced to ride for several hours down the West Road. When the ride stopped, her blindfold had been removed. She recognised the valley, known as the Wine Gate – because it was the best route into vineyard country – they waited a few minutes, then Lizzy was hustled into an enclosed carriage where she found another two men waiting. All through the journey her kidnappers were silent and hooded. They had travelled quickly at first, but then the roads steepened and the coach slowed. Lizzy heard the splash of water and the coach lurch downwards. A few seconds later the coach lurched upwards again before continuing, the sound of rushing water falling behind.

Her stomach rumbled and her eyes ached; she hadn't eaten, nor dared to sleep.

Lizzy closed her eyes; they must have crossed a ford. Concentrating, she tried to bring the maps of Albon that she had assiduously studied into her mind's eye, flicking through the files of her brain for one which covered the southern hill country. She knew they'd entered the Gate at sunset the day before and estimated that it was approximately midday – the coach had stopped an hour or so earlier for the men to change drivers and Lizzy had caught a glimpse of her location – so she was probably forty or fifty miles into the hill country. They'd been travelling uphill most of the time but there had been one descent, which she interpreted as reaching a pass in the hills. The map wouldn't settle in her mind; too tired, too hungry, Lizzy couldn't order her brain.

She nodded off, hoping that whomever had taking such a risk as to kidnap her wouldn't allow anything to befall her.

She woke some hours later as the coach jolted to a halt; Lizzy's eyes flew open. The carriage door opened; the man who had ordered her abduction smiled toothily at her.

"You!"

Chapter 3

"Michael, what news?" King John rose from his throne to meet his brother. A week had passed since Lizzy had disappeared. The Court still went on as normal, much to John's disappointment; he'd hoped some at least were worried about Lizzy's safety. The twins were doing their best to find their cousin, and their few friends had immediately joined the search, but nothing seemed to touch most of his courtiers. The Queen had deigned to join him on the throne today, and her gaiety when she heard the news had been sickening. If it weren't for their two sons he'd have sent the bitch home to her grandfather in Sumoast years before.

"We've tracked the horse they transferred to along the West Road, it seems they are definitely heading towards the southern hills. We have a witness who saw a hooded man riding double with a red-haired woman in clothes matching those Lizzy was wearing when she was abducted riding along the West Road at midday a week ago." Michael grasped his brother's hand in greeting and looked around. The queen was smirking at them. Michael was convinced she was behind the plot to abduct his niece, but despite all his agents working overtime he didn't have the proof he needed to send her to the gallows.

"How has it taken this long to get confirmation? Do we have any newer information?" John sighed in frustration and walked with his brother back to the throne.

Michael took a seat and accepted a glass of wine that the footman offered before answering, "Not yet. Come brother, let's go to your study, some things are better kept private." He flicked his eyes towards the Queen.

"Not yet."

"Of course."

The royal brothers sat back to observe the court. The courtiers were a subdued lot, Michael thought, ever since the Curates had started their campaign against 'vice and immorality'. The first thing they'd done was excoriate Lizzy and her set for refusing to attend chapel and for 'immodest' behaviour. Lizzy and his twins, Lawrence and Alex, had laughed, called them humourless and continued as before. It hadn't helped that Lizzy was a known backer for the newspaper, or that she publicly objected to the Curates Council's attempts to impose sumptuary laws.

"Did I miss anything at the Council meeting today?"

"Nothing much, the Navy are stopping and searching every ship in our territorial waters just in case Lizzy's on one of them and the Lord Commanders are sending out men every day. But that's not news to you, is it?"

"No, not at all. But is there anything from the Alliance?"

"Nothing, Calman and Umar send their best wishes and offered aid. Sumoast have yet to send a message."

"They won't; Holmgard doesn't recognise Lizzy."

"No he doesn't; they're sending a new ambassador

next year. Some cousin of my wife's."

"Oh, really? Must we have another Holmgard in our Palace?"

"Really, Michael, they aren't all terrible people."

"Just most of them." The brothers laughed, the Queen scowled.

"Ah, here we go." John nodded towards a group of courtiers who had just entered the Great Hall.

"Bold move." Michael spoke quietly, turning his head so none could read his lips.

"But to be expected?"

"Yes, you were right to wait. My agent hasn't been in contact in weeks, I'm assuming he's dead. If the Mortlakes get out of this alive I'll have a new agent in place."

"I don't intend to let them or anyone else involved in Lizzy's abduction get out of it."

"Even if I find evidence the Queen is involved."

"Especially then."

The Mortlake party advanced to the foot of the dais the thrones were placed on, variously bowed and curtsied to their monarchs and waited to be acknowledged. The Queen smiled and welcomed her allies, the king and duke ignored them a little longer, speaking quietly together. Eventually John looked them over.

"Evening Mortlake, where's your boy?"

Lord Mortlake bristled at being addressed so casually, even by his king but swallowed his bile, plastered on a sorrowful expression and answered, "Unfortunately your majesty, my son is sick and sends his apologies."

"I see; is he at your estate in the southern hills? I hear that part of our country is an excellent place to recover from a sickness."

"No, my lord king, he's at our town house."

A lie, but barely detectable. Only a slight twitch gave Lord Mortlake away to Michael's expert eyes. It was time to act. The king watched the Mortlakes as they spoke; for the most part they had always struck him as oily arrogance personified, but there was one who wasn't comfortable. Lord Mortlake's youngest son, kept glancing about; the boy knew something. His eyes kept flicking to the King's Guard. The duke rose, sneered at the Mortlakes, bowed to his brother and left to socialise. On his way to talk to some Commons Moot the Duke passed a message to the King's Guard, one of whom stepped out. John watched the youngest Mortlake blanch, and nodded to him. The boy leaned towards his mother and whispered something; Lady Mortlake looked mortified and whispered fiercely back. The boy started jiggling from one foot to the other. John let him suffer for a few moments.

"Mortlake, I think your lad needs the privy."

Lord Mortlake scowled at his son and sent him rushing away. "I do apologise your majesty."

"He's only young, excitement will do that to a boy. Your older lad, he's much more used to court life, isn't he?"

"He is indeed; I'm hoping to find him a position at court when he comes of age."

"I'm sure we'll be able to find something for him, provided he passes the exams of course."

"I'm sure he'll pass them with flying colours. Is

19

there any news of your daughter yet, your majesty?"

"Not yet, though we have our Lord Commanders on the case. We feel sure my daughter will be brought home safely and unharmed."

"I'm sure she will be your majesty; I can't imagine why anyone would wish her harm. Is it entirely certain she went against her will?"

"It is. Witnesses saw her once the abductors transferred to horses, she was restrained."

"How unfortunate."

"Indeed?"

"Unfortunate that nobody thought to assist her, or to send a message."

"Yes, yes it was, however, I'm sure they didn't know what they were seeing until our investigators thought to ask."

"And where was she seen last?"

"Near the Wine Gate. Don't you have an estate near there?"

"Yes, quite close by."

"It would be helpful if those with local knowledge would lend their assistance to our forces once they reach the area."

"I shall send a message by tower first thing tomorrow morning giving my steward instructions in the matter."

"Excellent. I've already asked most of your neighbours of course; the messages went earlier. Had I realised you were in the city rather than at your estates I'd have sent a messenger directly to your town house."

"These things happen; we arrived unexpectedly

and forgot to inform the Chamberlain. We've been so concerned about Maron."

"That I can understand. Sickness spreads so quickly through a family, why before you know it a plague can kill off a whole house."

"We hope to avoid that fate."

"Don't we all? Do excuse me, my brother need my attention for a moment." The king rose, the courtiers bowed, and then were left alone with the Queen.

#

"Well?"

"The boy has been taken to my study by a couple of the Guards. We should interrogate him before his parents realise he's not back yet."

"Anything else?"

"I've sent a troop to search the town house; if young Mortlake isn't there then we can confirm they're involved."

"They're involved, who else would do my wife's dirty work? Now let's go get a witness statement."

Chapter 4

Lizzy lay in the bed, pretending to sleep while she thought through her potential escape plans. So far she hadn't seen much of the house, but she knew it wasn't large. It was probably an old dower house, tucked away from the main house. Her first plan was the simplest. Her uncle would have gathered in his agents by now, he was bound to have troops on the way to rescue her. All she had to do was wait and avoid Maron Mortlake for another few days.

It was getting harder to avoid the little tick.

The maid he'd sent to her coughed politely from her place by the chimney. Lizzy pretended to stir in her sleep. The maid walked to the bed and gently prodded Lizzy's arm, "Ma'am you must get up now, Sir Maron is on his way."

Lizzy rolled over, squeezing her eyes together and yawning, "What?"

"Sir Maron will be here to speak to you in a few moments, you must get dressed."

"Must nothing. He can wait in the parlour while I dress in my own time."

"He won't like it, ma'am"

"I don't care. When my father's men arrive he won't like what they'll do to him, and everyone else who's helped keep me here."

The maid paled, aware that her reluctance wouldn't be considered when the judgement fell on them all.

"Ma'am, this is wrong, but please get up so I can dress you. Sir Maron is violent."

"He's a thug, yes I know. I have dealt with him in the past. Can't imagine why anyone would want to work for the family though."

"Oh the Dowager-Lady Mortlake is lovely. This is her house."

"And where is she now?"

"In Essenmouth, having a holiday."

"How lovely for her. I'm going to Belinos with my uncle and cousins in six months."

"The capital of the Empire? Oh, how delightful, you are lucky ma'am."

"Don't weasel, it isn't becoming. Do we have any water? I need a wash."

"Yes ma'am."

Lizzy kicked the blankets off her legs and got out of bed; the water waited in the closet, with her clothes. Lizzy shut the door on her borrowed maid's face and stripped off her night gown. The water was lukewarm and the soap was a far cry from her usual smooth, rose scented choice, but they would do for now. Lizzy heard the banging on her bedroom door and the maid's attempt to prevent Sir Maron from entering. She hurried through her ablutions.

The maid's voice rose as their visitor got closer to the closet door; Lizzy dried off quickly and struggled into the breast support. Pulling her draws up and her shift over her head, Lizzy listened to the argument. There was the sudden sound of flesh hitting flesh and the maid's whimper. Enraged, Lizzy wrenched her trousers up and her shirt on. She buttoned it with shaking fingers, missing buttons so that it was lopsided.

Taking a deep breath, Lizzy calmed her shaking hands and tried again. There was a rattling at the door. Finally satisfied with the shirt, Lizzy stepped into her shoes and laced them securely. The rattling on the door got stronger, she knelt to look under the dressing table, where she had secreted her private possessions. She retrieved the pick roll and her pocket knife, stashing them in her support. Her bag and coat were hung in the closet, tantalisingly teasing her with prospects of escape. She'd left them there for the past ten days knowing they'd be useful eventually.

Today was the day.

She'd put aside the idea of waiting, Sir Maron wouldn't wait any longer for his answer. Her bag went on first, she didn't need him to see it, and then her coat. Ready, she opened the door. Sir Maron had his hand raised to the cowering maid as she walked out of her closet. Lizzy looked at him disdainfully.

"Well, if that's how you treat your servants then I don't think I'll marry you after all."

Sir Maron looked at her, processing the statement.

"You were going to accept?"

"It had passed through my mind, but I don't think we're compatible you know. I'm rather Progressive in my attitude to the lower orders. It simply wouldn't work. Now, do have a horse saddle, Maron. I wish to go for a ride, I've been cooped up in this dreary house for far too long."

"I'm not letting you out of my sight."

"In that case, have a picnic made up and we'll go out for the day together. Perhaps you'll be able to change my mind?" She tilted her head to one side and arched an eyebrow. "I hear you're an excellent rider."

Lizzy was flirting shamelessly, she knew, but the only way she could get out of the house with the means to escape was to let him think his gallantry might work some sort of charm on her.

"If my lady insists on a ride, I'm sure I could oblige."

"Oh, I do insist." She smiled coquettishly and walked towards the door. Sir Maron looked down at the maid contemptuously before turning to follow his prisoner out of the room.

"Dora! Have my room cleaned before we return, there's a dear." Lizzy called back over her shoulder, trying not to let the mask drop as she watched the beaten Dora crumple to the carpet in pain.

"Don't concern yourself with such things, my love, the servants know exactly what to do. They don't last long in our service if they don't."

"I see; and how do they make a living when you turn them off?"

"Why should I care? They're not my responsibility."

"That, I fear is where we differ." She took his arm, "But I shall endeavour to convince you otherwise." She smiled at him sideways through half closed eyes.

"And I shall look forward to being persuaded." He waved a liveried servant over to them. "Have Cook prepare a picnic; I'm taking my fiancée for a ride. And have two horses saddled."

"Yes my lord." The servant looked at Lizzy

timorously before scuttling away.

"You shouldn't have told him I was your fiancée, not just yet."

"Surely I can persuade you?"

"Maybe." Lizzy smiled, eyelids lowered, "Let's go for this picnic and we'll see, won't we?"

Chapter 5

Alexander Fitzroy, the duke's bastard son, and his equally illegitimate twin brother, Lawrence, rode behind Lord Commander Summerton as the crossed the Mortlake Pass. Below them the lake spread out in a shining sheet and the hills were green with grape vines putting on new shoots. Interrogating Lord Mortlake's youngest son had proved profitable and the entire family were now under arrest. They blamed Sir Maron, who had intimidated them into complying; the boy however had told the king that he had seen Curates having private conversations with his father and brother. He didn't recognise them though; they hadn't been from the hill country. Armed with the new information the rescue party had left King's Ford in the early hours of the morning to avoid any news getting to Mortlake before they did.

Riding down into the valley proved easier than they expected. The only men about were working in the fields and didn't look like they wanted to put up a fight. They cowered from the Lord Commander when he told them their master had been arrested for abduction and treason. They seemed cautiously relieved. A woman with two small children begged a word,

"My lords, I think I know where the missing lady is. My daughter works up at the dower house; since the dowager went on her holidays my girl should have come back to help with the fields but she sent word two week ago to say she weren't permitted."

"So?" Alex barked, wanting to get on and find

Lizzy. They'd wasted enough time placating frightened commoners.

"Well, the only reason to keep a lady's maid is if there's a lady at the dower house. I just thought you'd like to know."

"Thank you, madam, that is a very useful piece of information," Lawrence nodded, it was useful information, "Where is the dower house?"

The woman pointed along the road to the main house, "Keep following it, until you cross the ford then take the first left had road. The house is in a small valley about two miles along that road."

"And the land?"

"Woods mostly, but there's a cleared area all around the house. The dowager has garden parties in the summer, I go up to serve sometimes."

"My thanks again, madam, you've been a tremendous help."

"Just you remember that, and don't let no harm come to my girl."

Lord Summerton promised that the servants would be unmolested, since the estates now belonged to the king. He would interrogate the staff though; they needed names of all the conspirators. The boy didn't know why his brother and father had abducted Lizzy, nor who their conspirators were. The information he'd provided would be enough though and of the whole Mortlake family he would probably be the only one not to hang. They rode on, following the route they had been given, sending scouts ahead, fast, nimble men known as Springers, to spy out the country.

Following the road down into the valley they

soon found and crossed the ford; the river was high and the banks steep, but the mounted troops managed it with more ease than the carriage that had brought Lizzy across almost a fortnight earlier. The road split a hundred yards from the ford. Lord Summerton called a halt before they left the main road, allowing his men and their horses a rest while the Springers ran ahead, spreading out through the woods looking for guards and assessing the lay the land. The first men reported back within the hour.

"My lords," The first Springer back panted out as he bowed to Lord Summerton, Alex and Lawrence, "The road runs through a narrow valley, the cliffs on each side are steep and wooded. Once through the valley opens out. There's a stream running though it and woods." He gulped another breath and continued, "But they're cut back in a large circle. The house is in the middle."

"And Lizzy?"

"We haven't seen her, I've sent men through the woods to spy out the back of the property, but they won't be back for another hour or two at least."

"Rest, we'll give your men another hour, then we move up the road." Lord Summerton waved the Springer Captain away to rest before turning to the twins, "Well, boys, it looks like we're on the right track, but getting her out is going to be difficult."

"Or not." Alex stood, walking quickly away from his brother and the commander, up, into the tree line where Lizzy waited, mounted and armed with Maron's sword. She was wiping blood off it.

Chapter 6

"Elizabeth Fitzroy, if you disappear like that again I will not be happy. You've taken ten years off my life. Look daughter, I have more grey hairs!" King John pulled at his hair.

"I do apologise father. I'd have come back sooner if I'd been able to." The king pulled his daughter into his arms in front of the entire court and refused to let her go. She had just returned and was still wearing the clothes she'd been wearing when she was abducted.

"And the traitor? Lord Summerton has him in his cells I hope."

"No father, he doesn't."

"Why not? I want that boy to hang."

"Too late father, I spit him on his own sword."

There was a murmur of surprise around the Great Hall.

"The idiot didn't actually wear his sword around you?" Duke Michael laughed.

"Yes, uncle. I don't think he knew about my fondness for edged weaponry. He thought it would subdue me into agreeing to his demands."

"What did he demand, daughter?"

Lizzy blushed, "I'd rather not discuss it here, father."

"In that case we shall adjourn to my private quarters and you can tell us the whole story in confidence. Wife, stay and oversee proceedings tonight, won't you, or little Michael can." He looked at the ten-year-old prince, "Here my boy, do you want to sit on Daddy's throne for a few hours this evening. I must talk to your sister and uncle urgently."

The Queen scowled at Lizzy's being referred to as her son's sister, but said nothing.

"May I really father?" the young prince gazed in wonder at the throne. The king stood and indicated his eldest son should take the place for the evening. He smiled at his son, who climbed into the seat and waved his legs because he was so high off the ground.

"You look marvellous sat there, dear brother." Lizzy smiled at her half-brother who blushed at her praise.

"Yes you do, now keep it warm for me and we'll be back before long."

"Yes father." Prince Michael answer solemnly, before looking down at the gathered courtiers as sternly as a ten-year-old can manage. Lizzy thought him too adorable, but remembered the first time she had met her half-brothers. Lizzy had thought them spoilt brats, their Mother's sons; she had to admit it though, her half-brothers were growing on her. It had only taken six years.

"Well?"

"Get me a whisky, I'm going to need it to tell you how I escaped."

"Are you getting squeamish Lizzy?"

"No, uncle, I'm not. But It is rather embarrassing to admit."

"Here," the king passed her a full glass of the

potent liquor, "now, tell us everything."

Lizzy took a couple of gulps, before proceeding with her narrative.

"When I arrived at that house, Maron Mortlake made it clear he intended to marry me, and that he planned to keep me at the house until he could force me to marry him."

"Good god."

"I know, the horrendous man thought he could get away with it. Anyway, I told him it wasn't happening, so he kept me locked in a room until I 'saw sense'. On the day I escaped, I suggested a ride in the woods might induce me to change my mind. He took that to mean, well, take a guess."

"Ah, yes, I see."

"And while you were out in the woods you took his sword and killed him?" Uncle Michael, Lizzy guessed, had seen where this was going and had decided to avoid any unnecessary pain.

"Basically."

"Did he ...hurt you?" If Mortlake had done her any harm he'd crucify the entire clan.

"No, he didn't get the chance. He insisted on bringing his guards with us but when we stopped for a picnic he sent them back to the house. I made sure he drank most of the wine and ate most of the food. He got sleepy, I didn't."

"And when he was befuddled you dealt with him?"

"Yes. I believe Lord Summerton is going to hang his body from the Mortlake gates, as a warning to anyone else who commits treason." Lizzy grinned.

"How did you know to suggest that day to go for a ride?" Michael was curious, it seemed too much of a coincidence.

"I just did; I woke up absolutely certain that that day was the day I had to escape."

The royal brothers looked at each other, concerned; prescience was condemned as witchcraft by the Curacy. Even if it was hereditary.

"You mustn't tell anyone that, tell them it was just good luck."

"Why?"

"Because, people, certain people, will misconstrue it."

"How so?"

"The Queen will be very pleased if she could get you hung as a witch by the Curates."

"Don't be daft, there's no such thing as magic." Lizzy laughed at her uncle's earnest concern. It was ridiculous, nobody believed in that superstitious nonsense anymore, not in Albon at least.

"The queen believes there is."

"But that's just Sumoasti superstition."

"The High Curate believes."

"Oh good gracious! What nonsense." Lizzy's bark of a laugh filled the room again.

"You're probably right, but don't draw attention to yourself, for at least a few months. I don't want any more attempts on your life."

"He was too desperate to marry me to kill me."

"We have his parents in custody; they've admitted that once you'd married Maron and I'd acknowledged the marriage they planned to kill you."

34

"I suppose it's a good thing that they didn't manage to carry out their plan; I rather like living."

"Yes, well, I'm having them hung in the morning. No need for a trial, they've given us a signed confession."

"Any idea who else was involved?"

"I have my suspicions, but nothing I can back up with evidence. The youngest Mortlake, Phillias, came to us with the information we needed to send the rescue party. He saw his father and brother conspiring with two Curates, but he didn't see their faces."

"So we know the Curates are involved, but we don't know which ones or who was giving the orders?" Lizzy drained her whisky.

"Essentially."

"What about the Agents?" Lizzy focused on her uncle; her father tried to stay out of their clandestine operations, officially.

"They've turned up nothing; our agents in the Curates Council and other areas have gone very quiet lately. I'm calling them all in for debriefing meetings."

"Anyone who doesn't come very likely can't."

"You look worried."

"A thought occurs."

"Go on."

"Uncle, why now?"

"What do you mean?"

"Everything that's happened lately seems to be connected. Why go to the trouble of abducting me? If something has happened to our agents, why now?"

"They're trying to weaken us?"

"Who though? Drat it, we need more people."

"Yes, Lizzy we do, but people are scared."

"Why?"

"The Curates are threatening the Guilds again, the paper is being harassed, accusations of heresy are being levelled at Progressives in the Commons Moot. Why wouldn't our allies be scared?"

"The campaign has intensified of late. Even I've noticed that." King John agreed.

"It's because the CMM elections are coming up, you know as well as I do, that the general antipathy between the Traditionalist and the Progressives gets nasty every two yours." Lizzy shrugged.

"There have been accusations made in the CC that you are supporting Radicals."

"Not as far as I'm aware. I didn't know we even had Radicals."

"Neither did we, and we don't. It's a game to legitimise their Fundamentalist faction."

"Oh dear, it's going to get unpleasant this time 'round isn't it?"

"It already has; the Mortlakes were the key public supporters of the Fundamentalist Party."

"Why did I not know this?" Lizzy looked from her father to her uncle, wondering what else they'd kept from her until now.

"You were busy with your own projects, and too young to get involved in politics."

"Until those politics, which I knew nothing about, tried to kill me. What else aren't you telling me?"

John leaned back, "Oh so much. But Lizzy, you didn't need to know."

"What else?" Lizzy felt her face harden into an

36

angry mask.

"The Queen is threatening to divorce me and take your brothers to Sumoast."

"She can't do that!"

"It would be difficult, but the High Curate has already agreed to sanction a divorce on the grounds of infidelity."

"Who with?"

"Your mother."

"But everyone knows Mother's been in East Marsh for twenty years, even before you married Jocinta."

"They're saying it's retrospective and my continued affection for you is evidence that I'm emotionally unfaithful."

"But that's nonsense."

"I know, I know, but she's using the boys as leverage against me."

"So we deal with the Queen and the High Curate in one go."

"How?"

"I'll think of something." Lizzy left, scowling, and thinking, hard. The queen was almost certainly involved in her abduction, but they needed the evidence to prove it. She certainly wasn't going to let that bitch take her brothers to her barbaric island.

Chapter 7

Lizzy laughed quietly to herself as she read the interview in the Rest-day edition of her paper. 'Women in Focus' was her favourite spot in the paper, so far they'd interviewed nuns and guild leaders, fashion icons and novelists, but not the Queen. So far they'd had three invitations to attend palace events and interview Jocinta, as yet Lizzy hadn't accepted. Her father's wife didn't need to know who was behind the Ford Daily.

"You aren't that funny, Lizzy." The Duke commented over breakfast.

"I'm not laughing at myself, I'm imagining the Queen's face when she hears 'Maggie Harford' has interviewed me, but still hasn't agreed to an interview with her."

"You're a wicked girl niece, I'm glad it is Jocinta and not me who has angered you."

"Oh, auntie, I'm not sure you ever could upset me." Lizzy smiled at the Umari wife of her uncle, Catherine. After seven years in King's Ford she still carefully enunciated her Albonese; Lizzy found her slightly staid conversation endearing.

"Only because you know I'd throw you out if you did."

Lizzy rolled her eyes at them both and returned to reading the paper and eating her breakfast. The twins barged in to join them at the table, knocking their sister, the youngest Fitzroy, seven-year-old Elenor, as they took their seats.

"Sorry El, here have another sausage. Father,

have you heard, the CC are denouncing the Mortlake's execution." Alex righted his sister and passed her another sausage. She wrinkled her nose at the stale beer smell on his breath.

"Are they?" Michael asked, not seeming surprised

"Yes, we heard it in the Royal Square Sermon." Lawrence nodded enthusiastically.

"What were you doing there?" Their step-mother laughed, the family did not attend any services. As she was Umari she wasn't a part of the Faith of the One that almost all the population of Albon professed. Her husband was a confirmed atheist and the children had been allowed to make up their own minds. Little Elenor, who she had raised from almost birth, had started joining her in their household temple to her own gods. The twins and Lizzy followed her husband's convictions.

"Coming home. Can I have more bacon?"

"Of course Alexander. Eggs, Lawrence?" The boys were already helping themselves. They weren't boys anymore, Catherine mused, they would come of age soon, like Elizabeth. There was only weeks to go. Catherine was beset with the planning of her Ball; luckily Lizzy's mother was keeping out of the arranging, and Caro was working on a suitable garment though all three despaired of getting Lizzy to wear a ball gown, even for one night.

"We saw the paper, it caused a bit of a stir, especially when people started reading it during the Sermon."

"Bet that upset people."

"Only the Curate. Everyone else was pleased for the distraction I think. They had Colvile out on the plinth today."

"Really?" Lizzy feigned disinterest, Colvile had once worked for the Queen but had been sent to a Seminary to teach as punishment after an incident several years before; he had slandered Lizzy and her father had not been happy. "I didn't know he'd been allowed back in the city."

"Michael let him come back a couple of months ago, if he stayed away from Court. I hear he's very bitter about his demotion."

"And what was he doing before that?"

"It's funny you should ask, because I had an interview yesterday with my agent at the Seminary. He tells me Colvile went on pilgrimage six months ago intending to visit all the sites of the Visitation."

Lizzy looked at her uncle in confusion, trying to fit together the information he was telling her.

"He went to the Wine Gate at some point?" Alex put it together before she did.

"So I understand."

"And...do we know when he was in the Southern Hills?" Lizzy skimmed the politics pages for news of the CM elections to cover her embarrassed blush; there's no way a hungover Alex should have worked it out before her.

"Funnily enough, about the time Phillias Mortlake saw his father and brother talking to two unknown Curates."

"How strange that there should be so many unknown Curates in the area, the Lake is only a minor shrine, after all." Lizzy folded the paper, pretending to give the conversation her full attention finally.

"Indeed, indeed." Michael smirked, he knew her game, but it would probably have fooled anyone who didn't know her as well.

"Perhaps, as a potential witness, we should bring Colvile in for questioning?" Catherine suggested as she finished her toasted crumpets and wiped her elegant hands on a fine cotton napkin. The twins had tucked a couple of those napkins into their shirt collars and were happily stuffing their faces; she really needed to talk to them about table manners.

"What a marvellous idea, dearest. I've sent the Guard to get him."

"So, Palace after breakfast?" Lizzy dropped her napkin on her plate starting to move.

"Yes, but let's not rush, I'm sure Colvile can wait a few hours for us. He can use the time to pray for forgiveness, if he's withheld evidence of course."

"Can we have a bath at least before we go to the Palace?"

"And a couple of hours sleep? It's hard work pretending to be layabouts."

"If you must. I'm going for a ride; I need some exercise." Lizzy stood, pushing herself away from the table.

"Where are you going?"

"Don't worry uncle, nobody's tried to abduct me for almost a month." She kissed his forehead, "I'll stay on the estate though."

Chapter 8

Colvile wasn't happy to be arrested in front of the crowd listening to his sermon. The Guards loudly announced his crime: failing to provide material evidence in a treason case. He turned red while the crowd had looked on in amusement. A few had suggested the Guards add 'poor sermonising' and 'wasting an hour of our lives' to his arrest warrant.

Half an hour after his arrest, Curate Colvile found himself in the cells of the Information Office, beneath the former City Palace, which had been converted for government use. Compared to the cells in the Guard Houses, and especially those in the King's Ford Gaol, these cells were positively luxurious. The usual prisoners at the I.O. were high ranking – or they were until their trial, at which point they went to Gaol minus their titles, fortunes, and, on occasion, not long after, their heads – so the walls were clean and the bedding fairly fresh. The bucket had a lid on it, and if they had the funds then a candle and decent food was available to purchase.

"What are you doing? Don't you know who I am? The Queen must be informed, at once!" Colvile rattled at his cell door, the iron bars clanking against his manacles.

"Shut up mate, we're not allowed to cut out your tongue until after you've given your statement." The Sergeant who'd brought him in ambled down from his desk, where he was filling in the prisoner's details in the book.

"What statement? What is this about?"

"I'll read your arrest warrant out to you again if you'd like?" The Sergeant pulled the parchment from his breast pocket and pointed it at the curate.

"No thank you. I think I can manage to read it on my own." The Curate snatched through the bars to grab his arrest warrant. The sergeant danced backwards, keeping the warrant just out of reach as the Curate squashed himself against the bars, failing to force his body out enough to grab the warrant.

"Now be sensible, Mr Colvile, you'll hurt yourself doing that."

"It's Your Reverance, sergeant."

"Not 'ere it ain't. If you're 'ere it's 'cos you committed treason. No titles for traitors."

"I am not a traitor."

"Yeah, you are. Else you wouldn't be here would you? Now, shut it, the Lord Commander will be along just as soon as he has time to speak to you."

Colvile kicked at the bed to check for vermin before taking a seat.

It puzzled him; Lord Summerton was still in the Southern Hills, so which of the Lord's Commander was he waiting for? He tapped his feet on the floor, counting the names of possible Lord Commanders, searching his memory but nothing occurred to him. He knew why he had been arrested, of course; ever since the youngest Mortlake brat had spilled his guts he'd been expecting to be called into answer questions. He rehearsed the story the High Curate had given told him to use should he be arrested. Bits kept flitting away from his mind until he became agitated. The curate stood and paced the room, mumbling quietly to

43

himself, though he did not realise it at first. The story got better and better every time he told it to himself. If only he could remember it when the tine came.

Eventually, the clatter of hooves from above caught his attention. He looked up through the glass of the tiny window that allowed sunlight to filter through. The lighted fluttered in and out as people passed above. The shadows suggested it was late in the afternoon. He'd been pacing for hours. Colvile returned to his bed to rest. If the courtyard was busy, he surmised, then the Lord Commander must have arrived, or help. He hoped it was help.

Colvile woke with a start; the cell door swung open, but he couldn't see anyone other than the sergeant who had locked him in. Colvile swung his legs off the bed and stood. The muscles and bones in his back cracked as he stretched.

"I hated to wake you, Mr Colvile, you were sleeping like a baby, but you are wanted in the Office."

"I see, by whom?"

"Never you mind, get a move on though 'cos she won't wait."

"The Queen!" Colvile leapt to his feet, grinning. Of course her majesty wouldn't leave him in this mess, after all he had done for her. Admittedly, the plan hadn't worked out the way they'd wanted, but he could hardly be blamed for that.

"Now, now, yer rev'rence, not so fast." The sergeant grabbed Colvile's collar, and dragged the man back. "You're still a prisoner; no running." He left the cell open and marched his prisoner between rows of empty cells, past the sergeants' desk and up a set of stairs. Here a heavy metal door blocked the path. The sergeant drew level with Colvile and hammered on the door. A flap in the door dropped and two eyes squinted through.

The door opened. Colvile was dragged through and along another corridor. Half way along they turned left then immediately right into an office. A woman sat with her back to the door, her hair covered by an embroidered black coif, popular among the more devout ladies at court; at the desk sat the Duke of Albon. He knew now who the 'Lord Commander' the sergeant talked of was, one of the few men who could sit in the Queen's presence.

"Your Majesty! How kind of you to come, I don't know why this fool has arrested me." Colvile bowed repeatedly.

Lizzy turned in her seat and grinned at the curate as she removed the coif from her hair, "Not quite, Colvile, but it's interesting you should assume the Queen would come to help a mendicant preacher. Why would that be?"

Colvile gulped and realised he'd been tricked. He slumped in the sergeant's arms. "I, I, I, used to be a part of her household, she was very fond of me."

"We know; but then she repudiated you. I can't imagine my sister-in-law would want to be associated with a traitor."

"I am not a traitor."

"Really?" The Duke looked at the papers on his desk, "We shall see. Sergeant, place the prisoner on the chair, if you'd be so kind."

"Of course yer grace. Excuse me Miss Lizzy."

The sergeant was a large man, all muscle and bone, he took up space, so manoeuvring the prisoner between Lizzy's chair and the wall wasn't the easiest task. Especially as Colvile had started to struggle. Lizzy stood, moving her chair out of the way; she closed the door, locking it to be certain, and returned to her seat. The sergeant had the prisoner in the metal chair and was struggling to pin the worming man down. The Duke stood to assist. The prisoner lashed out, clipping the sergeant on the head with a manacled wrist. Lizzy was impressed, first with the sergeant who didn't so much as blink, and secondly by Colvile; who'd have thought the scrawny creature had that much gumption?

The Duke solved the problem by punching the curate, who's head snapped backwards and hit the wall. The duke and sergeant chained the dazed prisoner to the chair. The sergeant, satisfied the chains would hold took up a place by the door to observe.

Colvile's eyes blinked twice and then he tried to stand. Lizzy smiled at him. It was a toothy, almost shark-like smile. Colvile shuddered.

"Edward Colvile, you are here today because we have reason to believe you were involved in the abduction of the king's daughter; aiding and abetting Lord Mortlake, Lady Mortlake and Sur Maron Mortlake in their actions; and acting as a messenger between the Mortlakes and the originators of the abduction."

"I deny it absolutely."

"Really? And can you explain why you were in

46

the Southern Hills in the weeks prior to Lady Fitzroy's abduction."

"Nothing to do with her I can assure you. I was on pilgrimage visiting the sites associated with our One True Lord. As you should be aware, the lake country was where the One found solace in his search for Being."

"Then, how is it you were seen in Lord Mortlake's house. As far as I am aware, no shrine exists there."

"I don't know what you mean."

Lizzy had been watching the exchange between her uncle and the hated curate, and was absolutely certain that he was lying. She'd guessed before, but now she just knew. A vision started to cloud her eyes. She blinked; this was no time for daydreaming.

"You're lying crow. You met Lord Mortlake at the Lake, in his carriage, and then returned to his house where you and your companion, a shorter, red-haired Curate, plotted to abduct me."

"How do you," Covile recollected himself, "That's conjecture, you have no evidence any such thing occurred."

"We have witnesses."

"How could you, we were careful not to...oh." Colvile sank in his seat, head in his hands.

"Is that a confession?"

Colvile grabbed at a remaining straw, "No it is not! What I meant to say was, my companion and I were careful to not disturb the residents of the lake country, knowing that they guard their shrine jealously and have accused visiting pilgrims of robbing their

47

relics in the past. I know nothing about your abduction."

"Tell the truth and you'll receive a lighter sentence; I'm sure you were only following orders."

"I have nothing further to say." The Curate crossed his arms and waited.

"You really would be better off confessing Colvile, you'll save yourself a lot of pain."

The curate blanched, "You can't torture me! I'm a curate."

His bluster left his interrogators unimpressed, "You must have missed the news," Lizzy drawled, "My father has declared forfeit the rank, lands and properties of anyone involved in my abduction, and we have more than enough evidence to show you were present at the meeting and acted as ambassador for the originator of the plan."

"So, tell us, Mr Colvile, ex-curate of this parish, who sent you?"

"If you have the evidence you say you have, then I'm a dead man anyway; there's no reason I should take more people to the grave with me, on her account."

"And if I told you your life would be spared if you gave us the names?"

"Why would I betray them? I've lost everything as it is; what point would there be in continuing to live?"

"Very well. Sergeant, return the prisoner to his cell. Full treatment."

"Of course your grace."

The prisoner wondered what 'full treatment' meant, but had not time to ask before he was led away, considerably less defiant than he had been when he arrive.

When the sound of chains had receded and the first door had clanged shut, Lizzy looked at her uncle,

"Well, that didn't go as well as it could have."

"He admitted to being involved."

"But not who sent him. We need to find that out." Lizzy pushed her chair back to stand. She paced the room, agitation and impatience coursing through her, and impatience. She was sure the queen had ordered her abduction and eventual death, but she couldn't prove it.

"And your agents?"

"Nothing at the moment. Summerton is searching the Mortlake properties for evidence and I sent a team to Colvile's lodgings when we arrested him. Unless one of them has been stupid enough to keep letters, it'll be difficult to follow the trail."

Lizzy stared across the courtyard, through thick glass that made all sights indistinct. The lamplighter was out, each dot of light flaring then settling into a gentle pool as he moved on. Each person in the palace was a cog in the machine that kept the place running, as Colvile was a cog in the conspiracy. If one cog broke the whole mechanism stopped. But, Lizzy realised, sometimes just the rumour that a vital piece was broken could stop the machine.

"I don't like that grin Lizzy; it means someone is going to get hurt."

"Oh they are. Uncle, I think I have an idea."

Chapter 9

A week passed with little obvious activity in the cells. An announcement was made in the Moot, the King's Council, and to the Curate's Council, that the conspirators had been identified, including the ring leaders, and arrests would follow shortly. The caveat was added that anyone who had been involved and would turn King's Evidence would receive a lighter sentence. The announcement was repeated in the Ford Daily. Colvile's name was kept from all reports, although his arrest had been trumpeted loudly in the days following it.

In Court, the day after the announcements were made, Lizzy started to hear the whispering. Gossiping courtiers silenced themselves when she passed them in the Great Hall as though afraid that they would be the next to be arrested; Lizzy smiled her shark-like smile, nodded and passed them by, joining her father and his wife on the dais.

"Good evening father, you look well."

"I am my dear, I am. Now that we know who was involved in your abduction I have little fear for your safety."

"Where's the High Curate this evening, ma'am, I thought you never went anywhere without him?"

"I think that's a little exaggerated Elizabeth, I often attend Court without the company of the High Curate. He has other duties, you know."

"Indeed yes. I suppose he must, especially now."

"How do you mean?"

"Well, ma'am, it was two of his own Curates who

acted as go betweens for my abduction. He must be busy investigating his clergy for signs of treason."

"Oh, no, I don't think so. I'm sure Colvile and Snapson were the only ones involved."

"Snapson?"

"Oh, yes, he told me, the Curates were arrested. Didn't you know?"

"No, I've had little to do with the investigation. It wouldn't be appropriate."

"Of course not. His grace has handled it all?"

"I believe so; he said something about having the couriers sent to Gaol in a couple of days, to get them away from their co-conspirators, but that's all I've heard of the matter."

"Why the Gaol?"

"Uncle fears for their safety, in the cells."

"Quite right, too, you never know who might visit. Though, as we know everyone involved it would be rather pointless to hurt the witnesses."

"Just so father."

"All the conspirators?"

"Oh yes, ma'am, all of them."

"Well, good, that's good. When will the arrests begin?" The Queen looked at her husband.

"Oh, very soon, Michael wants more time to prepare the cells. There's going to be a few formerly-important people in residence there by the end of the week."

"I see." The Queen became quiet, staring at the courtiers milling about and chattering.

Lizzy looked at her father. He seemed pensive; she supposed that knowing his wife had plotted to kill his daughter was weighing on him.

"Father?"

"Yes my dear?"

"Where are my brothers this evening?"

"Oh, I believe they went to visit Elenor. Catherine thought it would be good for them to spend a couple of days out of the city."

"You mean I'm going to have to put up with three small children screaming at the dinner table, rather than one?" Lizzy was grinning.

"They're growing up; they need to socialise. I can hardly trust them with anyone outside the family at the moment, can I?"

Lizzy smiled and shrugged. The Queen seemed to startle out of her daze. She hadn't known the boys were at the Ducal estates outside the city.

"Dear, is it really safe for them to be there?"

"Of course, my brother commands the Guards and his own forces; it would take an army to attack his house."

"You're quite correct father, the guards have all been on high alert since I returned. Nobody will get into the house unless they're invited."

"That's reassuring news. Elizabeth, where will you stay tonight?"

"I was planning to stay here, it's far too late to leave for home now. You know how uncle is, he insists I return before dark if I'm going out."

"It's probably for the best. I'll have my personal Guards outside your door, just to be certain. With the news of the arrests your enemies may try again before the duke arrests them."

"Possibly, your majesty, but with your Guards on the door I shall feel quite safe. Are you sure there will be enough to spare?"

"How do you mean Lizzy?"

"Well father, I noticed there are a few less in the Hall this evening; are they sick ma'am?"

"Oh, no, I believe there is some sort of celebration going on, one of them is getting married, or something."

"Ah, well I suppose that explains it." Lizzy smiled sweetly and rose from her seat, "Father, ma'am." She bowed and left the dais, looking for Lady Tessa Barnum, one of her few friends, and also an investor in the Ford Daily. Tess was almost a year older than Lizzy and ran her family estates for her aged mother and indolent brother.

"Lizzy, there you are." Tess darted out of an alcove where she had been keeping an eye on proceedings, to grasp her friend's hand.

"Hello Tess, how's things?" Lizzy smiled, at her enthusiasm. It had been a while since she had seen anyone who really wanted to talk to her, other than family.

"Not bad, dear, how are you? It's been an age."

"I'm tired mostly, and you visited us last week." Lizzy grinned.

"Help me find a table so we can sit down; be sociable for once."

"I'll try. I've got things on my mind."

"I know dear, I know. Why don't you tell me about it?"

"I really can't, not yet."

"Oh, the arrests? Well, I suppose you have to keep it secret or people will fly off in the night."

"Something like that. But let's forget it for now; who's here tonight?"

"Henry, Beth, and Charley. Phil and Gos couldn't get away from some family do."

"Poor them."

"I don't know, I rather enjoy family parties, at least at home I don't have to wear quite so many skirts."

"Don't wear them then."

"Just because you get away with wearing odd combinations of clothes doesn't mean the rest of us can. Mother tried to make me wear a coif tonight."

"But she didn't succeed."

"Well, yes and no. I took it off in the carriage. I'll have to put it back on again on the way home."

"How ridiculous. I didn't think your mother was religious?"

"Only about fashion."

"I see."

"Your interview in the Daily sparked a run on shirt dresses, you know."

"Did it? Caro didn't say anything."

"Of course she didn't, she mainly caters to the merchant classes. They have no idea about fashion."

"Tessa your snob is showing."

"Drat, sorry."

"And how do you know what's popular anyway?"

"Marie tells me. She's an excellent dressmaker."

"I know; she works with Caro. I'm going to set Caro up in business as soon as I come of age."

"How generous!"

"Maybe Marie can work for her?"

"She never would. Marie's a terrible snob."

"I know, but Caro will be able to pay more than the Guild."

"That is a generous gift, why?"

"Well, you know, we've been friends ever such a long time, and she was my Companion my first year in the city."

"Of course, you two were very close."

"And you were very jealous."

"That's not fair Lizzy."

"I'm sorry." They continued their tour of the Hall, trying to find a free table. Eventually, a group of three women and a man waved them over.

"Cooee! Liz. Tess. Here!" Charley called, "We got a table!" Charley was a large, intelligent woman, with eyes like chocolate and darkly tanned skin. She was half-Belenosian, the daughter of an Imperial Ambassador and an Alboni Countess.

The pair threaded their way through to their friends.

"Where's the twins tonight Liz? I'm surrounded by hens." Henry Fitzhaven laughed as the women punched and poked him in the ribs, "Ouch, you've got sharp fingers you know Charley." Henry was short and red-haired; he burnt easily in the sun. Despite years of teasing at the Royal School he had survived with his humour and confidence intact. Mainly because he was extremely popular with the girls. He was continuously surrounded by 'hens' but not a single one had persuaded him into their beds. Rumour had it that he was deeply in love with Lizzy, a rumour they both took care to spread.

"They've gone back to Mortlake to help with the investigation."

Henry's face fell.

"I thought it was all done with?" Beth asked. She was a quiet, mouse-like woman, with blond-brown hair and a terrible dress sense. Her mother had also insisted she wear a coif. Unlike Tessa, whose own mother never came to court, Beth's was watching them closely, so she couldn't take it off.

"Mostly, all bar the shouting, I mean."

"Can't wait to see who gets the chop, can't you give us a clue Lizzy?"

"You have such a morbid sense of humour at times." Beth admonished Charley quietly.

"But I'm not the one with a cow pat on my head." Charley reached over to snatch the coif off her friend's head.

"Give that back, mother's looking."

"Oh really Beth, you're twenty-five, I'm pretty certain your mother shouldn't be dictating your clothing choices still."

"Well, she can be very sharp at times. And she's worried."

"What about?"

"She doesn't like us being friends, not after Lady Mortlake's execution."

"Oh, yes, your mother and the late lady were cousins, weren't they?"

"Something like that, not close enough to drag us into their plotting but close enough that mother resents you now that they got caught."

Lizzy looked over at Beth's mother, hovering a few tables away; she smiled. Beth's mother pretended not to see and spoke to her own friends instead. The lady was in mourning, obviously for her cousin Lady Mortlake, since she'd long since stopped mourning her husband.

"Doesn't she know showing sympathy for traitors is likely to get her investigated?"

"I've told her that, but she insists on wearing black, for the next month."

"I'll tell uncle she's just being stubborn, rather than traitorous, then shall I?"

"Please do, as much as she's a nuisance, I'm sure Beth doesn't want her mother sent to Gaol as a traitor."

"No, I really don't. The Duke won't really investigate her, will he?"

"Probably not, but he's paranoid at the moment. I'm to stay here tonight, it's too late for me to ride home in the dark and all that nonsense."

"Oh, but the duke means well Lizzy."

"I know, but it can be stifling. I had to take an escort into town earlier! Me!"

"Well you did get abducted last time you went to town without one."

"Thanks Henry, I needed reminding about that. Oh, that reminds me, has anyone seen Walter Northwood recently?"

"Hasn't he been to call?"

"No."

"His mother found out you were meeting. You know what the dowager's like; she banned her precious

Wally from stepping foot in the capital for a year."

"He's twenty-eight."

"And a mummy's boy. Give up on that one love, and find yourself a man."

"Darling Henry, if only it were so simple. There are so few suitable men in Albon."

"So very true. I've looked so hard."

"Perhaps we should take a tour of the Empire instead?"

"Could be fun, when did you have in mind?"

"I don't know, next summer? I'd have to talk to uncle first though."

"Why?"

"Well, he wants me to be responsible."

"Oh dear. Doesn't he know responsibility is bad for you?" Harry passed a bottle of wine to Lizzy.

"I know; it's shocking that he thinks I might suddenly become sensible just because I've reached twenty-one."

"Ridiculous."

"Utterly." Lizzy drank from the bottle, before passing it back to Harry.

"We shall have to inform him that it is impossible for you to be responsible for at least ten years."

"We will, we will."

The conversation continued in a similar vein for some time before they became distracted and the conversation went elsewhere. Eventually, slightly inebriated, the group broke up.

Lizzy continued her pretence of drunken silliness all the way to her room. Once inside she collapsed on the sofa long enough to kick her court slippers off. She washed and changed into a different outfit, replacing her silver silk with brown cotton before pulling on dark leather boots, tightly laced. The silk was discarded on the floor by the bed. Lizzy arranged her excessive cushions and pillows into a vaguely human lump and pulled the curtains round the bed. It would only fool her attackers for a few moments, but a few moments were all she would need. With any luck.

Retreating to the other side of the bed, Lizzy slipped through the door into her closet. It was dark, but she knew it well enough that she could navigate to her desk in the dark. She settled into her writing chair to wait for the next move in the game.

Lizzy sat up, startled by the knock on the hidden door. The knock came again, then three quick raps. Lizzy sighed, the twins had arrived. She got up to let them in, opening the wall panel that lead into the narrowest of tunnels. Lawrence then Alexander slid into the room on their bellies.

"I don't know why you don't have that entrance widened Lizzy, it's getting harder to get through every day." Alex brushed dirt of his brown shirt and trousers.

"I can still manage it. And keep your voices down."

"Who's outside?"

"No one in my room at the minute, but there's five Queen's Guard out in the corridor, to 'protect' me."

"Another five have been arrested trying to kill Colvile, and some of the Curate's Enforcers were seen entering the lodgings of the formerly-reverend Snapson."

"Father got the message to you in time then?"

"Straight after you went to play you part for the court. How're the gang anyway?"

"Henry was most put out by your absence and Beth is worried uncle will investigate her mother for wearing mourning. And it's been suggested we should all take a tour of the Empire next spring, for our education."

"A grand tour?"

"That sort of thing, yes."

"It could be fun. We'll have to ask father though. He might need us here."

"We'll see, but life can't be all work, we need some adventures."

"You just got back from a big adventure."

"Oh yes, and it was so exhilarating. Not. Now, are you two going to hide or not?"

"If we must."

"We've been shot at tonight, you know."

"I'm sure you have. And as soon as we've dealt with the Queen's Guard and father has delivered his ultimatum we can all have a holiday."

"You're certain they'll attack tonight?"

"It's their last chance. The Queen will have guessed we're going to start arresting people soon."

"If she's going down she's taking you with her?"

"Something like that. For all that she's a malicious, jealous sow, she isn't stupid. Taking the boys to uncle's tipped her hand. She can't run and take them with her, so she may as well stay and see me dead."

"Twisted."

"Extremely."

"Shush, they're going to start moving soon."

They stood in silence, contemplating the irrational nature of human jealousy for a few seconds before the sound of the outer door opening, and chain mail rattling as intruders tripped over Lizzy's discarded slippers by the door, seeped into the closet via the air brick over the door. The floor creaked a little, then a muttered curse signalled that someone had stepped on the silk clothes and slid across the polished wooden floor. There was furious whispering, orders to remain silent, as the intruders crept closer.

Lizzy waved the twins to the door, which opened with a slight click, muffled by a wall hanging. They slid out and crouched behind the bed, waiting for the Guards to attack the pillows. Lizzy waited behind the door, holding it slightly open so she could slip out while her attackers were engaged in fighting the twins.

The Guards had righted themselves, to reach the bed without further accidents. The curtain rings scraped over the wooden rod; Alex pulled back the far curtains in time to see the blades of four swords slice downwards, glinting of the lamp light. The Queen's Guardsmen stepped back, away from the feathers billowing from the now ruined pillows. The twins jumped on to the bed and across the mattress ready to attack. Their drawn knives reflecting the lamp light back at the Guards.

"Really shouldn't have drawn swords in here."
Alex grinned, as he slid off the bed and under the
reach of the first sword.

"There's really not enough room for that."
Lawrence dived at another guards, pushing him
backwards. The Guard tripped as he scrambled
backwards. Lawrence followed him down and plunged
his first blade into the guard's eye socket. Wrenching
it out with a twist, Lawrence stood, smiled at the
remaining two guards and asked,

"You next?" He pointed his dripping stiletto at
the Guard nearest himself. The man shook his head.

"Doesn't he want to play brother?"

"Not at all."

"Well this one does, so come give me a hand."

Lawrence sighed and drew a throwing knife from
his belt. "Duck." Alex dropped to the ground as the
knife whirled over his head to bury itself in the
Guard's sword arm. The sword dropped from his numb
fingers as Alex returned to his feet and sliced forward
with his own blade, putting his opponent down,
although not permanently out of the fight.

"Try to keep one or two of them alive Lawry, we
need evidence."

"I will, don't worry."

The bedroom door opened, the Guards left
outside on watch had fetched more of the Queen's
Guard. Five men joined the remaining two.

"I think we're outnumbered."

"Possibly."

They returned to the fight, their knives an
advantage in the tight confines of Lizzy's bedroom but

were beaten back, cornered behind the bed.

"Whatever Lizzy is planning she better get on with it."

A pale green smoke started to seep through the air brick above the door to the closet. Alex pointed upwards, smiled at the guards and opened the closet door, covering his face with a sleeve. The twins stepped through the door, grabbing the smoke bomb on the desk and hurling it into the bedroom. They shut the door behind them, before wriggling into the tunnel.

The space was cold, granite lined and dark. The twins pulled with their hands and pushed with their lower legs braced against the walls. There were grooves carved into the walls every foot or so giving them some grip. Alex felt something catch his hip; he couldn't move forward. Unable to reach his arm back he wriggled slightly on to his side before continuing through the tunnel. After five yards it opened up, enough that they could stand full height. Lawrence was waiting for his brother, tapping his foot on the undressed stone floor.

The tunnel tilted upwards. The twins ran, coughing slightly from inhaling the smoke, one behind the other, towards the exit, the tunnel dipped again before turning back on itself and starting to rise. They passed three doors before opening the forth. This lead into a linen cupboard. Pushing the shelves back into place behind them, the twins opened the outer door, peering out, looking for other Queen's Guards. Further down the hallway they could see Lizzy hanging on to her door handle.

"Stop lurking, would you? I need help." The door

63

was rattling.

The twins ran down the corridor to hang on to the door with her.

"How long is that bomb supposed to take?" Alex grabbed the handle, standing next to Lizzy.

"Two minutes."

"It's got to be more than that now." Lawrence pushed her out of his way and took her place on the door. They braced themselves against the wall and held on.

"There were more than I expected, the bomb wasn't enough to knock them all out."

"Damn. Plan?"

"We wait. It'll work eventually, just more slowly."

"Do we have time?"

"The Queen isn't going anywhere, not until she knows Lizzy is dead."

"Father won't let her leave her quarters, he's got most of his guard with him. The rest are on the way here."

"Good, father was going to send some of his men too, but he needs them to arrest the Curates Enforcers and the High Curate."

Chapter 10

A fortnight later the Queen sailed off to 'visit her family', alone, and the Curates found themselves in need of a new leader.

The trial, before the Moot and King's Council was short and sweet. When the Duke arrived to arrest the High Curate he found the man burning documents from Lord Mortlake and his son. Unfortunately, they couldn't find evidence that the Queen had been involved directly. Her Guard were executed for attempting to murder Lizzy, but she claimed to know nothing about the conspiracy. In the absence of direct evidence, the King's Council were forced to accept her explanation that the Guards had been bought by the Curate to get rid of Lizzy. Colvile and Snapson received the lighter sentence of life in Gaol, to contemplate their crimes.

Lizzy waved the Queen off from the Royal Hythe, seething with anger,

"Precisely why are we letting her go?"

"I've told you already we don't have enough evidence to execute her."

"But she'll come back!"

"Not for a few years yet."

The young princes were waving to their mother's ship still, though it was out of the harbour.

"Uncle, how long will Mama be away visiting Tarjan?"

"Oh, I should think it'll be a while. Don't you worry, Auntie Catherine and Lizzy will look after you."

"Are we staying at your house tonight, uncle?"

"Afraid not Michael, Dad wants you back at the palace."

"Oh, is it safe now?"

"Probably."

"Are you staying at the palace too, Lizzy?"

"I might."

"Please." The boys bounced up and down, hands together, begging. Lizzy laughed at them.

"Alright then, I suppose I must, if only to stop your noise. Boys come away from the edge."

She grabbed for the capering children who'd got a little too close to the fence that ran long the top of the Hythe.

"Uncle we really must get a proper wall built along here. Someone could fall in."

"People regularly do. Now boys, settle down, what would your sister tell the king if you fell into the bay and drowned?"

"Back to the coach with you both. And stay in the centre of the Hythe."

The boys ran along the Hythe towards the carriage. It was an open topped carriage; they'd never ridden in one before. They'd travelled to the Hythe in the ducal carriage and met Lizzy who'd travelled in her own conveyance. Dawson waited to lift them into the carriage, but the boys insisted on getting themselves in, clambering around the door.

Lizzy watched the pantomime, as the boys struggled to reach the first step, not realising that Dawson carried a stool to help them up.

"Do we have any agents at sea?" She smiled and

66

spoke out of the side of her mouth.

"Yes, but we can't use them."

"No?"

"It'd be war."

"If the queen's ship was attacked by pirates?"

"Indeed. Tarjan is not a stupid man."

"I suppose you are right, but I don't like it. Something tells me when she returns that woman will be trouble."

"How so?"

"I don't know, just a gut reaction."

"Well, we'll keep an eye on her and if she looks like causing trouble then we might act."

Still uneasy, Lizzy went to rescue Dawson from her brothers.

Chapter 11

Compared to the preceding months, the following weeks were rather dull. Had it not been for the excitement of her upcoming Coming of Age Lizzy would have been inconsolably bored. Since the arrangements for the Ball were being made by her aunt Catherine, Lizzy was left to get on with dealing with a more important problem; persuading Caro to accept the gift of her own business.

"Caro." Lizzy advanced one morning, while she was being fitted for a new dress.

"Umphf?" Caro mumbled through a mouthful of pins.

"I have an idea."

Caro removed the pins to the pin cushion. "Oh?"

"I think I'd like to invest some of the money uncle's been looking after for me, in property. What do you think?"

"Well, it could be a good move. What would you do? Buy the buildings and rent them to people?"

"Yes, something like that. I don't know where to start though. I think I'd like to invest in business properties."

"There's that new parade of shops on Water Market, I'm sure I saw something in the paper about them."

"I'll have to look into that. If I bought some of the shops there would you like to rent one, at a nominal rent, of course?"

"Lizzy I couldn't possibly afford my own premises at the moment."

"But you're doing so well, and if you didn't have to give half your earnings to Mrs Brasckett you'd be doing so much better. Besides, I can always cover the bills for a year or something until it gets off the ground."

"Lizzy."

"Yes." Lizzy looked down sheepishly, she knew that tone of voice.

"Is this business venture an elaborate ruse on your part to give me money?"

"Not just money, your own business." Lizzy blushed.

"Why?"

"Seemed appropriate, considering I have so much cash now and you need your independence."

"I wouldn't be though, would I? People in the trade would say I was only successful because you bought everything for me."

"But you have loads of customers!"

"And in another three or four years I'll have enough saved to open a shop on my own."

"What if I gave you it as a loan?"

"People would say I wasn't paying the right interest."

"Why do you care?"

"Reputation is important. And if enough people in the Guild decided I've got ahead unfairly I could be thrown out. Then I wouldn't be able to work."

"People aren't that petty, surely."

"Don't you believe it. There's only so much work to go 'round and the older Guild members hover over their rights like a hawk over a kill."

69

"Petty, petty, people. Well if you won't accept a business of your own, would you accept a position as my private seamstress?"

"Maybe, what about my other clients?"

"Oh, you could keep those if you wanted? I mean, as my employee if you should be asked to take freelance seamstress work it would be acceptable, if I don't have work I need you to do."

"Hmm, I could give Mrs Brasckett my notice tonight but she'll want her half of the fee for this dress."

"Tell her I rejected the dress today. She designed it, didn't she?" Lizzy started to strip out of the dress pieces before Caro could answer her.

"Yes, mostly it's based on the latest Southern Belanosian patterns we've received."

"Interesting, that does explain the flounced skirt though. Do you have any ideas for my outfit?"

"Of course. The Southern Belanosian patterns are far too ornamental but they are the latest thing."

"All over the Islands?"

"Even in Sumoast."

"Well, I don't want anything that everyone else already has. What did you have in mind?"

Lizzy went house buying the next morning and found a small, but clean and light, establishment not far from the Palace which her uncle bought in Lizzy's name. A week later Caro moved in and took up her position as Lizzy's seamstress. The house was rather perfect, Lizzy thought, when she viewed it the day after Caro took up residence.

"More tea Lizzy?" Caro poured a cup from her (brand new) teapot as they sat in the front parlour. The windows were open to relieve the gathering summer heat. The city seamed far off, to Caro; the rumble of carts and the cries of traders were faint, and the buzzing of insects in the garden reminded her of the Marsh where both women had grown up.

"Thank you."

"You look like you need it."

"The boys are running me ragged. They've decided that after I come of age I won't be able to play silly games, so they are getting in as much as they can before next Secondday."

Caro chuckled, looking away. She noticed a faint cobweb in a corner of the ceiling where the light bounced through the window and off a mirror. Caro stood and flicked at it with a rag."

"Didn't the maid clean the house before you moved in?"

"Some of it, but I think she needs better training."

"But she's thirty if she's a day."

"No, she's a child, no older than we were when we came to King's Ford."

"Really? Ring the bell Caro, something's not right."

Caro clanged the bell hanging by her chair. Down the corridor a door opened, slammed shut. Feet hurried to the parlour door. There was a knock.

"Come in." Lizzy called.

A girl, thin and sallow, sidled though the door. She curtsied awkwardly, unsure who she was curtsying to.

"You're not Maggie Richards."

"No ma'am, that's my mistress."

"I pay your wages, not Mrs Richards."

"No ma'am, you rent me off of her."

"That is not the arrangement I made. What is your name?"

"Sandra Fawks ma'am." Sandra curtsied again.

"And how long have you worked for Mrs Richards?"

"Ten years, ma'am."

"So she's 'rented' you to other households?"

"Yes ma'am."

"In what capacity?"

"Maid servant, mostly."

"And how much does she pay you a week for your work here?"

"Pay ma'am? She doesn't pay me; I get my bed and board."

Lizzy drummed her fingers across the table.

"Now Lizzy," Caro warned, she knew the signs, "It happens all the time."

"It's slavery Caro."

"No ma'am, indentured servitude."

"That's another way of saying legal slavery. Sandra, how long do you have left on your indenture?"

"Don't know ma'am, never seen the paper. My Mam signed it when I was little."

"It must be registered with someone?" Caro mused.

"Yes Miss, Mrs Richards says it's with Twerps and Fosset, the notaries on the Little Market."

"And you've never been to check for yourself?"

The girl shrugged. "Didn't seem worth the beating."

"What do you mean?"

"One of the other girls got it into her head to go see the notaries, cos she wanted to get married but caunt cos of the indenture. When Missus Richards found out she beat her black and blue. Couldn't work for two weeks and the Missus went to Twerps and tol' 'em to add another two years to the indenture to make up for lost earnings."

"That's terrible." Caro was aghast.

Sandra shrugged, "Everyone does it."

"So? That doesn't make it right. Lizzy, we have to do something?"

"I'll talk to uncle. But first, I think I should visit Mrs Richards."

"She'll be ever so mad at me if she thinks I've got her into trouble."

"Don't do anything rash, Lizzy."

"I won't." Lizzy stood, "I shan't be long, though; we really need to get to work on my clothes."

The woman was half risen from her seat, startled by the banging of the front door as Lizzy entered the town house secreted in an older, less than respectable part of the city. It had once been an elegant area, about two centuries before.

"Mistress Richards." Lizzy took a seat in the parlour uninvited, her driver glowering by the door, "You have defrauded me. I demand the return of the wages I paid you."

That stung Mrs Richards into action. She stood, seeming to consider advancing on Lizzy with a scowl, until Dawson, armed with a small crossbow, moved away from the door. She noted his movement and looked away. Mrs Richards turned an ingratiating smile on Lizzy and diverted to the bell pull.

"Tea?"

"No thank you."

"Of course." Mrs Richards returned to her seat by a side table, "How can I help you?"

"You can return my money. I paid in good faith for an experienced, mature housekeeper for my property in Spring Hill, and I visited today to find a chit of a girl who should be in school clattering about the place. You have defrauded me; if you don't return my money I shall have to report the matter to the Watch."

"Ma'am, you must be mistaken, Sandra is a competent housekeeper, small for her age I'll admit, but reliable and hard working."

"But not what I paid for. Is the girl indentured to you?"

"Why?" Mrs Richards asked suspiciously, then seemed to remember Lizzy's connections, "Of course, the papers are with my notaries, Twerps in Little Market. She's been with me a few months, poor girl comes from a family of brewers, but times have not been kind."

"Can I see her papers? If she is going to work in my house on a long-term basis, then I need to know when her indenture ends. I wouldn't want to be party to illegal contracts; it would be so embarrassing for father if I did."

"Well, of course you wouldn't want to upset the king; I'll have the papers sent to you as soon as possible."

"Don't you have a copy here?"

"Not at all; I find that for safe keeping it is better to store such things with Twerps."

"But what of Sandra's copy?"

"With her family."

"Indeed; come Dawson, let us visit the Little Market." Lizzy stood as her driver opened the parlour door on to the street.

"But Ma'am, they won't be expecting you!"

"It doesn't matter, if they are a respectable firm then there is no reason why they shouldn't show me the contract. I am the one paying the girl's wages after all."

"But ma'am, how will they know you've come from me?"

"Easily. I shall tell them."

"But, ma'am, please, wait. Don't trouble yourself, I shall have the documents sent to Spring Hill as soon as possible." The woman clutched at Lizzy's sleeve.

"I'm impatient Mrs Richards," she removed the woman's claws, brushing the silk of her sleeve, "I have other things to do. Good day."

Dawson shut the door on the astounded woman,

before climbing on to the carriage.

"Do you know where we're going Dawson, I think we'll have to get there quickly."

"Aye, miss, it's not far to Twerps. That woman will have one of those poor kids scurrying there already."

"Well, we'd best be moving then."

The carriage pulled into the Little Market minutes later; Lizzy looked around. She'd never visited this part of the city before. The buildings were of plaster and lathe, the shop fronts were open to the air; a bench showing the available goods was formed from a part of the front wall, on hinges and lowered down. These wall/tables were held in place with leather brackets during the day and bolted up at night. The streets were crowded, but Lizzy noted she was the only one in a carriage. The air creaked with wagon axles and the shouts of purveyors. Lizzy heard hooting above her; on the second or third storey of every other building, above the shops all around the square, women hung out of windows showing off their own wares.

"Whores, miss, ignore them. This is it."

Dawson pulled up outside Twerps. The notary office was the only shop with glass windows, small and green tinted. Lizzy climbed out of the carriage, looking for the door. It was also green tinted, the paint peeling and the wood warped along the bottom. Above the door hung a metal sign, once painted gold

76

but now tarnished and rusting.

"Want me to come with you?"

"No, stay here and watch the carriage."

"Yes miss. If you need me just shout."

"I will. See if you can collect up a few Watchmen while you're waiting; I have a feeling we may need them."

"Yes miss. You do remember what his grace said about you starting fights don't you?"

"Of course Dawson." Lizzy smiled then wrenched the swollen door open with a shove.

Inside, Lizzy found that despite the general air of neglect outside, the notaries kept their desks tidy. The floor looked like it had been swept recently and only one or two cobwebs hung from the corners. Two men, in black suits worn to a shine, and loud ties sat at desks that faced each other, surrounded by filing cabinets. They seemed startled to see the eccentrically dressed lady whose carriage had pulled up outside and about whom they had been speculating until the moment she shoved open their door.

"My Lady, how can we help you?" Both men stood at once and hurried to take her hand, to lead her to the client's chair.

Lizzy put on her best austere aristo voice and looked around, her eyebrow arched and nostrils flaring. She flicked to two men away from her and took the more comfortable looking chair that one of the notaries had just vacated. On the desk was a letter, just opened. She recognised the writing and smiled slightly; it was going to be so easy.

"Do you know who I am?"

"Lady Fitzroy, it's a great honour for you to visit us. How can we be of service?"

"Mr?"

"Twerp, my lady, and this is my cousin, Mr Fosset."

"And have you been in business for many years?"

"Twenty my lady." Mr Twerp fiddled with his tie, "How can we be of service?"

"I understand you specialise in indenture contracts; I have a girl in my service."

"And you wish to indenture her?"

"I wish to see her current indenture. She is contracted to Mrs Richards, of Dorathea Street, I believe. Mrs Richards has defrauded me, I paid for a mature, experienced housekeeper and found she had sent a child who barely knows how to sweep the floor."

"Ah, yes, my lady, that does seem rather unfortunate. I'm afraid we can't show you the contract though, client confidentiality is important in our trade."

"You are materially assisting Mrs Richards in fraud. I will be forced to take the matter to my uncle, the Duke."

"But ma'am, we weren't aware of her intention to defraud you."

"Really? Then why do you have a note from the woman on your desk." Lizzy picked up the letter and read it out. "'Lady Fitz going to visit, hide S. Fawks papers'. How obviously incriminating." Lizzy folded the letter and placed it in her bag. "Gentlemen, show me the contract or I will have you in the Gaol before you can breathe."

"My lady, really, this is hardly fair!"

"Neither is forcing young children into unending indentured servitude. You know the law; anyone under sixteen cannot enter a contract, yet I have evidence that Mrs Richards is doing just that. If you have knowingly been party to her illegal activities, then you can expect a hefty sentence."

"We never saw the indentured servants." Mr Fosset spoke quickly, his face pale.

"No, never, my lady, I assure you, we took Mrs Richards at her word that the girls were all sixteen." Mr Twerps pulled at his tie, sweating.

"Don't you have a copy of their birth certificates?"

"Most of these girls don't have them. Their parents are too lazy to go and register their births. Really ma'am these people can't expect much out of life and an indenture gives them security." Twerps seemed more confident in this answer, as though he'd rehearsed it a thousand times to clients.

"Be that as it may, I wish to see the contract."

There was a knock at the door. The notaries looked away from Lizzy as a couple of Watchmen pushed open the door.

"Ma'am, your coachman alerted us. You have evidence of a crime?"

"Ah, Sergeant, what a pleasure to see you again; I

hadn't realised Lord Summerton had posted you to the Little Market this week?"

"And next; we've got a lot of people on their summer holiday week just now."

"How lucky for me; yes, to answer your question, I have evidence of a crime. About a week ago I made a contract with one Maggie Richards of Dorathea Street, for her to provide housekeeping services in my property at Springhill Street. I specifically understood that she would be the housekeeper. I visited the property today to find a fourteen-year-old indentured servant acting as housekeeper. I ascertained that the child had been in Richards' service for eight years, having been sold to Mrs Richards by her parents. I have visited Mrs Richards to ascertain the truth and was told that the girl was legal but small for her age. When pressed, she admitted that the contract was in the possession of these notaries. I believe these men are aiding and abetting illegal indenturing of underage servants, and extending their indentures indefinitely. I also have testimony of abuse."

"Well, that's a serious charge my lady; we should call in our Commander. I'll have men sent to Dorathea Street. Mrs Richards is known to us, with so many girls living in her house there have been accusations of prostitution without a license."

"I quite understand; be so kind as to arrest these men, and ask my uncle to send his Investigators."

"Of course my lady; you've done a grand job of tracking down the evidence I'm surprised you need the Investigators. I don't suppose you'd like to join the Watch would you? We could do with intelligent people about the place."

"Ah, as much as I would love to pound the streets of our fair city with you, my dear Sergeant, I'm afraid my father is quite set against my taking a profession."

"Shame." The sergeant sighed at her smile and turned away, "You two," He called two more Watchmen lurking at the door. "Got the wagon with you?"

"Yes Sergeant, waiting outside."

"We're taking these two to the Gaol. Pop by Dorathea Street and collect that baggage Maggie Richards on the way. And Corporal,"

"Yes Sergeant?"

"Have two men guard the house. Keep everyone in it inside. I want it intact when the Investigators get there."

"Yes Sergeant. I'll send a runner up to the Investigations Office, too?"

"Already done, I suspect?" The Sergeant looked at Lizzy, who nodded slightly. She'd sent a messenger as soon as she'd left Caro.

"They're probably already in Dorathea Street; you'd better send the wagon along."

The Sergeant nodded and returned to his task, "Mr John Twerps and Mr Marshall Fosset, I'm arresting you for aiding and abetting the illegal indenturing of children, being party to abuse of minors and to the running of an unlicensed brothel. You do not have to say anything, anything you do say will be taken down and used in evidence before the magistrates. Corporal, remove these men."

Three Watchmen manhandled to notaries out of

their office and into the cage on the back of a heavy wagon outside. As they were scuffling out another knock shuddered on the door. Two women, in smart dark blue dresses entered. The Investigators had arrived.

"My Lady, your message arrived." Investigator Murphy, well known to Lizzy, saluted, "The Duke is rather perturbed that you are involving yourself in these matters. You should have come to us with your evidence."

"And if she had Maggie Richards would have got away with another crime."

"Am I missing something?" Lizzy looked between the officers.

"You just happened to stumble into a crime ring we've been trying to take down for years." Investigator Murphy sighed, "Every time we get close we lose our grip on her. Everyone is scared to talk."

"Nasty piece of work." Sergeant Tailor concurred, "There's rumours of beaten girls but we couldn't get any evidence to arrest her."

"And yet I managed to. Did anyone think to just ask?"

"We tried, the girls clammed up. How did you run across her?" The second Investigator asked. Lizzy had never seen this one before. There was something sharp about her eyes.

"I needed a housekeeper for my dressmaker."

"Johnson, you will find Lady Fitzroy has an uncanny knack of finding the information we need. It's almost magic."

"Magic is an abomination." The new Investigator

scowled.

Lizzy sighed inwardly, her 'skill' wasn't magic, magic didn't exist. She was just clumsy. "Murphy is of course speaking metaphorically. Everyone knows there's no such thing as magic; it's superstitious nonsense."

"The Curates teach otherwise."

"I know. That doesn't make it true."

"Assistant Investigator Johnson, start with those files." Murphy interrupted before the conversation went any further. She pointed to the cabinets behind the desk formerly belonging to Mr Fosset. "My lady, if you are finished here I would prefer it if you returned to the Palace."

"I need the contract of indenture for Sandra."

"Who?"

"The housekeeper?"

"Oh yes, I see. You won't be keeping her on though?"

"Probably not. There must be a school she can go to. All of Maggie Richards' girls are going to need rehousing and educating."

"You've found yourself a project then. That should keep you out of trouble for a while, you're giving his Grace grey hairs."

"He's had them for years. You have met the twins, haven't you?"

"Of course."

"Then you know that compared to them I'm a little angel."

"You really are not." Murphy laughed while Sergeant Tailor grinned.

"I have to find that indenture though. And you need this." Lizzy fished the letter out of her bag.

"Where did this come from?"

"It was on this desk," Lizzy tapped the cracked wood, "when I got here. It must be evidence of something. Prior knowledge maybe?"

"Indeed. Sergeant if you'd stay to assist? I'd like men to investigate this building from cellar to attic."

Lizzy realised she'd been dismissed and stood. "Well, now I've got your job started for you I'll be getting back. You might want to send someone up to Caro's to interview the girl and Caro. Caro was witness to the girl's story."

"We sent someone there as some as we got your message. I'm not joking about the Duke; he really needs to see you at the Office as soon as possible." Murphy looked back over her shoulder.

"Well, I suppose then there's nothing for me to do except answer the summons. And I really wanted to get my dress started." Lizzy sighed, grinned and left for the Office.

Chapter 12

"Are you even a little jealous that they got all the credit?" Alex asked his cousin as they watched the ceremony, there to show their appreciation for the work of the gallant officers of the law.

"Not particularly; Murphy and Tailor found more than enough evidence at the notaries and in Dorathea Street. All I did was find them a way in. Anyway, Father doesn't want people to know."

"Really?"

Lizzy shrugged, "Maybe a little bit. Like I said, Father didn't want people to know. And it would be petty"

Alex nodded, "And you can't be seen to be petty. Did Caro ever make your dress?" He changed the subject.

"I'm going to collect it later. You have got a new suit, haven't you?"

Alex grinned, "Of course; it's green silk, from Belenos."

"Mother's glaring at us." Lawrence nudged his brother

They looked over at the Duchess, falling silent. There were speeches, of course, about civic duty, another by the new High Curate about treating the lower orders decently. The new High Curate rambled on; he had droning voice that sent Lizzy into a trance. She found herself covering a yawn as her eyes fluttered closed, earning another glare from her aunt. The Curate looked at her, a slightly hurt expression rumpling his beard. He coughed and continued.

It had been decided that Lizzy's part in the arrest of the people traffickers should be kept out of the papers. The Daily had covered the story in detail, praising the Investigations Office and the Watch for their undercover work and the officers involved were pronounced heroes for rescuing thirty-five women and seventy children from slavery.

Lizzy was nudged out of her daze by Alex at the end of the speeches; the King had risen from his throne and waved her forward. Lizzy looked at her uncle, who grinned and shrugged. She stepped towards the dais, a puzzled frown creasing her forehead.

"Today we not only honour these Officers for their lifesaving work; we are also celebrating the coming of age of my daughter, Elizabeth. Twenty-one years ago today I became a father for the first time, and after all the trials and tribulations of those years, I have decided that her Coming of Age gift should acknowledge my love and devotion to her. With that in mind, I am adopting my daughter. Henceforth, Lady Elizabeth Fitzroy will be known as Her Royal Highness, Princess Elizabeth of Albon."

There was a smattering of applause, with cheering from her friends and family. Lady Mary Val, Elizabeth's mother, cried out in shock. Lizzy hadn't even realised her mother had arrived at the Palace. She turned to help her step-father, Sir Philip, with Lady Mary, but her waved her away. Around the hall whispers broke out among shocked courtiers; the Sumoast Ambassadors stood but were waved back into their seats by the neighbouring Umari Ambassador, Greta Van Smelt. Lizzy heard her fierce whispering, silencing the outraged Sumoasti.

Lizzy blinked back tears as her father held his hands out to her. Shaking, she mounted the dais and took the throne next to her father. The boys, Michael and John, grinned happily, bouncing in their seats. Lizzy heard a rustle behind her and turned, the High Curate stood behind her throne, holding a light coronet. It had belonged to her great aunt and namesake. Now the High Curate placed it on her own head. He read out the official adoption record, as entered in the Roles, and presented the new princess with her signet ring. She looked at the ring in confusion then slowly reached out to take it from the High Curate. It slipped on to her finger with ease. Lizzy sat back and smiled slightly.

The courtiers, led by her uncle and aunt, approached the dais to congratulate her. She nodded and smiled but it was all rather a blur. Lizzy sat in stunned silence, the voices around her drowned by the pounding of blood in her ears; her eyes became cloudy and her head felt full of wool. She tried to speak, to thank her father, but no words would pass her lips.

"Bit unexpected?" King John whispered to Lizzy.

She nodded in response.

"Well, had to do something. I would've adopted you years ago, but Jocinta objected."

"She's gone now." Lizzy felt as though her voice was drifting to them from far away, it didn't belong to her.

"Don't know how long for, but there's nothing she can do about it. I've had your adoption papers ratified by the KC, the CC and the Moot. Can't argue with that, can she?" Her father smiled indiscriminately at their well-wishing courtiers, even those officially in disgrace for being associated with the plot to kill Lizzy.

The last people to approach the thrones was the Sumoasti ambassadorial party; they looked less than happy. They ambassador, a cousin of Queen Jocinta's bowed to King John.

"Your Majesty, my I extend my High Lord's congratulations to your Officers; they do a great service to your nation."

"Indeed they have done; we hope to see through reforms, after the summer recess of the Moot, regarding indentured service. The notorious Richards ring will help us make the case for its abolition, I'm sure."

"I wish you success."

The ambassador turned to leave but was stopped when his host spoke.

"Doesn't my daughter look well? It's such a pleasure to be able to give her this gift."

"I'm sure Lady Elizabeth looks lovely."

"Princess."

"Of course, a slip of the tongue your majesty. Do forgive me Your Highnesses. I shall send the news to my High Lord at once. I'm sure he will wish to send his congratulations."

"Well, you can if you want. I don't see how it's really Tarjan's business."

"The Queen?"

"Will find out soon enough."

"I see." The ambassador bowed again and

returned to his seat.

"That wasn't wise, was it?"

"Bating the Sumoasti? No, father, it probably wasn't."

"High Lord Holmgard is just looking for an excuse to start a war with us. Did we just give him one?"

"I don't think so; but it won't help. He already thinks that you've slighted his granddaughter by sending her to Tarjan indefinitely."

"It's not indefinite, just until she learns some sense."

"We should have sent her to Umar then."

"On what grounds? No, visiting her family is much more acceptable than exile."

"I hate politics already."

"You've been playing politics for years; it's not a game anymore and you can't back out."

"I suppose not. Game or not, I have things to do."

"The children?"

"Yes, we need to set up a school for those unfortunates. And a refuge for the women. They can't go on living in the Watch Houses."

"Well then, announce it. You have full control of your fortune now."

"Right now?"

"Yes. Start as you mean to go on, girl. And then get your dressmaker up here. We've got a party to prepare for."

"Yes father."

Lizzy stood and waited for the silence. She thanked people for their well wishes and added her own thanks to the Officers of the Watch and Investigations for their work, before announcing the founding of a school for those children who had escaped indentured service, and a refuge for the women. There was further polite clapping as Lizzy returned to her throne.

Chapter 13

"So now what?" Lizzy shifted from one foot to the other as she stood for her dress fitting.

"What do you mean Lizzy?"

Caro made the last tiny adjustments to the long tunic dress, fitting it perfectly around Lizzy's bust and hips.

"Well, what does father expect me to do now he's officially adopted me and I'm a princess."

"Act like one?" Caro shrugged; her friend was complaining when she should be celebrating

Lizzy sighed, "It's so much easier being a bastard. I could come and go whenever, now everyone will know who I am."

"Darling everyone knows who you are as it is. You've hardly kept a low profile."

"I don't want things to change,"

"Coward. You're being ungrateful."

"I am not!"

"Yes you are, you're so frightened of responsibility that this honour from your father is a burden to you. You are young, wealthy and influential; think how much good you could do. You own the only newspaper in Albon."

"That's not technically true. I own fifty-one percent of it."

"Well, and so? The rest is owned by the twins. You have a voice. You want to change things here, don't you? Well, now you can."

There was a knock at the door, interrupting the conversation.

"Come in."

"Are you decent?" It was Lawrence.

"Of course."

The door opened and the twins trooped in, dressed in their finest suits. Lizzy looked them over and sighed. Someone really did need to tidy them up.

"Alex, why are you wearing a lime green tie?"

"It matches your dress."

"But not your waistcoat." The waistcoat was embroidered with flowers in a riot of pastel colours. "Caro, do something with them."

"I haven't got time. I really don't understand the fashion for dressing like peacocks."

"We feel like it. Plus, the traditionalists would prefer everyone in black."

"It's a political statement." Alex slumped on to the sofa, crossing his legs at the ankles, showing hideous socks as his trousers rode up above his black dancing shoes, polished to a high shine.

"It's also a statement that you have no concept of refined taste."

Lizzy laughed at Caro's observations; as fond as she was of the young woman, Lizzy often found Caro to be a little conservative, and snobbish at times. The twins looked fairly tidy, even if their ties were a little loud. For once they had even washed their hair, and brushed it.

"Well, are we ready to go?" Alex shifted around the room.

"I'm just finishing this hem," Caro said from her knees, "then you can go and enjoy yourselves."

"Aren't you coming Caro? Lizzy, you did invite

her didn't you?" Lawrence asked, a wrinkle of confusion on his face.

"Of course I did." Lizzy looked down at Caro "I thought you were going to the ball?"

"I can't; it wouldn't be right."

"Nonsense. You've been my friend for six years, of course you should come."

"She's right, you know, Caro."

"Well, when it was just a few of us at the Residence I didn't mind going, but I can hardly come to a royal ball, can I?"

"I don't see why not? It's my party and I'll invite whoever I want."

Caro sighed, "I'm not getting out of this am I?"

"No."

"You do realise I have work to do don't you?"

"New commission?"

"Yes, your friends all want dresses like yours. The long tunic dress has become the fashion item of the season. And since no one knows how to make them except me, I'm really busy."

Caro's 'dresses' were a full, pleated skirt under a contrasting three quarter sleeve tunic top. Lizzy tended to wear hers with trousers rather than a skirt. When she wasn't wearing a shirt. Women traditionally wore subdued, long-sleeved and full skirted dresses, requiring a corset and multiple underskirts. The arrival from Umar of boneless bust supports (a sort of vest tailored to support the female breast) had radicalised women's fashions. Lizzy had been an early adopter of the garment; it had caused quite the stir at court.

"See, I knew setting you up as my personal

dressmaker would work."

"I need extra help. I was going to ask Sandra if she wanted to learn basic skills, putting the skirt waistbands and collars on."

"Doesn't she have to learn it all at the Guild?"

"Only if she wants to set up as a seamstress herself. She can't for another couple of years yet anyway."

"Well, see if she wants to; she's still living with you, isn't she?"

"Yes, and still keeps trying to be my housekeeper. I've told her she's too young to be working and that you're giving me an allowance to educate her."

"She must find it very strange." Alex said from his seat.

"How so?"

"Well, so far she hasn't had a particularly easy life and then suddenly a princess is paying for her education and she lives with a respected dressmaker."

"Bit of a shock to the system." Lawrence explained

"I see what you mean." Lizzy tried to step down from the stool. She was stopped by a yank to her clothes.

"Lizzy, stand still or your hem will be wonky."

"Is this going to take much longer?"

"Almost done. There. Last little bead on."

"Give us a twirl, cuz."

Lizzy was finally able to step down from the stool. She slid her feet into soft grey leather slippers and danced around them all, laughing. The grey silk of her tunic dress floated around her knees. Slit up to her hips, with a contrasting green underskirt, and drawn in beneath her bust, the dress accentuated her figure while releasing her from the confines of traditional Albonese ball dresses.

"Very pretty. Makes a change from men's clothes."

"Aunt insisted I wear a dress for my Ball, she didn't specify the exact pattern."

"I don't think she meant you to wear an extended shirt though."

Caro harrumphed in irritation. Lizzy had insisted on a rational garment that allowed her ease of movement, so she'd based it on the thigh length tunic tops she liked to wear, made longer, with capped sleeves.

Lizzy turned to hug her friend, "It's perfect, if I have to wear a dress. Are you sure you won't come?"

"No, I'm tired and there will be more commissions after they see this creation. Oh, I have a message for you from one of my colleagues. Mady Clair's setting up to make the breast supports. Just breast supports, nothing else. She asked me to let you know; she takes commissions if you want something special."

"Tell her I said thanks, and good luck." Lizzy smiled. Caro's contacts were always sending messages through her; Lizzy's custom was known to bring all the modern ladies to a business.

"I will, now go and make my fortune with that outfit, would you."

"Yes Caro. And enjoy your quiet night in; don't strain your eyes."

Caro laughed and packed her work box away as the bright young things fluttered off to the ball. She had a good reason for not going, other than embarrassment; Robert was expecting her for dinner.

Chapter 14

"Deep breath, cuz, it's just the Court." Lawrence reassured her as they were announced.

"But they're all going to be looking at me."

"Well? That's hardly unusual, is it?"

"It is. Normally they look at me, smile and ignore me. Tonight, I have to pretend I like being starred at."

"Yes, well, it happens to all of us at some point. We'd better get a move on, Father and Uncle are waiting."

Lizzy, her cousins on each arm, stepped out on to the red carpet to walk the length of the Hall to their fathers. They smiled and nodded politely and pretended to care. Their friends – identified by their bright clothes in a room of blacks and greys – waved and cheered, drowning the polite applause.

Eventually - it felt like the longest walk in eternity – they arrived before the dais and bowed to the King. A band struck up as her father stepped down, took Lizzy's hand and lead her out to dance. The Duke and Duchess followed, Lady Mary and Sir Philip joined them. Young Elenor and Prince John – both only seven – joined them, determined to show off the results of their lessons. Alex and Lawrence shrugged and danced with each other, while their friend Beth asked Prince Michael to dance. The rest of the court joined them in the dance.

Lizzy danced with an endless series of courtiers and ambassadors, some who said they'd come 'especially for her Ball' though she knew they were really there to make trade agreements and political alliances. Eventually she had to decline a dance, bowing to the under-secretary to the Belenosian ambassador who had asked her for a further dance, even though she'd just danced three with him and was getting 'looks' from her mother, Lizzy hurried away to find her friends.

They weren't in the Hall, because that was filled with the be-corseted, grey gowned conservatives and their parents, the majority at court. The doors to the garden terrace were open though, the glass reflecting the flickering torches and fluttering crowd back into the ballroom. Beth's laugh became clearer as she got nearer; Lizzy grinned. Beth only laughed like that when she was drunk and flirting; her mother mustn't be around.

"Evening all, shove up Harry, I need to sit down."

Lizzy burst into the conversation laughing.

"Finally got sick of dancing with idiots then?"

"Well, after I danced with you I managed to cope with their conversation quite well."

"You wound me, my dear friend, wound me grievously." Henry grasped at his heart and pretended to faint.

Lizzy elbowed him in the ribs, "Very mature. And this is why I am not marrying you. Ever."

"Glad to hear it, we'd kill each other eventually."

"So, any news?"

"Mother is angry with me." Beth volunteered with a satisfied smile.

"What did you do?"

"Refused to dress like a widow for your party."

"Good god, I wondered how you'd managed to

get away with a new dress."

"I had Marie measure her up last time she came to visit."

"I like the colours. Why do people keep calling them dresses though? They're two separate garments."

"Our mothers would have screaming fits if they thought we were wearing two piece outfits. It took me long enough to convince mine that I really didn't need a corset." Charley's mother was known for being more modern than most of the older women at court, but even she still wore a corset and coif on occasion. Charley found it very embarrassing.

"I like your dress, is it new?" Tessa asked.

"Caro finished it just before the Ball started. I'm losing beads already." Lizzy lifted the hem of the green over dress to show her friends. The pale gold-green beads danced with firelight and the silk slid over her fingers.

"It's not too bad. You should have it taken up a bit to keep the beading off the floor."

"And show more of my underskirt? What a shocking thought." Lizzy gave Tessa a look of mock-horror.

"I don't mind seeing more of your underwear Liz." Gos laughed.

"Well, you know, very few people get to see my underwear."

"We all have."

"Only when I'm drunk."

"You were quite sober last time."

"That's quite enough of that, thank you." Lizzy blushed. She'd known sleeping with Gos was a bad

99

idea when they'd fallen into bed together, but she'd been incredibly horny at the time. She just hoped he didn't think it meant anything; they were friends and friends alone.

"Stop teasing Lizzy, Gos, it's her birthday." Phil, Gos's younger brother, shoved him gently, "And now, my lady, what do you intend to do with your life?"

"How should I know? I don't know what I'm doing tomorrow, let alone the rest of my life. I just hope it isn't as exhausting as the last few months have been. I can't quite face another abduction attempt yet."

"Well, if you're going to be boring..."

"Very funny Phil. No, I think I want a quiet few months, just pottering around with the paper, being a fashion icon and learning this princess lark."

"Yeah, about that, did you know?"

"What that dad was going to officially adopt me? No, no clue. Biggest shock of my life. Other than the time I realised just how tiny your cock is, Gos."

"Thanks."

"We don't need to know." Beth flushed, with wine and embarrassment. She didn't need to hear about Gos's cock.

"No we don't; Beth, will you stay at my house tonight? Your mother looked awfully grim earlier, she probably won't like it that you're drunk as well as immodestly dressed." Charley asked.

"That's what she said?"

"Yeah, we're all dressed like whores and pimps apparently. How she would know about whores and pimps I don't know."

"She does charity work in the city with the Ladies

100

Purity League." Beth volunteered.

"Oh lor' those old bats? They're practically crows, except the Curates don't let women in."

"Except nuns."

"Except nuns. How dull life must be for nuns."

"Drudgery and prayers, no fun times."

"Sad, very sad."

Tessa and Lizzy nodded at each other in agreement, then fell about laughing.

Lady Mary interrupted the silliness half an hour later.

"How much have you had to drink?"

Lizzy looked at her glass as she mentally counted up, "Five or six glasses, not much at all. Compared to this lot I'm sober."

"I see. Beth Warren, your mother wants you, she says she's leaving now, so you'd better get along."

"She's staying at Charley's tonight, mother."

"Does the Countess know that? Or Lady Warren? You children can't go making plans without telling people."

"Mother, we're not children. Every single one of us is an adult. I think we're capable of making our own decisions."

Affronted, Lady Mary glared at her daughter, the daughter she'd seen little of since she'd sent her to the capital as a fifteen-year-old. She still saw the wilful girl who liked to climb trees.

"I should go and speak to mother." Beth muttered quietly.

"I'll come with you, don't want her browbeating you again." Charley stood up and followed Beth back into the ballroom and over to the tables around the edges of the hall where the matrons sat delicately drinking wine and gossiping about their social rivalries.

Out on the terrace, the young people had fallen silent as Lizzy and her mother stared angrily at each other. Lizzy broke her gaze first, feeling guilty about winding her mother up; they hadn't seen each other in two years and it was probably a shock to see her little girl grown up, especially after her father's announcement.

"Come on mother, sit down and have a drink with us. It's my birthday, I'm officially a grown up now, with access to funds."

"And responsibilities. Don't forget the responsibilities. I never do; you're lucky you're not the heir, I have to help run our estates and visit tenants and stuff. It's all very dull." Henry laughed.

"It's your duty to do those things. Oh, Lizzy, I haven't had a chance to tell you, Curate Albert sends his regards, and asks you not to cause too much trouble. He's only just settled down again after the inspection five years ago."

"That wasn't my fault. It was Colvile and the queen."

"And the High Curate."

"Yes." Lizzy hissed, she still hadn't forgiven their much more recent abduction/murder attempt.

"The new boy seems harmless enough though."

"Don't speak about High Curate Cosgard like that Philip Val, or I'll tell your mother to stop your allowance."

He smiled and looked at his brother, their mother couldn't stop his allowance now that she was the Dowager-Lady Val; Gos controlled the family fortune.

"Well, I think I shall leave you young people and return to Sir Philip, he's discussing hounds with the king."

"Really? Why am I not surprised?"

"Because they are both obsessive old men."

"That you love dearly."

"It is fortunate for them both that I do. Perhaps I should leave them to it and hunt down some old acquaintances?"

"That could be fun. How long are you in King's Ford for?"

"Another few days, I'll come and visit you? There must be a lot we need to catch up on?"

"Of course mother, I shall probably be staying here for a few days at least." Lady Mary gave the 'children' a tight smile before rising with an insane amount of grace to return to the ballroom.

"Aren't you coming back to the Residency?" Alex asked when the group were alone again.

"I don't know; I think father would prefer it if I lived here for a while."

"If you bought your own place it would be so much easier." Henry laughed.

"I don't want to just yet; I have a few other things I need to do before that."

"The school and refuge?"

"Yes; I have no idea where to start."

Chapter 15

Lizzy groaned, shifted the damp cloth slightly further over her eyes and sagged further into the settee cushions.

"I am getting too old for drinking."

She reached out blindly, flailing for her water glass and the willow bark pastels. Her ring clinked against the glass, which toppled off the table edge and soaked the rug beneath. Lizzy shifted the cloth once more, rolled slightly on to her side, groaned, and flopped back on to the settee again. She'd have to ring for a servant. Which meant standing up. Lizzy considered just taking the willow bark dry but it tasted vile and her mouth was drier than a desert as it was. She sighed and prepared to stand up. It was a complicated manoeuvre requiring coordination of all her limbs. She couldn't quite manage that, so fell off the settee on to the wet rug and crawled across to the bell pull by her bed. Since she was there Lizzy decided to climb back on to her bed.

She passed out for a few minutes but woke up when a servant arrived carrying a tray with water, more willow bark and a message. Lizzy hadn't seen the servant before; she was tall, and appeared about ten years older than Lizzy.

"Your Highness." The young woman curtsied expertly, "You have a message from the Duke." She handed the single sheet of folded paper to Lizzy while pouring out a glass of water and dispensing two pills from the box.

Lizzy put the letter on the bed besides herself.

"Thank you. I don't know your name."

"I'm your Lady-in-Waiting, Sarah Carnavan, my father is our ambassador to Calman."

"That explains the curtsey. Wait, I get a Lady-in-Waiting now?"

"Yes Your Highness."

"This feels wrong."

"Why?"

"You're a peer acting the servant?"

"So? Aren't we all? You bow to the king and the duke. Everyone else bows to you. It doesn't make any difference. Princesses don't deal directly with servants, Your Highness."

"I think I preferred it when I wasn't."

"Well, you are, so buck up, you've got things to do today."

"Like what?" She'd planned to spend the day wallowing in agony.

Sarah, pulled a small diary out of her pocket and flipped to the first page.

"At midday you have lunch with the Sumoasti ambassador, at three you have a meeting with your father and the duke, I think that's what the letter's about, and this evening you are having dinner with your mother and Sir Philip."

"Do I have to?" Lizzy said, stunned

"Yes. Tomorrow you have a breakfast meeting with the King's Council, at midday you're having lunch with the High Curate and at two you are meeting your estate manager and legal advisor, about your property portfolio."

"One house is not a property portfolio."

"There's the estate in the highlands and several city properties, I believe."

"How do you knew that when I don't?"

"I've spent the last few days with Duke Michael getting up to speed with your legal and business matters. He thinks it's time someone other than him dealt with your finances."

"I can manage."

"Do you know anything about banking? Or rents? Or estates?"

"No, do you?"

"Of course, who do you think runs our family properties while my parents are off visiting the world?"

"Good point."

"And I speak five languages, so you won't need a translator. Now, get up, you have to go to lunch in an hour."

"Urgh. I hate being a princess already."

"Yes, being wealthy beyond imagining and living in luxury must be such a burden."

"There's no need to be like that. I'm grateful for all that, I just meant I'm used to making my own schedule and not having to go to meals with ambassadors I can't stand."

"Well, that, I'm afraid, is called growing up. You're officially an adult member of society now, these burdens are placed on all of us. The One wouldn't give us more than we can handle."

Lizzy looked sideways at her Lady-in-Waiting, "You're not a conservative, are you? Because we might not get on."

"No, I was mostly brought up in Calman, they worship trade, above all else, so I never got the indoctrination. I saw you last night, looking at everyone with such contempt."

"It isn't contempt, it's confusion. Why on earth would people shackle themselves to beliefs that keep them in mental chains?"

"Because they can't see the chains?"

"Then we need to show them the chains. Is there any room in my schedule for property searching? I need to get moving on the school and refuge project."

"I've pencilled in the day after tomorrow, your uncle suggested meeting your manager and legal advisor first, that's why you have a meeting with them tomorrow."

Lizzy looked at Sarah, noticing the slight tension around her eyes, "Thank you, you've got me organised."

"Only because the Duke thought about all of this in advance. He's been making arrangements ever since we got you back from, ever since you were abducted."

"He could have told me."

"You were busy."

Lizzy nodded, it had indeed been a busy few months.

Finally convinced she needed to get up, Lizzy ordered a bath and found some clothes to wear. Sarah did not approve.

"You can't wear your riding clothes for lunch with an ambassador, they'll think we're slighting them. Look this is much better." She pulled out a white blouse with fine, almost transparent lace sleeves and a long pale blue skirt.

Lizzy grimaced but nodded agreement; she could always change later.

"Where do you keep your underskirts and such?"

"Knickers and vests are in that draw. Stockings are in the one below it."

"No shift?"

"No need, it's too hot."

"But an underskirt at least?"

"Don't start. It's too hot for more than the absolute minimum. Now, I'm having my bath."

Sarah rolled her eyes and went to find the clothes. At least she'd be able to get dressed quickly; they'd be late if she was prone to wearing full skirts and corsetry.

Chapter 16

"That's it, no more official business this week, I'm going on strike." Lizzy threw herself into a chair at Caro's house. Sarah rolled her eyes.

"You're being over dramatic Lizzy; it can't be that bad. I've spent the last three days sewing clothes for your fan club, I've had to ask Maria and Mady Clar to help."

"I thought Mady was going into the vest business and Marie Clar only works for the Warrens."

"Beth Warren has asked for a whole new wardrobe, now she's living with the Countess and her daughter."

"I didn't know that, why hasn't anyone told me this?"

"You've been busy. Now let me get you both some tea. No Sandra, sit down, and carry on with your lessons." The girl had risen from her table at the window where she was practising her hand writing, "You know that's not your job anymore. If you really want to get into a Guild school, you need to be able to read and write." Caro shook her head and rang the bell.

"So, tell me."

"Gossip."

"I need to keep up with my friends somehow."

"Lady Warren made a fuss the day after your party about Beth associating with you all and said if she wouldn't come home and go to a convent or get married, she shouldn't come home at all."

"I'd have thought Lord Warren would have had

something to say."

"He did; he transferred a hundred thousand into Beth's accounts and handed all control of her fortune over to her."

"At last."

"They've cut her off though." Caro grimaced at the injustice.

"Ah; it's fortunate the Countess took her in." Sarah said.

"Countess De Narvel wouldn't let her god-daughter suffer. She fostered with her before Beth went to School." Lizzy told her Lady-in-Waiting.

"How on earth did a new family like the Warrens get a daughter fostered with the De Narvel's?" Caro asked.

"Hey, my family are 'new', you know." Sarah protested.

"Service to the Crown for several generations counts, I've never heard it said the Warrens did anything other than lend my great grandfather cash during the second civil war."

Sarah snorted, "It was enough to get them a knighthood and work up from there."

"Fair enough; I'm going to have to remember things like that aren't I? It was so much easier when I could be happily ignorant and just play the game my uncle taught me."

Caro looked pointedly at Sarah.

"It's okay, I'm one of his agents."

"I see. That explains why you're her Lady-in-Waiting."

"I'm still in the room, you know."

"We know, but sometimes you get in the way."

"Thanks ever so, the pair of you."

The tea was brought in and the women were silent as they imbibed.

"So, how went the property search?"

"Nothing."

"Not in the city at least. I think we should look at the monastery the High Curate mentioned. Master Thompson did say he thought it was a good investment." The subject had come up during the various meetings Lizzy had had in the previous days and her estates manager was enthusiastic about the property, an abandoned monastery that the Curates had been hoping to reopen for fifty years and had failed to do so.

"It's out in the wilds."

"Hardly! It's just off the main road ten miles out of the city."

"The land would be valuable too. Does it come with much?"

"A thousand acres."

"Wow, I'm surprised they haven't sold it to developers, that'd be a nice country estate close to the city."

"They were hoping to restore the Sanctuary."

"Ah."

"The new High Curate seems like a fairly sensible, modern man. Better than that martinet who bullied everyone before."

"I suppose there may be hope for us yet."

"They do keep complaining that hardly anyone enters the Seminaries anymore and Lastday service

111

attendance is down."

"It's been falling since the second civil war, in the cities at least."

Lizzy and Caro looked at this unexpected statement from Sarah.

"What? I did a study during my training for the Investigations Office. If you look at the pre- and post-war registers you'll see a marked decrease in Seminary entrants, and a marked increase in those with an exemption from Observance. I show you if you want, there's copies in the Royal Library."

"Well, that's news to me. I was always told if we didn't go to Chapel we'd be fined and imprisoned."

"Without an exemption you could, two hundred years ago. The laws were repealed by the king's father."

"Good man, my Granddad."

"Yes, and unobservant."

"He was not! I remember him being very clear sighted."

"Now you're just being silly."

"Someone has to. And the last few days have been so serious. Send a messenger to Thompson and the High Curate, we'll get the details of the monastery and visit, but not tomorrow."

"Tomorrow you're supposed to be visiting the Old Guards."

"What time?" Lizzy sighed.

"Mid-afternoon, for an inspection."

"Really, can't I have a day off? I want to see my friends."

"You'll see them at Court tonight. But don't get

too drunk."

Lizzy bashed her head on the table with a thud, the tea cups and spoons rattling with the impact.

"You're being a little dramatic."

"I haven't started yet."

"It'll slow down in a few weeks, everyone wants to see the new Princess Royal."

"I have other things to do."

"Like what?"

"The paper?"

"Runs itself quite happily now, actually you're making quite a profit on it. They like your 'Maggie Harford' pieces but don't need them every day, there's all sorts of things happening to write about."

"I think 'Maggie' might be coming for a visit, to interview the new Princess though, and to talk about the school she's founding." Caro suggested.

"Is that such a good idea?" Lizzy wasn't sure, her uncle had been quite adamant about keeping her role in the arrest of Maggie Richards a secret.

"Yes, there needs to be a small announcement anyway, or people will make things up for themselves."

Time, being the contrary creature it was, passed incredibly quickly and the long summer turned into blustery fall-of-leaves quickly, and before she knew what was happening Lizzy was officially opening 'The Princess Elizabeth School and Refuge for

Unfortunates Escaping Illegal Indenture', generally
known as The Princess's School. The wind whipped
her coat about as she climbed down from the carriage
with her father and brothers. The children who hadn't
been returned to their parents and the women who
needed somewhere safe to live had been installed a
month before, teachers, nursing staff and a Matron had
been employed and lessons had already.

The Court had reluctantly travelled out of the city
for the opening; they were huddled in cloaks and coats
around the steps leading up to the main doors. A
lectern had been erected and the High Curate was
performing a service for the residents and any visitors
who cared to listen. Most of the younger members of
Court and a few of the older Unbelievers huddled
together waiting for the royal party to arrive. When the
Duke stepped down from his carriage with his wife
and children to meet the King, the waiting courtiers
tidied themselves up and followed them to the doors.

The High Curate smiled at his congregation and
ended his sermon, bowing to the King as he arrived.
Lizzy had held his arm all the way to the lectern, now
he loosened her death grip and pointed her in the
approximate direction of the crowd.

"Good afternoon, I won't keep you long, the
weather is awful and those children look eager to go in
and get at the food." There was a giggle from the
audience. Lizzy felt herself gain some confidence,
"The circumstances that lead to the founding of this
school have as you all know, been fully reported by
the papers, and resulted in the arrest of several terrible
people. I am far from believing that there are no other

such slavery rings operating in our city and our country. I can only wish that this school and refuge were not necessary, however as they are then I hope this place will provide sanctuary for those who escape such horrors. And with that, allow me to welcome you to The Princess Elizabeth School and Refuge for Those Escaping Illegal Indenture." Lizzy looked around to her father, "We really should have come up with a shorted name, Father."

She stepped back as a pair of servants removed the lectern and led the children and women resident at the School towards the doors. Another servant handed her a pair of scissors; she cut the purple and green ribbon – which matched the children's uniform – and pushed open the doors. As expected, the children high-tailed it to the dining room. Lizzy and the Matron, a small, smiling woman in a severe dress, called Agatha Binns, shook hands with the courtiers who came in to look around.

Tired but happy, Lizzy eventually left, pleading her exhausted brothers who fell asleep at the dining table. There had been compliments from even the most conservative courtiers regarding the restoration and conversion of the monastery into a school. The children were pronounced poor, dear little things and Lord Summerton celebrated finally getting his Watch Houses back.

Chapter 17
Summer A.E. 1334

"Well, this is a disaster." Lizzy said to her cousins at the Residency a day after they received the news that the High Lord of Sumoast had died. Her brothers had joined her on the visit and Michael, at fourteen, was convinced he was an adult and therefore joined their conversation in the parlour. John and Elenor were far too busy helping Catherine to make decorations for an important Umari festival the Duchess was hosting in her temple in a fortnight. Adults, they decided were very silly and worried about the wrong things.

"Why?"

"Don't exaggerate Lizzy. You'll upset the children." Catherine scolded.

"I'm not a child, father says kings don't get to have a childhood."

"Of course Michael. And it's a disaster because your mother hates me."

"Does she? I can't imagine why?"

"I couldn't when I was your age, but since I'm responsible for her being sent home in disgrace for four years, I think we can agree that she probably has good reason to now."

"It's not your fault Lizzy, she tried to have you killed."

"But she hasn't tried since. Maybe she's mellowed?" Michael suggested hopefully.

Alex and Lawrence looked at each other. Lizzy caught the look, "What?"

"Yeah, about that, not so much."

"What do you mean?"

"Well, you know how uncle has had you on official duty for four years?"

"Yes, four incredibly dull years. Some days I never want to hear another fake compliment or attend another gala until I die."

"Yes, well, we've been dealing with a few potential assassins. The Queen, or someone in Sumoast, sends at least three a year. The king wanted you in plain sight until we dealt with them all."

Lizzy paled at the thought, although it did explain why she'd been kept out of Investigations.

"Oh, there haven't been any sent for six months, it's a record. We think she's planning something now that she's able to return."

"Talking of, I though her exile was permanent?"

"Uncle had to renegotiate to stop old Lord Holmgard sending his fleets. Some of the northern Sumoasti are nasty fighters. We wouldn't have won."

"So now my mother's grandfather is dead she's coming back?"

"'Fraid so little brother. And your mother's uncle is High Lord of Sumoast now."

"Yes, I know." The teenager looked thoughtful. "He has a daughter and a son, and mother's mother and he have another brother, younger, who only has one son?"

"That's right. I heard that the Holmgards aren't a particularly pleasant family, but the youngest married some lord's daughter in the north so he could escape the family." Lizzy wracked her brain for information

117

about her enemy's family.

"Is that true Alex?" Michael liked the idea of a cousin brave enough to argue with the war-like Holmgards.

"Oh yes, he was sent on a diplomatic mission, and ended up married. But not to Lord Arun's daughter."

"No, his son." Lawrence laughed at the blush on his royal cousin's cheeks. That sort of thing was not allowed in Albon; the Curates had long disapproved of same-sex attraction and the Moot still refused to acknowledge such partnerships as legal entities.

"Stop teasing my brother; you're embarrassing him."

"I'm not embarrassed, I'm confused. How is that legal?"

"They have different laws in Sumoast, though I hear Lord Holmgard is not amused."

"He never is; the entire clan are miserable wretches."

"That's my family you're talking about."

"You've never met them."

"So, technically they're family."

"Unfortunately they are. Hopefully the Queen won't feel the need to bring any of her cousins back with her."

"She won't; the Holmgards are busy fighting a minor civil war with their northern and eastern provinces."

"Why does nobody tell me this stuff?"

"We didn't want to worry you."

"You were busy."

"Poor excuses."

"Probably. But Father was adamant you weren't to get involved."

"He's so overprotective at times."

"We know. He took the key to the wine cellar off us when he left for the north."

"Cruel. Cruel indeed."

"Incredibly."

"We've been sober for a week. It's terrible."

"I'm sure you'll survive another week until he gets back."

"I don't think we will; take us out won't you?"

"Even I can't afford your bar tab."

"Oh but Lizzy."

"Oh but nothing. You kept me in the dark about attempts on my life. I suppose my Lady-in-Waiting is a bodyguard?"

"Well, you knew she was from the Investigations Office."

"I did; she told me the first time we met."

"Why did you think Father sent one of his Officers to be your Lady-in-Waiting?"

"Because he's nosy and over-protective."

The children stopped playing their games with paint and pens to watch the three of them fighting. Michael sat in his chair, quietly observing his sister and cousins. The atmosphere became tense as the argument continued. Finally, the Duchess interrupted.

"What's done is done, Lizzy, there's no need to keep on about it. You know now and that's all there is to it. Michael did what he thought was best and so did your father; you can't blame them for wanting to give you a few years of peace. Now, supper will be served soon, and I want there to be no fighting or shouting. John, Elenor, tidy up, then go and wash your hands."

The two eleven year olds reluctantly put their creations in a box, desperately jealous of Michael who got to stay and hear the rest of the conversation.

"Hurry, or you'll be late to supper."

The children nodded at the Duchess and rushed out of the room. The faster they washed their hands the faster they would get back to the parlour.

"Now, I think we all need to take a deep breath." Catherine returned to her seat, and started picking up the bits of material John and Elenor had left on the floor and table.

"Yes auntie." "Yes mother." "Of course, mother."

Michael smirked to see his sister and cousins so roundly defeated, until Lizzy glared at him.

Chapter 18
Winter A.E. 1334

"Father." Lizzy dozed in her comfortable chair in the family parlour at the palace. The boys were out playing in the gardens. A fall of snow overnight had turned them into heaven for children (though Michael was adamant he was just keeping an eye on John). Lizzy had had a late night; Caro had announced her engagement to an innkeeper called Robert and there had been a free bar; Lizzy was suffering.

"Yes, my love?" The king had been up late with his council discussing the Sumoast situation, and was also dozing, and waiting for his lunch.

"I want to go on the Belenos trip with uncle and the twins." Lizzy cracked an eye open to see how her father reacted to her request.

"But you've got so much to do next summer."

"Really? Jocinta will be back before then, and quite honestly I don't think I can stand being around her for too long."

"Ahh, yes I see. Look, I know you two don't have the best relationship."

"She keeps trying to have me killed."

"Yes, I know. I'm going to speak to her about that."

"The stupid Sumoasti bitch won't listen."

"Lizzy, that is my wife you're talking about."

"So, it doesn't change anything."

"Try, for once, to understand the position I'm in. She is my wife, the mother of my sons, your brothers. I can't divorce her because Lord Holmgard will declare war if I do, I can't keep sending her into exile, because Lord Holmgard will declare war if I do, and I can't send you away because I love you."

"Well? Have her done in, it's not as though she's popular here."

"No Lizzy, because, Lord Holmgard will' Declare war?"

"Yes! At last, you get it. We're in a bind, that, at the moment, there is no way of escaping. Until we do, you play nicely with the queen. I understand your hatred. To be entirely honest I find the woman impossibly difficult to live with too, but we are in a difficult position."

"We have allies."

"The Umari are too far away to help and the Calmani won't disrupt their trade network for us, unless they're getting something out of it."

He'd been through all the possible options with his Council a dozen times in the six months since the news that Jocinta would be returning after her period of mourning. He personally considered it lucky that the coming of winter had extended the time frame available. Wait and see had become the only possible response after the Sumoasti fleet had sailed into Albon waters; their own fleet was nowhere near large enough to defeat the interlopers.

The Council meeting had been fraught with debate, the night before. Now Lizzy was arguing with him too.

"Am I the King here or not?"

"Of course you are father."

"Then why does everyone keep arguing with

me?"

"Who else is arguing?"

"The Council. For hours, and hours."

"What about?"

"Fleet wants new ships; Foreign Office doesn't want to provoke our enemies."

"They don't have to find out?"

"How do you mean?"

"We have ship yards all 'round the coast, not all of them belong to Fleet."

"Civilian yards?"

"Why not? The Marsh yards build new ships all the time, how would anyone find out of the ship was a merchantman or a man-o-war?"

"It's an idea. I'll suggest it at the next meeting."

"When's that?"

"Next Fifthday."

"I'm not doing anything; I could come to the meeting?"

"Why not? It's about time you learnt to run a country."

"Because I don't have a dozen other things to do." Lizzy smiled.

"Lizzy, are you coming to the Council meeting?" Her Uncle Michael stuck his head round the door.

Lizzy looked up from her notes; Daily Ford had a new rival, the Albon Informer, and were struggling with sales.

"Oh, yes, of course, I just need to put these away." She put her pen down and closed the notebook, sliding it into a draw and locking the draw.

"What are you up to?"

"Nothing much, it's just a few ideas."

"That is a frightening thought."

"Not really. Come on, we have to go to the Council meeting."

"One thing, the Curates are joining us today."

"Why?"

"The High Curate is sick."

"Ahh."

"Yes; I have reasonable suspicion he's been poisoned."

"Right. Who else knows this?"

"John, so far, and the High Curate himself."

"Hmm. Can I see the evidence?"

"Why?"

"Just an idea I had."

"You scare me when you say things like that."

"Well, as long as I'm scaring other people too, what's the problem? Let's go to the meeting."

Lizzy had only ever been in the Council Chamber after a meeting, usually to remind her father that beds were for sleeping in, so it was a refreshing change to see the echoing room swarming with life. The King's Council, sat in their accustomed places around the table, while the visiting Curates Council, and, unusually, a delegation from the Commons Moot, took seats around the edge of the room. The susurration of hundreds of important papers clutched in the sweaty hands of council member and delegates filled the air.

"Take a seat next to John, I'll be back in a moment." Duke Michael whispered under the noise.

Lizzy nodded and walked across to the throne at the head of the table. Lord Summerton stood beside her father talking urgently in his ear. King John noticed her and motioned the Lord Commander of the Watch, and Lord Marshal of the Kingdom, back.

"Explain it to my daughter, Summerton, she'll handle it."

"Yes, of course, your majesty."

"Afternoon, my lord, do you mind if I take that seat?" Lizzy smiled and insinuated herself between the Commander and her Father to sit down.

"Now, what are you bending Father's ear about?"

"We have a slight pirate problem."

"Again? I thought Fleet cleared them out last winter?"

"We did," The First Lord of the Fleet, Lord Jonesey, interrupted, "But they've come back."

"Where are they now?"

"In the Rocks."

Lizzy nodded, the Rocks were a group of tiny islands, little more than sea stacks, a hundred miles to the north of Albon. They were used as a staging post for ships heading to points beyond Umar, but only in extreme bad weather. The Rocks formed a ring, joined at the base. There was one narrow channel in. In poor weather, it was some shelter, when some was

125

marginally better than none.

"It's a hundred miles from our north coast, how are they hurting us?"

"They're right on the shipping lines. We've lost twenty merchantmen this year."

"The year is almost over."

"Two a month, Your Highness, we can't afford to lose ships at that rate, or the trade with the Camari and their allies."

"What do we trade with the Camari for?"

A Moot member, who Lizzy vaguely recognised had heard the conversation in passing, and tentatively offered, "Furs, and whale oil."

"So, it can't be that big a business."

The man blushed, "Well, Your Highness, we, that is the oil merchants, buy the oil from the Camari and sell it to the Belenosi. It's rather profitable, and our control of the trade routes between the two continents help get favourable agreements from both."

"I see, Merchant?"

"Uil, Your Highness. I have a half share in the King's Ford Oil Company, five of our ships have been taken by the pirates."

"And that's why you and the rest of the delegates are here today?"

"No ma'am, we're here because we don't want the Queen back, but we can't afford war with Sumoast either."

"Thank you Master Uil, allow me to think on your problem." Lizzy dismissed the man and sat back to think, though she already had an idea.

"That grin is going to take us to war."

"Not unnecessarily, Lord Summerton."

"But you have an idea?"

"One may be forming, that will solve all of our problems. When is bitch face due to return?"

"In the spring?" Lord Summerton shrugged; there was no definite timetable, everyone was guessing.

"How long will it take to build enough ships to clear out the Rocks?"

"I don't know, next summer at the earliest, probably longer, the shipyards are busy replacing the lost merchantmen." Jonesey nodded.

"Could we do it now with the ships we have?"

"No, the fleet are all at sea or out of the water being overhauled."

"So, we need more ships, and presumably more men to sail them?"

"We've got the men; we could pull in the fishing fleets and merchantmen for a short period if we need more."

"Thank you gentlemen; I presume you'll be bringing the matter up to the Council?"

"Of course. I can't afford to send any more men north to stop the smugglers, nor can Fleets put any more ships to sea to deal with them. We're not desperate yet but we will be if many more of our ships are taken."

"I understand, Lord Commander. I think you should both bring the problem up, and I shall present a small idea."

"This could get nasty."

"It might, but we need to solve these problems, and I think I have a way to do it."

The meeting was called rapidly to order once Duke Michael returned from wherever he had been, and took a seat on the other side of King John.

The Lord Chamberlain stood to welcome the Counsellors and their visitors.

"Gentlemen if you would take your places, the Council of John, seventh of that name, King of Albon is now in session."

He sat back down as King John stood.

"My Lords of the Council, learned Curates, and members of the Commons Moot, we are here today because our island faces a difficult choice. As you know my wife will return from her exile after the winter. She is neither popular nor welcomed by our people. We are a moderate nation, of a secular nature; my wife belongs, as we are all aware to the Fundamentalist branch of the One Light. Honoured and learned High Curate, I ask for your comments at this moment. What is the state of the faith?"

The High Curate, haggard, pale leaning on two younger men and a cane tried to stand.

"Please, learned High Curate," Lizzy gestured, "Return to your seat, we will think it no insult."

"Thank you Your Highness, with His Majesty's permission I will?"

The king nodded.

"My thanks. I have recently taken a survey of our clergy. We have a majority of seventy-three percent who identify as moderate, um, now where's that paper gone, Josh? Oh, yes, thirteen percent who describe themselves as progressive, and, ah, yes, here we are, fourteen percent who describe themselves as fundamentalist or conservative."

"So, most of you are reasonably decent people?" Fleet laughed.

"Yes, of course. Even my conservative colleagues may be described as reasonable people, with a little less flexibility in their approach to Unbelievers. The Queen is a convert, and was under the influence of Fundamentalist clergy before exile. I understand from our records that a young curate called Lucal attends her in Tarjan now. We have no record of his beliefs however."

"You're being very generous, High Curate, considering someone has poisoned you, and the I.O. has traced it back to my father's wife."

"Yes, well, the One will judge her actions and mine, Your Highness. I do not have the energy to hate, merely to set the Faith in order before I am called to Him Who Made Us."

"I wouldn't have so much generosity, High Curate," Lord Summerton grimaced, "I'd treat her as the criminal she is."

"Summerton do try to remember you're talking about our queen."

"Doesn't stop her from being a criminal, does it? It's not like I don't have enough on, dealing with smugglers and pirates, as well as our usual criminal classes."

"Smugglers, Lord Commander? What about our

129

ships?" The Elder of the Moot, Master Johnson, stood from his place. "What are we going to do about that? It's all very well arguing over the queen and the clergy, but real people are suffering because of the pirates."

"Elder Johnson," The Lord Chamberlain stepped forward, "We will proceed in the order of our agenda. The pirates will be dealt with next."

The old man grumbled and took his seat again.

"What about our voice?" A younger man, in rich furs stood, a few seats down from the Elder.

"Your voice?"

"Yes, the Moot have met and we have decided we don't want her back here. She caused difficulties for the Guilds ten years ago when she had them shut down, we've only just got ourselves back up and running again. How do we know she won't try to control the merchants again?"

"Sit down Rod, we're not here to discuss whether the queen returns from exile, we're here to make our case for help with the pirates." Elder Johnson lifted his cane to prod at the young man.

"Gentlemen, please, there's no need for violence. May I summarise the collective opinion so far?"

There was a general murmur of consent, as Lizzy stood, she gestured to the King's Council members, "My Lords, I believe that you are not in favour of ending the queen's exile, is that correct."

The Lords nodded.

She turned to look at the Curates, "Learned Curates, you are in favour of forgiving the queen's previous criminal behaviour but are wary of her influence on the clergy?"

The High Curate looked at his Council members and nodded in agreement.

"And you, honoured delegates of the Commons Moot, you do not wish to see her return because she damaged your Guilds?"

"That's right."

"Thank you. We have a problem then. The queen is unwelcome in Albon, except among a small minority of Fundamentalists and Conservatives. However, we cannot deny her return, because her uncle, the High Lord of Sumoast will declare war. We cannot afford a war; is it not the case, Fleet, that we are short of ships now?"

"Yes, the entire fleet needs overhauling and refitting."

"And, Lord Marshal, what is the state of the Regiments?" Lizzy addressed Sommerton.

"Honestly Your Highness, they need overhauling too. We're so used to fighting at sea I don't think they'd be able to muster on land at all."

"So our fleet and our regiments are not prepared for war. The purpose of this discussion should be to determine what action we should take."

"We've been over every possible solution, there is nothing that can prevent the queen returning."

"Uncle, you're being pessimistic. We'll think of something."

"You already have."

"Elder Johnson, please keep your delegates in order."

"It's fine Lord Chamberlain. Master Reg?" The man bowed, "What makes you think that?"

"You were speaking to Master Uil, Lord Fleet and Lord Watch before the meeting started."

"Indeed I was. And indeed, I do."

"So, daughter, tell us."

"We can't stop her returning without starting a war, but we can delay her return."

"I don't see where you're going with this Lizzy."

"Well father, it would be terribly irresponsible of us to expect the queen to travel in pirate infested water, wouldn't it?"

"Of course, I couldn't possibly risk her life."

"Until we can clear the pirates out of the Rocks we can't possibly send a ship for her."

"They'll realise it's a delaying tactic."

"But they won't be able to declare war."

"And we do need to clear the Rocks. We rely on the oil and fur trade." Elder Johnson added.

"We don't have enough ships to clear the Rocks." Fleet insisted.

"Let's build some."

"The ship yards are busy replacing the ones we've lost to the pirates." A Moot delegate pointed out.

"So they are. I suppose Fleet will just have to wait for his ships until after the merchantmen are complete."

"But that could take months."

Lizzy smiled.

"You conniving wench, Lizzy Fitzroy." Lord Summerton laughed. He finally got it! "We send a message to the Queen to tell her we'll send our best ship as soon as it's safe to do so. Sorry, sea lanes are pirate infested, we need to clear them first."

"Then we build more ships to clear the Rocks, and oh look we have a brand new fleet. How fortuitous."

"And what are the regiments doing?"

"Training? Organising? If any of the others object, we've got a pirate and smuggler infestation to deal with."

The First Lord of the Chancery laughed, "It may work, but how do we pay for it?"

"We have funds, do we not?"

"Some, but a new fleet and regiments will cost money."

"Gentlemen of the Moot, Curates, we may need to increase taxes, on land and goods, if we're to improve our fleet and regiments enough to destroy the pirates and keep the routes with the Camari and Belenosi open." King John spoke, finally, after leaving everything to his daughter and ministers.

The merchants in the Moot delegation were perturbed by royal pronouncement. Jowls wobbled, there was scowling. Someone cried out, "Now hang on a minute, why should we pay for it?"

"Do you want these problems solving or not?" Duke Michael growled, "Either we raise the funds for a new fleet and regiments, or the pirates continue to destroy your ships and damage our trading arrangements."

"His Grace is quite right," the High Curate spoke for his Council, "There is no other choice. We have to find the money somewhere, and I've no doubt a tax on all land and income will be implemented."

The King's Council looked uneasily at one other.

"Of course. Everyone must contribute." King John declared.

And so began the campaign.

Chapter 19
Spring A.E. 1335

Lizzy banged her head on her desk.

"Elizabeth, what are you doing?" Sarah asked, after five years she was weary of Lizzy's displays.

"Sorry, I fell asleep."

"Again? How late were you up last night?"

"Too late."

"It was after midnight when I left, how long did Charley stay for?"

"Another three or four hours."

Sarah raised her eyebrow. Lizzy blushed.

"We had to discuss the itinerary for the cruise, then we got distracted. Discussing history."

"You're not going on that cruise until next year, why worry about the itinerary now?"

"We wanted to get the basic outline sorted."

"Uhuh, I believe you, thousands wouldn't."

"What precisely are you implying?"

"You and Charley are very close."

"We've been friends for years. Now Beth and Tess are married and hiding at their estates with husbands and babies, I don't get to see many of my friends. Gos is in Belenos playing diplomat. Phil and Henry are busy with their regiments; it's nice just to spend some time with an old friend who doesn't expect me to be a princess all the damn time."

"You need new friends."

"Everyone at court either avoids me like the plague because they think it'll help them when the

Queen returns or they fawn all over me."

"It happens dear, it happens. Come on, leave your writing for a while and have a nap."

"I'm not a child Sarah."

"No, but sometimes you act like one. And tonight, we have another meeting with Fleets and Marshal. You can't afford to be distracted."

"I suppose so. Wake me up in time for supper, will you?" Lizzy scraped her chair back, making Sarah wince at the sound, and the damage to the wood of the floor. She left the room to find her rather comfortable bed. Someone had made it for her so she threw herself on top of the covers and was snoring in minutes.

Sarah tidied Lizzy's desk, trying to organise the jumble of notes she would need for the meeting that evening. Sarah sat back down on the sofa and started writing her own reports for the Duke. Once finished, she started on the translations he had sent her to do. There were reports from their Calmani office mostly. She was the most fluent in the language that the Investigations Office had. It was getting dark when she finished and the sunset bell was ringing in the city. Rubbing her eyes and folding her papers back into their case, she stood, creaked, stretched and went to wake a princess for dinner.

"Well, gentlemen?"

Lizzy had assembled the committee in her rooms. Sarah stood by making notes while Jonsey and the

Secretary of the Fleet took one sofa, and Sommerton and his Secretary of Regiments took the other. Papers were spread around them.

"We're starting the construction of the second dozen soon." Fleet took a sip of his wine.

"How soon?"

Fleet looked at his Secretary who handed him a sheet of paper, "Midsummer."

Lizzy breathed a sigh of relief. They'd spent the winter hurrying the merchantmen through the shipyards and by spring had got the first dozen keels laid for the new fleet. The ship builders had gone on strike for more pay because they were being forced to work longer hours. Once that was agreed the work had restarted but was three weeks behind schedule.

"And the regiments?"

"We've started to overhaul the system. A lot of the lords don't like it."

"They're used to having complete control of their men."

"Well, the men are soldiers of the crown, not the lords. They'll just have to wind their necks in a bit."

"They don't like the standardised uniforms. Lord Gordon asked me how he was supposed to know which were his if they weren't wearing his colours."

"I hope you suggested something useful."

"I told him to stop being a ninny."

"I'm sure that's exactly what you said Sommerton. How are we doing financially?"

The Secretaries rifled through their papers. The Secretary of the Fleet answered first.

"We could do with more money for outfitting the

ships we already have. Most of it's going on the new ships."

"You'll have to wait for the midsummer tax return."

Fleet Secretary nodded. He'd known that would be the case. "But you will factor it into the budget then?"

"Of course. Regiments? How are you doing?"

Secretary of the Regiments looked down at his notes again and shifted his spectacles into place.

"We have twenty full regiments so far, and another five being formed, but I think that might be our limit for now. We haven't enough officers to form any more regiments."

"Ask for volunteers?"

"Tried that, nobody will play."

"Promote officers we already have?"

"Done that already; about seventy-five percent accepted their promotions."

"I see. Well, we'll just have to keep working on it. Have you asked any women?"

"We can't have women in the regiments."

"Why not?"

"They can't fight. Women get squeamish and faint at the sight of blood. And what if they get captured?"

Lizzy looked at Sarah, who shrugged.

"You're making quite a few assumptions there, Fleets. Women in Umar fight." Lizzy glared at the Secretary.

"And in Belenos."

"Do they really, Sarah? I didn't know that."

"If you're lucky, when you visit next summer you might get to see some of the Blood Maidens. They're very impressive."

"And scary. I've seen them."

"When Secretary?"

"I was Secretary at our Embassy in Belenos before I joined Regiments. There was some rioting one year over the bread dole. The Maidens stopped it."

"Against unarmed civilians? Anyone, even women, can seem impressive then."

"No, not just civilians. Some of the legions had joined the riots and were organising the rioters. I don't blame the Belenosians for rioting, the bread dole was particularly stingy that year, especially when the Empress had spent so much on her son's birthday games."

"How decadent."

"Very. But the Maidens destroyed the legions and the civilians."

"So, women can fight. Sommerton, I suggest you start recruiting."

"We'll do what we can."

The meeting continued with Sommerton grumbling about women in his army and Jonsey wanting to know where the money was coming from. By the time it had wrapped up, Lizzy had a headache and Sarah's hand was cramping from writing.

"Good evening gentlemen, come back if there's any urgent news before our next meeting."

"When are we meeting again?"

"Three days before midsummer, to finalise the budgets and progress report. Now, if you'll excuse me

139

gentlemen, I'm exhausted."

The four men bade her good evening and left to return to their own offices and argue.

Chapter 20

Midsummer came and went, and soon another fall-of-leaf was on them. The budgets were set and recruitment increased. A surprising number of women had enlisted but they were still short of experienced officers until the Duchess called on her family in Umar during the summer. A group of older, battle-trained women arrived in the months that followed and were integrated into the regiments. Sommerton, while surprised by their arrival, had been impressed and at the first opportunity had expressed his admiration, thanking the Duchess gratuitously for her help. Lizzy merely wondered how they would pay the higher wages their only experienced troops would expect.

The addition of women to Albon's traditionally male regiments had caused a stir among the Curates, some of whom denounced it as a wicked innovation. It had another, more surprising, effect, which came to Lizzy's notice one morning, late in the year.

"Miss Lizzy, nice to see you this morning." The editor of the Ford Daily, Peterson, stood as Lizzy dripped into his office over the print room below. She could hear it thumping through the brick walls.

"I'm Maggie here, you know that." Lizzy shut the door and took her accustomed seat, looking out of the window at her enterprise.

"Aye, but only when I print the paper. You got anything for us?"

"Yes, a report from the parade last Holyday. I thought it might encourage a few more to join, and court gossip about the Queen. We had a message from

141

Tarjan a few days ago, the High Lord is fretting because we haven't let her come back yet." She pulled out various papers from her bag.

"Nobody wants her back."

"I don't, certainly, but." Lizzy shrugged, she couldn't speak for the other four million people who call Albon home.

"Your pamphlets are selling well, especially the one about universal suffrage. The Moot aren't happy though."

"Ignore them, they just don't like the idea that beggars might get to vote as well as burghers. Anything else going on that I should know about?"

"Yeah, it might interest you to know there's a petition going around. The nuns want to preach."

"Really? But aren't they supposed to be shy and retiring?"

"Only officially."

"Interesting. And how did you hear about this petition?"

"We got a letter," The editor rubbed his chin, "Last week, from one of the Sisters of Mercy, asking for our support. By which she meant you."

"Hardly."

"Lizzy, everyone knows this is your paper."

"I hardly have anything to do with it."

"But it is public record that you own the paper, for those who care to find out."

"Yes, it is. So, what do the sisters want?"

"Support against the new High Curate."

"I'm not getting involved. It's an internal matter."

"What about the Regiments?"

"I'm head on the committee for recruitment. That was my business; this isn't."

"I'd have thought you'd be in support of this?"

"I'd rather not have any of them; we don't need their ridiculous god."

"Really Lizzy? That's not very egalitarian of you, is it? They tolerate atheists but you won't give them the time of day?"

"Why should I? The clergy are the ones who've tried to kill me."

"They were working for the queen."

"Well, their religion should have told them that killing is wrong."

"You're being very childish, for a grown woman. Stop it and think for a change."

"How dare you!" Lizzy stood quickly, her chair clattering to the floor as she stormed out of the room and slammed down the stairs.

Outside, still wrathful, she climbed into her covered carriage, ordering Dawson to drive her back to the palace.

"What is the matter with you?" Sarah looked up from her notes.

"Nothing." Lizzy stared out of the window of her carriage, fiddling with her hat.

Sarah kept quiet; experience told her that Lizzy would tell her about it eventually. She lifted her notes again and returned to work; the Office had intercepted some messages bound for the Sumoasti Embassy, written in Calmani. Naturally everyone at the Office was suspicious; if the Sumoasti were trying to work on the burghers of Calman, there was a chance the Calmani would stop supporting Albon's efforts to winkle out the pirates still infesting the Rocks. The last thing they needed was the other two large islands in the archipelago allying against Albon.

Her work was interrupted just as they left the city for the royal road that lead to the palace, a mile long winding gravel track-way leading uphill, away from the noise of the city through manicured countryside – minus all the normal things found in the country such as sheep, cows and untidy trees. It was a pretty illusion, like so much else in life. Sarah sighed at this reflection and returned her attention to Lizzy; she was in the middle of a sentence.

"...then he said I wasn't very egalitarian because I wouldn't talk to the nuns. What do you think?"

"What do the nuns want?"

"I just told you that, would you listen for once? The old bats want to be able to preach in public."

"Oh, right, is that all?"

"No, I told you, Peterson said I wasn't egalitarian enough. I can't believe he said that, after everything I've done to help."

"You live in a palace and receive more in a year than most people earn in a lifetime, I think that might just be colouring your views."

"I don't see how it matters where I live, my politics aren't affected by my income."

"Yes they are. You don't have to worry about where your next meal is coming from, so you have time to sit around arguing with your equally wealthy and privileged friends."

"Sarah, do you have a heretofore unexplored republican streak?"

"I was brought up in Calman, technically a republic, mostly an oligarchy. I can't imagine Albon would be any better. We'd have to completely take apart society and rebuild it if we wanted any different outcome."

"What are you saying?"

"You and your well-meaning friends are fiddling around the edges. Yes, we need to enfranchise the entire population, that would be great, and we need access to education and medicine for everyone, I'm not arguing with that; in fact, I'm rather proud of your efforts to spread free schools and hospitals. What I am saying is, our efforts are no good if in the end someone is still being exploited."

"So, what, we shouldn't bother trying to change anything if we don't remove the old system altogether?"

"That's not what I said." Sarah sighed; why did the Duke have to give her the job of teaching Lizzy politics? "I said you're doing good but we haven't got to the root of the problem, we're attacking the symptoms, not the cause."

Lizzy stared at the neatly cut grass passing by outside her window. Eventually, after she'd turned a few things over in her mind, she said,

"Everyone works for someone. Even me."

"But you have a choice in the matter. You don't have to work at all. You choose to spend your time this way, because you don't have to live on what you make from writing. If you did you'd starve and we

145

both know it."

"Or I'd be in prison by now."

"That too. Think about it, how many people, ordinary, working people do you know, who get to decide how they live their lives?"

"No one."

"Right. And if they could?"

"Well, I suppose they'd rather not work eighteen hour days?" Lizzy seemed hesitant.

"Quite probably." Deciding she'd given the princess enough to think about for one day, Sarah returned to translating intercepted messages. She could do with not working eighteen hour days too.

Chapter 21
Early Summer A.E. 1336

Lizzy sighed over the reports in front of her, her back burning as early summer sunlight streamed through the great windows of her study; the ships were built, the men, and women, trained, the supplies paid for and aboard, now they were just waiting for the right moment to strike, it seemed.

"Well, gentlemen, and lady?" The committee had been joined by a distant cousin of Duchess Catherine's (it seemed everyone in Umar was related to the Duchess), Commander Shahanna Armanno.

"My regiments will embark in three days, Commander Armanno will lead her regiments north tomorrow."

"Thank you, Lord Sommerton. Lord Jonsey, are the ships ready?"

"Oh yes, and the Royal Swallow will be my flag ship."

"Does father know you're taking his favourite toy to war?"

"Indeed he does. It was all I could do to stop him coming with us."

Lizzy smiled, she'd missed that meeting because she'd had to go to a free schools' committee meeting. It seemed she'd missed the fun.

"And do we have enough ammunition?"

"Yes, I hope it won't take all that much cannon shot to bring them to their senses but you never know."

"And your men, are they used to the cannons

yet?"

"They are, though I'm taking them out to play in the bay tomorrow. Cannon fire below decks can be a bit disorientating if you aren't used to it."

"Good, I expect with you three in charge of the expedition, I can finally go on my cruise without worrying."

"I see, leaving us to do the hard work while you swan around Belenos."

"Oh yes." Lizzy grinned, "I think I may have earned a holiday. Thanks for releasing Phil and Harry from command so they can come on holiday with me."

"I'm not releasing them from command. They're going as your bodyguards, with a dozen men each, and you know it. Anyway, our Umari ladies are much better soldiers and officers." Lord Sommerton grinned.

"Yes, yes, I know. And aren't we lucky that auntie has so many relatives willing to help us."

"You pay well." Commander Armanno laughed, "Better than the Calmani and Camari at least."

"That is a relief; I wouldn't want us relying on unreliable officers." Lizzy laughed; the loyalty of the Umari who had joined the regiments was to their queen and by extension their queen's representative in Albon, Lady Catherine, Duchess Alboni.

"You're not getting a holiday Lizzy; you know Duke Michael is sending us both for his own reasons." Sarah hinted.

"We don't want to know, if the Office is up to something, the Regiments and the Fleet need to keep out of it."

"It has nothing to do with the Office. He's trying

to marry me off."

"Lizzy!"

"What? If I can't trust the Lord Marshal and the Lord Admiral, who can I trust?"

"Me, and possibly Caro. I have my doubts about everyone else. Including Duke Alboni."

"Thanks Sarah."

"So, who does he wish you to marry?" Commander Armanno asked.

"Some Belenosian prince. How dull!"

Commander Armanno filed the information away; if it had finally been decided that Princess Elizabeth Alboni should marry – something everyone had discounted by the time she was twenty-five – then the Umari Queen might be interested in offering her son or daughter as a match. Everyone knew Lizzy wasn't choosy.

"It could be useful, if the Sumoasti decide to attack."

"Thanks Fleet, because that's a reason to marry."

"Hey, some of us married for strategic reasons and it turned out well."

"You're forgetting my father's disastrous marriage of course."

"Well, yes. Sometimes it's best to."

"I don't intend to marry anyone; I'm having far too much fun being single."

"We've heard."

"Not all the rumours are true you know; I keep her out of the worst trouble."

"And we, as a nation, are truly grateful for that Sarah."

"Thank. You. Now, if you've finished speculating about my apparently not so private life, is there anything else?"

"Yes, the twins are going to Belenos with us."

Lizzy groaned, her cousins, trouble-makers-in-chief and current embarrassment to the kingdom, would not help her avoid marriage.

"They have a job to do for the Duke. That is Office business, so unless there's anything else you need to discuss I'd recommend the Commanders and Secretaries leave."

"Anything?" Lizzy looked around the room.

The three commanders and their so far silent Secretaries, shook their heads and stood to leave, bowing on the way out.

"So," Lizzy asked over lunch, "Why are the boys coming to Belenos with us? I thought Uncle needed them to find evidence when the fleet attack the Rocks?"

"He's sending some of the others to do that. I think he just wants to keep them safe; I could do the job he needs doing in Belenos."

"Which is?"

"Oh, yes, our under-secretary has gone missing."

"Isn't that Gos Val?"

"Yes." Sarah looked at her plate, carefully setting down her knife and fork before facing Lizzy. She was pale.

"How long has he been missing?"

"Two weeks."

"Where has he gone missing? Why was he there?"

"The Duke needed someone to collect a few messages from one of our agents in Belenos. Lord Val is less noticeable than any of our other staff in Belenos."

"So they sent Gos."

"Yeah. His horse was found in the stable of an inn, just outside the city, on Imperial Highway East. His servant was unconscious in the straw next to the horse. The only information we have from the man is that they stopped at the inn overnight and he was drugged at breakfast the next morning. He has no idea what happened to Lord Val."

"Damn it Gos!"

Taking just one servant had been foolish, but Gos probably thought he'd be fine. The idiot always underestimated the circumstances, in Lizzy's opinion, and eventually something was going to teach him caution, but not this.

"The twins are to accompany you to the imperial palace, and make delicate enquires. If anything turns up they have to follow the trail. They will find something. While you've been busy being a princess, they've become rather good Officers. No wonder the Duke won't adopt them; he'd lose two of his best weapons."

"I think their mother is stopping him, actually. Lady Eleanor has been a possessive bitch for as long as I've known her. She doesn't want my cousins, but she'll be damned if Uncle and Auntie can adopt them officially."

"Yes, well, either way, they're good at what they do, so don't worry, we'll find your friend, one way or another."

"Yes, that's what I'm worried about. Oh! Has anyone told Phil?"

Sarah patted her hand, "The Duke is telling him today, and the Dowager. Were you two ever?"

"Lovers? No, not really. I haven't slept with all my friends you know."

"Well, Beth isn't interested in women, and neither is Henry, so I suppose that's the pair of them discounted. But the others?"

"On odd occasions. We got drunk a lot when we were younger. Growing up has made us boring, except on rare days when we get to not be adults once in a while." It wasn't really as simple as that but Lizzy found it hard to articulate her feelings; she loved her friends, some of their friendships had a physical aspect, but it wasn't the most important part of those friendships. Love was.

"You sound sad."

"I am; life has been too serious these last few years. I miss my friends, I miss the twins, I miss not having so many responsibilities. Or so many enemies."

"You have a total of one enemy."

"But she has so many friends."

"Not as many as you'd think."

"Here, no of course not, except a very few fundamentalist curates and their flocks, but in Sumoast? I'd have thought she would have a few."

"The Holmgards are only popular among the Tarjani, their own tribe. The rest of the Sumoasti can't stand them."

"Of course, the three tribes. But haven't there been alliances and such for centuries?"

"We've had alliances and such for centuries with different nations; does that mean we actually trust each other?"

"Politically? No, of course not, everyone is out to get the best for themselves."

"Something like that. I'm glad you've been listening to my politics lectures. It's only taken six years."

"I listen, I don't always understand, but I listen."

"That's good, it'll help when we're in Belenos; especially if we want to find Lord Val quickly."

"Oh poor Gos!" Lizzy despaired, the chances of finding him alive were small. It would take two weeks to sail to the Imperial capital, after so long could there possibly be any chance of finding him alive? "How far has the investigation in Belenos got?"

"Other than finding his horse and servant? Nothing much. He was heading out of the city but we don't know where to, he'd been in contact with our agent but their communications haven't been found in the Embassy."

"So we contact the agent."

"Tried, she's been out of touch for almost as long as Lord Val has been missing, her last message arrived two days after he left, asking why he hadn't met her yet."

"Damn. Do we know where she's based?"

"She isn't based anywhere."

"I didn't think uncle approved of using itinerants?"

"She's reliable, and a former Officer."

"I see."

"Our Officers already in Belenos are tracing her movements but she's good at her job."

"Have I ever met her?"

"Once, long ago. You remember the indenture case?

"Yes, of course."

"The junior Officer who met you at the notary's office?"

"I see; I didn't take all that much notice of her at the time." Lizzy remembered sharp eyes and not much else about the woman.

"No one ever does, it's why she's so good at her job. If we lose her as well as Lord Val our network in the Empire will be in ruins."

"Why are we reliant on two Officers for the whole of the Empire?"

"They're the only two who know who everyone in the network is."

Lizzy dropped her head in her hands as the enormity of the situation became obvious to her. Albon relied on the network of Officers and their informants to pre-empt their enemies' actions. The Empire wasn't much of a problem, they were too busy focusing on their own intrigues to be a threat, but everyone had embassies in Belenos. The current situation in the Isles made their network in the Empire essential; diplomats that wouldn't talk to each other in

154

the islands mixed freely in the Empire.

"We are screwed." Lizzy looked up, staring at her bodyguard/Lady-in-Waiting.

"Not yet. We don't know what the Commanders will find when they get to the Rocks, and by the time we get to Belenos there might be news about Lord Val and our Officer."

"That's a hell of a thin thread to hang the nation by."

"Yes, well it's the only one we've got. The Umari can't send us any more help and the Calmani are keeping out of things."

"How many more ships do we have in the yards?"

"Three being made in the north and there's one almost finished in the Marsh. Your step-father has been overseeing it himself."

"Really? I'm surprised he's prised himself away from his dogs and his crops."

"I think your mother might have had something to do with that." Sarah laughed briefly, then became serious again, "We can keep the Sumoasti at bay if we have to, but I think everyone would prefer it if we didn't have to go to war at all."

Lizzy nodded, her features grave. "So, are we leaving early for the Empire?"

"No, it would look like we were panicking if we did; whomever has Lord Val will be watching us for a reaction."

"It has to be Holmgard." Lizzy pushed her empty plate away from her, leaning back to think, "They're the only ones with any reason to start a fight with us at the moment."

"Not necessarily; it could just be a coincidence."

"It's not a ransom abduction, we'd have had a demand by now. The Calmani won't let anything interfere with their trade routes, same goes for the Belenosians." She ticked off their neighbours and rivals on her fingers, "The Camari don't have a presence in the Empire, and the Umari have no reason to hurt Gos, or their links with us."

"Leaving only our 'friends' in Tarjan. The Duke has come to the same conclusion but we have no proof."

"That's why we're really going to the Empire? To get proof?"

"Yes. I know you and Charley were looking forward to a holiday, but we have work to do."

"What does uncle want me to do?" Lizzy was resigned to her path now; there would be no holiday, no sightseeing. The road she had started on before her legitimation had returned beneath her feet. She'd lost six years though, being a Princess.

"You are going to flirt and dance, and act the flighty fine lady."

"Won't people find that a bit suspicious? My friend has just disappeared."

"No-one knows that yet, as far as we know, except those responsible."

"And what is the purpose of my acting?"

"Distraction. We need the Empress and her court to be looking at you while we investigate. Flirt with her sons, and ambassadors. Pretend to be ignorant and silly."

"I'm not sure I can do that."

"Spend a bit of time around other court ladies and you'll work it out."

"But they're so dull."

"Then be dull."

"No."

"Lizzy, you have a job to do, just like everyone else; don't be a brat about this."

"Sarah, I'm not being a brat. I can't be what I'm not. You and uncle have done a fine job of teaching me to be serious; how can I act like my only education is in dancing and embroidery?"

"Don't shout Lizzy."

"I apologise; I can't do this Sarah. Why can't I just be myself? That usually distracts people enough."

Sarah laughed, the tension easing slightly. "Yes, I suppose it does. But, we still need you to at least dress like a court lady."

"Not the corsets, please?"

"I'm afraid so, and three petticoats."

"Make it one and I'll agree."

"No. You can wear your normal clothes except when we're at the Empress's court or attending official events. Your father has already ordered five full outfits, in variations of our colours."

"Oh dear, please tell me Caro is making them? She knows my sizes and has some taste."

"Don't worry, I approved the designs myself."

Lizzy looked Sarah up and down, assessing her dress for the first time. She nodded, accepting Sarah's expertise; you'd never notice the knives and hidden pockets unless you knew they were there.

"Well, what next?" The day was passing; despite

the news there was nothing much they could do from King's Ford.

"You have a meeting with the Decency Committee this afternoon."

Lizzy groaned; she'd met them a couple of times, and each time she had laughed at their proposal for reforms meant to bully people into conforming with their ideas of 'decency'. She wondered what they wanted this time.

Chapter 22

"Your Highness, it is very kind to see us at such short notice. We know you must be busy, especially as you are leaving for a pleasure cruise soon." The committee chairman said 'pleasure cruise' as though it meant 'orgy'.

Lizzy smiled, "Well, we do have other commitments in the Empire but as you say, it will also be a holiday. We anticipate many pleasures. Now, what can we do for you today?"

"Our members have collected a petition; we'd like to present it to the King's Council for their consideration." The chairman, a Curate from one of the small villages to the south of the capital presented a small roll. Sarah swooped into take it from him and unrolled it.

"To what does the petition pertain?" Lizzy looked at the committee but asked Sarah.

"The extraordinary sexual licentiousness of the Court and the deleterious effect it is having on public morals." Sarah read the heading on the petition gravely.

"Really?" Lizzy nodded, her eyes widening slightly in innocent interest. She was really quite good at this acting lark. The committee members seemed to think she was taking them seriously, if their earnest nodding was anything to go by. Lizzy lay back on her couch, lifted her feet from the floor. She reclined as waved for the committee to continue, sipping from a glass of wine.

The chairman seemed a little distracted; Lizzy put

it down to her dress riding up slightly, revealing a pair of black trousers and riding boots. She hitched the dress up around her knees for a little more comfort, and if Sarah hadn't coughed discretely would have removed it entirely.

"It's getting rather warm this early in the summer isn't it? I must talk to my dress maker about some lighter clothes. Now, you were saying something about a petition."

"Well, yes, but I'm not sure you're the right person we should be speaking to." The Chairman made to rise, his committee members following suit.

Lizzy watched with polite interest as they collected their papers, no doubt evidence of the corruption of public morals, until Sarah prodded her in the shoulder. Lizzy rolled her eyes at her Lady-in-Waiting and sat up straight.

"I really am interested in your petition; is that your evidence?" Lizzy gestured to one of the women, a mature merchant's wife in a black dress and coif.

The woman coughed and reddened, looking at the Princess suddenly addressing her and the committee chairman determined to leave.

"Mistress?"

Sarah leaned down and whispered the woman's name in her ear, "Mistress Launston, please, answer me."

"Of course Your Highness. Yes, this is a list of the courtiers attending a late theatre."

"A late theatre?"

"Yes, they are open until midnight, playing most scandalous plays."

"Ah yes," Lizzy looked through the list, "I see my cousins the FitzAlboni twins are on your list. When was this made?"

"Last Sixthday, Your Highness. We were most shocked to see Duke Alboni's sons there, though I don't know why, they are well known dilettantes."

"They do enjoy life don't they? Last Sixthday, now let me think." Lizzy tapped her lips with the paper, "Sarah, didn't the twins invite us out to the theatre that night?"

"Yes, Your Highness, to see 'The Maid of Umar', an historical tragedy I believe."

"That's right. We couldn't go because I had a meeting with the Fleet Board about rations. Such a long dull meeting, and we could have made the second half if we'd rushed."

"You didn't attend, surely, Your Highness?"

"No, not at all. By the time I got out of the ration meeting it was far too late to be gallivanting across town to see half a play."

"And you had a visit to the School early the next morning." Sarah added.

"Of course, the uniform meeting." Lizzy smiled at Mistress Launston, "Those poor children, their parents can barely afford shoes, but we supply the uniform, so that helps a little I suppose. Sarah, that reminds me, have a note sent to Matron would you, I want a report of the needs of our students."

"Of course Your Highness, I'll send it immediately."

"Thank you dear. Now, this play, I understand is an historical work. How is it lewd?"

"The acts of murder and adultery are glorified."

"Yes? How odd, as I understand it the real Maid of Umar was forced into a marriage with an abusive chieftain; she was in love with another. One night she fought back and killed her husband. After her husband's death she married her love and united the tribes of Umar into the present kingdom. I don't see the adultery there. Is the play somehow different?"

"No, Your Highness, I've read the script, as has Duchess Alboni, we both agree it is as accurate as possible after a thousand years."

"Thank you Sarah. You see, there is nothing scandalous in this play that I, or my aunt, can see. What precisely do you find offensive about it?"

"She murdered her husband and married her lover, how can that not be immoral?" The chairman blustered while Mistress Launston gasped for an answer.

"In the context of the time and place, and in her position, it was perfectly moral."

"There is also the nature of her lover."

"You mean that she was a woman?"

"Of course, it's unnatural!"

"How so? How is love unnatural?"

The Curate and his committee seemed taken aback, his mouth flapping in the air. Lizzy gave them a few minutes to recover and then waited for a counter argument. When one wasn't forthcoming she stood and bowed to her visitors.

"Well? You have yet to present a reasonable argument, so I don't think I'll help you put this before the King's Council. Maybe you should try the Curate's

Council, trying to regulate individual freedoms is more their area of expertise. Good afternoon. Sarah be so kind as to have my guards show our guests out, please."

Lizzy smiled, turned her back on the committee and left the room.

Back at her desk and running through final arrangements for the trip to Belenos, Lizzy barely looked up when she heard her study door open and close.

"Sarah, get me a glass of wine would you, I need it after dealing with those bigots."

A loud click disturbed the flow of her writing. Lizzy looked up, and quickly rolled off the chair and under her desk as the wine bottle flew. The angry matron, Mistress Launston, red faced and breathing hard, screamed incoherent slurs. Outside, Sarah wrestled with the door, which Launston had locked quietly as she entered the room.

Lizzy assessed her situation. She could probably stay under her desk for a minute or two while the older woman found other things to hurl, and Sarah was outside. She'd be in in no time. But on the other hand, the woman was clearly unbalanced and would probably try to get at Lizzy under the desk. She would have to move, do something. More glass smashed above her head, and wine dribbled down the legs to the floor. The woman was getting more accurate.

Rolling out from under her desk, Lizzy sheepishly raised her head above her temporary parapet to survey the scene. Mistress Launston was closer, riffling through the books on her shelves, pulling them off and discarding some but keeping others. Lizzy slid the draw open, silently thanking her conscientious servants for their attention to minor details. She kept a letter knife in the draw that looked more dangerous than it was. Lizzy looked again, the woman's arms were burdened with books now.

Thus armed, the Princess rose to her feet and spoke, knife behind her back,

"Mistress, if you wanted to borrow a book, you should have asked first. Please tidy up the mess before you leave."

"Bitch. Whore. The Queen should have made certain you were dead. You're spreading filth and corruption all through the kingdom. This is why the One has cursed us with a surfeit of enemies. He demands your blood."

Lizzy yawned; the Queen's pet Curates used to say something similar, but blamed it on her accepted and acknowledged bastardy.

"Oh dear, you're one of those sorts of religious are you? How unfortunate. I was going to try reasoning with you, if only for the sake of my books. Do put them down, you ridiculous creature. But now I shan't bother."

There was a clink from the door as Sarah finally succeeded in pushing the key out from her side of the door and inserted her own key. Sarah stepped into the room moments later, an armed guard waiting behind her.

"Bitch! Do you fuck your maid as well? Corrupter of youth! These filthy books should be burnt!"

"No, no, they really should not. Sarah, be so kind as to remove this woman, to the Hospital would be most appropriate I think. She's clearly suffering some sort of religious mania."

Sarah smiled and advanced on Mistress Launston, who smirked, her arms still clutching the stack of books.

"You trifling whore, let me by." She barged into Sarah, who gripped Mistress Launston's arm as she fell backwards, taking the over-balanced woman with her to the ground. Lizzy followed up the move as the two women wrestled for dominance by picking up a heavy book of plays and slamming it down on Launston's head. It was a victory for literature everywhere, as the impact dazed her attacker for a while and Sarah took control of the fight.

Finally, subdued, the guards entered to remove the intruder from the royal study. Lizzy looked at the dishevelled Mistress Launston as should stood between two guards – the other five were busy re-shelving books – and smiled.

"You really should threaten my library; I do take it so personally."

The woman hissed and spat. "You don't deserve this, you robbed it from the rightful queen."

"Go away, you're a tiresome woman." Lizzy waved the guards away, including those stacking books, they were doing it wrong, and righted her fallen chair.

"Wine Sarah?"

"I think we need another bottle." Sarah had found the bin and was using a paper file to scoop the fractured glass into it.

"And new glasses. Father will be upset, that was from the set he gave me for my twenty-fifth birthday."

"The engraved ones?"

"Yes, Charley and I used them the other day to celebrate finally leaving to visit her grandmother in Belenos."

"They were supposed to be for the first toast at your future wedding."

"Never going to happen my dear." Lizzy laughed then looked at the mess on her desk. She was going to have to re-write her clothing list for the trip, and the first three pages of her current monograph (on education reform).

"Nice move with the Shaply." Sarah pointed at the book that Lizzy still grasped.

"I do have a certain reputation to maintain, you know." Lizzy spoke seriously, then collapsed in giggles as the adrenaline of the fight wore off. She placed the book on the desk, carefully avoiding the streams of wine and went to shelve books and check them for damage.

Chapter 23

"Really, I don't know why you're going, after the last attempt to kill you?" They rode in the carriage through the streets of the busy city, waving politely to onlookers. The boys insisted on riding their horses down to the Hythe, leaving father and daughter to some relative privacy.

"Do stop fussing father." Lizzy patted his hand, "You're turning into a worry-wart in your old age."

"Cheeky child, I'm not that old."

"Father, you're practically ancient." She laughed, they'd celebrated his fifty-second birthday only weeks before.

"Well, you're not getting any younger either. I wouldn't mind if you met a nice man while you were in Belenos. We could do with the allies."

"Thanks Father, and here I was thinking you wanted me to be happy?"

"I do, but also married. I'm getting on a bit; I want to know I have at least one grandson to take the crown."

"That's Michael's job, not mine. I'm only your daughter."

"Only my daughter? What rubbish is this?"

"I have no responsibility for filling the throne, you have sons for that, after all. And you know, sons are always favoured over daughters." Lizzy laughed. Women still lost all their property on marriage; she could deal with primogeniture when that particular travesty was dealt with.

But first to Belenos, and to rescue Gos.

King John, his sons and brother, watched as Lizzy and her cousins sailed away from Royal Hythe. The elder pair of brothers gave each other a look; Duke Michael shook his head then nodded. The king seemed satisfied by the answer, though saddened. The younger brothers, the princes, merely watched their sister until her ship was out of sight, lamenting their father's refusal to allow one of them, at least, to go.

"Home?" The king said, to his younger, twin brother.

"Come to the Residency, we need to talk."

John nodded and watched as his brother wheeled his horse around to lead his wife and daughter's carriage back up the Hythe and into the city again.

"Boys, come along, we have to go."

"But I want to stay and watch Lizzy's ship."

"We have business at the Residency. Mount your horses and come along."

The boys grumbled but returned to the carriage where their horses were being held by an empty faced groom. They mounted and the party finally left. They were quite dull now that the excitement of the morning was over and young John sighed in his saddle.

"What's up, m'boy?"

"Nothing father, I'd have liked to see the Empire."

"You will get the chance one day."

"Why's Lizzy going on holiday when we're

expecting a war?"

"She's got a job to do in Belenos."

"What job?"

John looked about him, assessing their privacy; he decided the least was best at the moment.

"Diplomacy of women."

"Huh?"

"He means the marriage offer from Prince Cthinnerthy, idiot." Michael rolled his eyes at his little brother.

"Oh that. Lizzy will turn him down."

King John looked askance at this statement from this suddenly certain Prince John.

"What makes you say that?" His brow crinkled.

"Elenor told me; she heard auntie and Lizzy talking about the Campaign for Women's Marriage Rights."

"The property campaign?"

"That's the one. Anyway, Lizzy said that while she was away could auntie look into the laws for the Islands and she'd get information in the Empire. I think Auntie is going to ask her friends in Umar to talk to their friends in Camar as well."

"And that's what Elenor said?"

"Yes, ask her yourself if we're going to the Residency."

"I think I'll talk to Catherine."

"Might be an idea dad, these children might have got the wrong end of the stick."

"We haven't. Anyway, if Lizzy is planning to help the CWMR then she can't be seriously considering marrying Prince Thinnery."

169

"His name's Cthinnerthy. You'll have to get it right if he becomes our brother-in-law."

"I'm telling you, it's not going to happen. Or the back-up offers from the Queen of Umar."

"How do you know about that?"

"Elenor saw the letters on her mother's desk."

The king sighed. He needed to talk to Catherine; nothing was secret among the family. Not that it ever had been, not with the propensity for twins in the family. It had come as a universal surprise to everyone when his sons had been born alone. When Michael had been born, there were questions raised about the Queen's loyalty, but the boy had grown a shock of red-blond hair just like his father, sister and everyone else for two hundred years. They'd been wrong about that instance but it was obvious now that the queen was not a loyal woman, or more correctly she was loyal to herself alone. And soon he would have to welcome her back.

King John sighed. He didn't want his wife back but the new Lord Tarjan was insistent; his niece returned to Albon or there would be war. They were ready if that were the case, but he'd rather avoid it.

"Father?" Michael's voice brought him out of his reverie, "There's a messenger for us."

"Odd."

"She's from the army, it must be news about the pirates."

"Good, they've been gone long enough without sending word." He waved the woman, sweat soaked and covered in road dust, to ride alongside the carriage.

"Your majesty, a message from the Commanders." She gasped, took a breath and continued, "The Rocks have been cleared. We found disturbing evidence of enemy involvement in their activities. The Officers have taken control of the encampment and are searching for further evidence."

"Has the Duke been informed?"

"My companion left me on the road to the Residency, sir. His Grace should know by now."

"Thank you. We're going there now, ride with us and tell me about the campaign."

The woman nodded.

Chapter 24

Aboard the fleet's flagship, the commanders of the expedition sat in gloom.

"So, Officer, what have you found?" Lord Admiral Jonsey asked.

"Nothing good my Lord." Officer Martins sighed.

"Good? I wasn't expecting any."

"Nor treason." Commander Armanno added.

"And yet treason we find." Jonsey sighed.

Lord Summerton growled. "We must bring them to justice." He'd arrived to join the meeting from the coast.

"You have arrested the conspirators on the northern coast?"

"Most of them."

"My colleagues have been searching their houses and businesses for further evidence. If there are any more conspirators, we'll find them."

"As always the Office is ahead of the Watch, Fleet and Regiments." Lord Jonesey laughed. He was proud of his new and untried fleet. They'd done a fine job of encircling the Rocks, pounded away with cannon at the exposed ships until their crews had given in. Then the Marines and soldiers, led by Marshal and Armanno had landed to mop up any resistance. It had been a model campaign. On land Armanno's countrywoman, Commander Laitano, had led her forces through the northern coastal towns, and with the help of some Officers, had rounded up the pirates' contacts on land. It wasn't until Officer Martins, in charge of the Officers on this expedition, had combed through the paperwork in the cave the pirates were using as an office did they realise the scale of their problems.

"Well, has a message been sent the King's Ford?"

"Yes Sir, I sent one of my officers and one of Commander Laitano's messengers south as soon as we found the first evidence."

"Good man. What else have you found?"

Martins looked sideways at Commanders Armanno and Laitano.

"None of that, Martins. We're equals here."

"Of course Lord Jonesey. Well, so far my teams have managed to find enough evidence to start a war."

"With whom."

"Sumoast."

The rest sat back in their chairs. The collective groan sounded like a zombie herd that had just seen lunch.

"We need to tell the king immediately."

"No, not yet." Armanno said, "We don't know how he'll react. We should wait until we're back in King's Ford with the fleet and troops."

"You're right, we have to protect the king."

"There's more."

"More?"

"I found a letter signed by the new Lord Tarjan ordering the pirates to join his own fleet at the end of summer, when they invade."

"What!?" Marshall shouted, "The duplicitous bastard."

"What did you expect?" Laitano asked, "The Holmgards have been trouble since they united the three tribes. Our queen refused a marriage alliance for the Princessa because we don't trust them."

"I wish King John had refused to marry Jocinta Holmgard." Sommerton muttered.

"Wouldn't have. We weren't ready to fight a war against them then." Jonsey barked a laugh.

"We are now, with the help of our friends." Sommerton nodded at the Umari commanders.

"My lords, commanders, may I suggest you return to King's Ford, I shall stay here with a small force to continue the investigation."

"We'll need your full report for the Duke, Officer."

"I shall write it as soon as we've finished our present interrogations. The evidence would be safest returning to the city with you. Commander Armanno, may I borrow your second battalion for the duration of our investigation?"

Armanno nodded in agreement, "They're already helping you so they may as well stay with you and the other Officers."

"Martins, when do you expect to finish your investigation of the Rocks?"

"Tomorrow we enter the furthest caves; I would say it'll be two or three days."

"Excellent. Ladies and gentlemen, I suggest we leave at first light four days from now to return to the capital. Officer Martins, have a coded message sent from the nearest tower. I want the Duke to be kept informed." Jonesey, as Lord Fleet, was in overall command of the mission.

"Agreed. I'll gather all the evidence we have and

write my report before then. I'll have someone from the coast bring their evidence and interrogation reports. Can you take the prisoners back with you?"

"I'll march them back with my battalions."

"We will leave the day after tomorrow, that way we'll not be long behind the fleet returning to King's Ford." Lord Sommerton decided.

"I'll get to shore then before it gets dark, we'll be ready to leave as soon as you are."

"What shall we do with the pirates' ships?"

"We've finished going over them, I suggest Fleet takes anything useful from them and burns the lot."

"Can we make use of them?"

"None 'ull sail again. They're not much use for anything except firewood."

"Let's burn them three nights from now. I have had a good burn in years, not since the Belenosian sixth fleet tried to force the Camari trade." Jonesey laughed.

"Anyone watching for Sumoast will know we're on to them." Summerton mused.

"They'll know anyway. The pirates had a small tower. I imagine they were supposed to report in every day."

"Who too? Sumoast is over the horrizon."

"A ship?"

"Possibly, I bow to your expertise Jonsey, of course, but I suggest we send out two or three of our ships to the edge of out territorial waters this evening. Just to have a look."

"Excellent idea. I'll have Captain Grey take his men for a trip out to sea, they could do with the

175

experience."

"And if they find anything?"

"We'll have to report it."

"No provoking them though, not yet."

"I think, Commander Armanno, they've done plenty to provoke us, why should we not offer something in return."

"My queen wishes it to be known that the Sumoasti started the war. She's sending a fleet, which should arrive in King's Ford in two days, but the Sumoasti can't know we have already supported you until the war starts."

"You're very certain there will be a war."

"My queen has Seen it."

"Argh, nonsense. Seeing doesn't exist."

"But the Duke Sees?" Armanno seemed confused; it was obvious to her that both the Duke Alboni and the Princessa Elizabeta were Seers of some sort, it was why the Queen wanted her for a daughter-in-law. But perhaps the Alboni didn't believe?

Laitano kicked her friend under the table and shook her head.

"I must have been mistaken, it is only that he seems to know so much. His network and Officers are very good at their work; I think?"

"Yes, yes, the Duke's network of Officers and agents is very well informed and so is he. It must seem like magic to some people." Lord Summerton, an old friend and distant relative of the royal twins knew the truth, but it was generally kept quiet; Lizzy didn't know about herself yet. He hadn't been in the least surprised when she'd appeared after her kidnapping so many years ago, just as they were about to attack. He'd had to fain surprise for his men and the Fitzroy twins. Someone should tell them.

"These cultural confusions make diplomacy so difficult at times."

"They do indeed, Commander Laitano. Now, are we agreed?"

"Aye." was repeated around the table.

"Well then, ladies and gentlemen, let us be about our business. We have much to do."

The ships returned to King's Ford two weeks later with their reports adding further to the busyness of the King's Council chamber. The Umari ships had arrived three days before with the Umari Prince at their head. A week after Commander Armanno and Lord Summerton marched into the city. The prisoners were immediately dispatched to the Gaol and Lord Summerton joined his colleagues – now much expanded by the arrival of the Umari – in the Council chamber. It had been a busy six weeks, summer had almost passed and the Sumoasti fleet would be leaving Tarjan soon, unless a peace deal could be arranged. He feared it was unlikely.

Chapter 25

The voyage to the Empire had been quiet for Lizzy. She had enjoyed the first few days but then, once out of sight of the Isles and not yet within sight of the Essenmouth, the great river delta that marked the opening of the continent and the road to the Imperial capital, she became anxious. This far out no messages could be relayed to their ship from the towers and she had to go without news of events at the Rocks or in Belenos for five days. She was relieved when the coast around Essen came into view.

Once through the tricky passages of the delta, they had to sail upstream through a narrow gorge, just wide enough to admit a small merchant vessel, for a day, then the river opened out and she had been enchanted by the mountains and their dark forests. They stopped every night to rest, restock and collect messages. The twins disappeared every evening at sunset and usually came back with clouded faces, and refused to talk all evening.

One night, a few days from Belenos itself, they came back laughing. Aboard the ship they gathered their friends in the stateroom. It was stuffy and overcrowded with all seven Alboni aristocrats packed in like sardines. They'd turned south three days before and the river had widened out, it seemed as though they sailed on a small sea during the day, but the expanse of glass sucked heat into the stateroom, and even late in the evening it was still sweltering.

"We've finally contacted Gos's agent. She's alive."

"Oh thank the One." Charley breathed out.

"What happened?" Sarah asked. She was pleased but the information was more important. She wiped the sweat from her brow.

"Our agent was to meet Gos in the mountains outside the capital. There's a spa town about twenty miles along the coast."

"I know it, my mother took me once, it's call Hercalia, or something like that."

"Hercalium." Lizzy idly corrected, fanning herself with a sweat stained piece of paper, a monograph she'd been working on until the twins returned.

"That's the place. She was due to meet him at dark moon except he didn't arrive so she started towards the capital. She got caught by the same people who have Gos, at a villa five miles outside the city. Since she knew you were heading towards the city she got herself out and walked up river until she met us."

"But what about Gos, and how did she get out?" Phil finally spoke. He'd barely said a word in all the days they'd been travelling. Now it seemed Lizzy could see guarded hope in his eyes.

"Gos was alive last time she saw him two weeks ago, but he was being kept in a cave in the hills behind the villa, guarded by a small army of Sumoasti. She was in a cellar in the villa itself. She escaped but couldn't get through the guards around the cave to rescue Gos."

"She knows how to get there though? We could send a force to rescue him?"

"We can't raise a force in Imperial territory, the

179

Empress would take it as a threat. No, Sarah, our agent, Alex and I must go ourselves, with half the guards. If you'll lend us them, Harry?"."

"I must come too." Phil insisted.

Lawrence looked from his friend to his brother and Sarah; they nodded in agreement.

"Alright then, just the five of us."

"Six, you're not leaving me out of this." Harry added, "Gos is my friend as well. And you're taking my soldiers with you. I have my responsibilities to them.""

The rest nodded, before Lizzy protested, "You can't leave me out of this if Phil and Harry are going."

"We are Lizzy." Alex sighed.

"I can come if I want." Lizzy said petulantly.

"No you can't Lizzy; we need you to smile sweetly at the Empress and her Court." Sarah reminded her.

"We can do that Lizzy; Grandmother is already planning who she'll introduce us to."

"We're a distraction?"

"And we're on holiday."

"I'm not, I'm working." Sarah muttered.

"If you want we'll handle it?"

"And face the Duke if anything should happen to his beloved boys? Never. I'm coming with you; Lady De Narvel will just have to find Lizzy a waiting woman for a few days."

"Grandmother has plenty of servants who'll do for a few days."

"Where's our agent now?" It suddenly struck Lizzy that they were talking about the woman but had yet to see her.

"In the hold hiding out until we leave in the morning."

"Send her to see me when we leave in the morning. I'd like to speak to her myself."

"Of course."

"It's a start, a start." Phil started to laugh. He'd been so strung out since the Duke had told him his brother had disappeared while on a mission for the Office; even the news that their agent was alive and had seen his brother two weeks ago was enough to give him hope, little as it was.

They went to bed more relaxed than they had in weeks and in the morning Lizzy interviewed their agent, although she seemed to be answering to Sarah more than Lizzy. It occurred to Lizzy afterwards that Sarah was more important in the Office than admitted to Lizzy. She would have to ask her about it.

But not until they got home; there was too much to do in the Empire first.

Chapter 26

The welcome party waiting for Lizzy and her friends was surprisingly large; not only had the Embassy come out in force to meet her, the De Narvel family arrived in a barge of their own to meet Charley. Charley stood on the deck of their modest ship, little larger than a merchant's vessel, looking out over the blue bay around which the great imperial capital rose. Ships and boats of all sizes clustered around the bay, but she was looking for one barge in particular; blue and gold with a silk canopied deck, rowed by a dozen slaves. She spotted it, beside the ambassadorial barge, pulling out of the private dockyard where the very highest in Belenosian society kept their private barges. Charley saw her grandmother resting regally among the cushions as the barge came closer. She bounced on the balls of her feet, waving and laughing.

Lizzy smiled at her profuse excitement; Sarah and the twins watched the bay around them, standing close to Lizzy protectively, though she was unaware of their formation. Phil and the agent, who seemed to have bonded over the missing Gos in the three days they'd travelled together, waited at the prow to welcome the Ambassador.

"And I was hoping we'd be able to arrive unnoticed." Lawrence sighed to his brother.

"We need Lizzy, Charley and Phil to be noticed. We three, and our silent friend, need to disappear."

"No, we need to be seen; it would be strange otherwise.

A Princess wouldn't travel with such a small entourage. I suggest we appear as we nominally are, if Callia will play at being Phil's lover?"

A laugh behind them signalled Harry's arrival on deck, "Believe me, my dear Sarah, there is no play-acting necessary."

Lizzy spun around, "Really?"

"Oh yes. Definitely." He laughed again and watched his friend and the agent down on the lower deck, "See, he's barely keeping his hands to himself." He took Lizzy by the shoulders and made her look, properly look, at their friend.

"They are quite close together." Lizzy mused, "But not unusually so."

"Watch his hands."

Lizzy did as she was told, though she had never realised Harry was so observant. His time in the regiments had matured him. It was probably the responsibility of a thousand soldiers expecting him to find them food, shelter and wages every day. Lizzy smiled. Growing up could be so dull. Laughing at the thought, she returned her attention to Phil and Callia. His hands were moving more than usual, describing something as he spoke. Occasionally one hand would wander close to the agent, a stray, sly caress, unnoticed unless you were watching them. Callia turned to look at Phil, reacting to a comment. Her eyes were larger than one would expect, outlined with dark brows, finely shaped. Lizzy was surprised she didn't remember the woman from the indentured servant scandal investigation, but Office agents were meant to be unremarkable. She smiled at Phil and leaned into him. They grinned at each other and looked up to their friends on the aft deck.

"We've been spotted." Lizzy laughed to Harry, "Hey, you two, are you coming up here for the view or not. It's marvellous."

"No, we'll stay down here and meet the ambassador. You be all regal and everything up there."

"Regal my backside, I'm on holiday." Lizzy grinned, getting into character. Voices travelled over water much more clearly and people would be watching, she knew.

"Indeed, we are, my lady, indeed we are." Callia laughed back.

Harry stepped backwards as Lawry nudged him away.

"Our Sumoasti friends have come to meet us." He whispered in her ear, "No, don't move your head, pretend we haven't seen them."

"What do we do?"

"Act. Everyone thinks we're idle and rich; let them continue thinking that."

Lizzy nodded. Lawry stepped back and smiled before starting his own act.

"If you love birds stay down there you'll miss all the fun."

"We can have our own fun."

"Not in public!" Alex laughed, mock admonishing them.

"Don't spoil the fun just yet, FitzAlboni." Calia laughed and caressed Phil's shoulders.

"I'll ban public displays of affection if you two

184

aren't careful." Lizzy giggled at them.

They were interrupted by a gentle bump as the embassy barge finally pulled alongside.

Chapter 27

The reception, on their small ship, was a cramped and rather hurried affair. Lizzy did her best to hide her impatience to be on land and desperate for the latest news about Gos. Sarah and Callia disappeared with Gos' aide about an hour in, while Lizzy was listening to the ambassador, drone about trade agreements and the difficulty of pinning Belenosian merchants down on a price and delivery date. Lizzy nodded, trying to concentrate, but her shoulders itched without Sarah's presence. Lizzy excused herself, disengaged from the conversation with the ambassador and went to find Charley.

"Lady De Narvel, you've found us then?"

"My dear Princess Elizabeth, thank you so much for bringing our dear Charlotta to visit us."

"Oh, well, I can hardly say no to Charley, and it's been an adventure so far. I've never been this far south or east. How do you cope with the heat?"

"Why, dear girl, it's only just after midyear and quite cool yet; next month it'll be delightfully warm. I don't know how you manage in your cold islands, at all. Won't you stay two months and really enjoy the sun?"

"Oh, I'd love to, but father is rather insistent I return before first harvest. We have a deal of politics on our hands at the moment. But Charley should certainly stay, if her mother allows it."

"Oh, I think she would; Charlotta dearest, I had a letter from your father three days ago. There are

186

rumours that there will be war between Albon and Sumoast; do stay with us until it settles down. I'd ask you all to stay, but I understand the FitzAlboni twins are needed by their father and young Sir Philip and Sir Henry command a regiment apiece, do they not?"

Lizzy smiled, "I'm afraid I can't say, Lady De Narvel, you never know who may be listening. Can I get you all a top up?"

"I'll come with you Lizzy; same again Grandmama?"

"Please dear. And another of these pastries. Your Grandfather would have loved to have met the princess."

"I'm sure I would have been honoured to meet him too."

The young women collected the food and drinks, and returned to find the ambassador talking to Lady De Narvel. They joined the conversation, though Lizzy listened more than she talked. Finally, bored of trade chatter she asked,

"Ambassador, have you heard any news from King's Ford lately?"

The ambassador turned red, and swallowed.

"I have, from my friends. I received a message early this morning, we tend to do business early in the morning here, when it's cool."

"Yes, ambassador, you've mentioned that already. The news?"

"Oh, yes, well. The expedition to the Rocks was a success. I understand you took part in the planning."

"A little, but what news?"

"As I said, gosh it's hot isn't it, perhaps we should

move into the shade of the canopy?"

"Ambassador!"

"Of course, well, there are rumours that the investigation found evidence that, that, oh dear, that Sumoast is behind the attacks on our ships and that they are planning to attack at the beginning of winter."

"Who are your friends that they would know so much, ambassador?"

"Peterson, the news man."

Lizzy rolled her eyes. "Idiot Peterson, I told him not to spread rumours without seeing the evidence. This could precipitate a war. It goes no further until you verify it with the Office and Duke Alboni directly."

"I sent a message, coded of course, first thing this morning. As soon as I have the response I'll let you know. Have you taken a house for the summer or will you be joining us at the embassy?"

"Of course they won't. My Granddaughter and her friends will be staying with me. The house has been far too quiet since my husband returned to the Fields."

"Yes, I suppose it must be. With all these young people you'll have no peace though."

"I'm sure I can accommodate the temporary change, Ambassador Conort. We have a ball planned for a week today; you and your wife must join us."

"My wife, I regret to say, has had a religious conversion and returned to Albon to take her place in a nunnery. But, I would be delighted, Lady De Narvel, if you would honour me with the first dance on the occasion?"

"Why, Ambassador, surely that honour should go to the Princess."

"Oh, but I am happy to concede it to our gracious hostess." Lizzy smiled as the Conort blushed.

"You have to visit the Court officially tomorrow evening, Your Highness, for your introduction to the Empress, and I believe her son Prince Cthinn-Erthy is happily waiting for your visit."

"Yes, ambassador, so I understand. Whose idea was that?"

"Oh, well, they may have approached me and I sent a message to Duke Michael."

"Thanks Conort."

"Oh, I thought you might, well, everyone says it's time you married and I thought an alliance with the Empire might be beneficial."

"I do wish people would stop doing that."

"My dear these things happen." Lady De Narvel patted Lizzy's arm, "You're not the only one who should be settled down and married now." She winked at Charley, who rolled her eyes at her grandmother.

"Lizzy, I was wrong, we should have stayed home; Grandmama will marry us off before we know what's happening."

"Now, now, ladies, you shouldn't mock such a wise, and I must say, elegant, lady; she's quite correct. After the excitement of youth, nothing gives quite so much content as a settled and companionable life with a beloved mate."

"Oh lor' ambassador, you sound like Father." Alex had joined them, a glass of cherry wine in his hand and a silly grin on his face.

189

"And your father would be right. When is he going to legitimise you two?"

"Three. We have a fourteen-year-old sister, too." Lawrence hugged his brother and laughed.

"That's quite an age difference. You must be twenty-five or twenty-six by now. I remember your name day. The Court was in uproar and the Curates couldn't decide on the right thing to do."

"They, and I are twenty-seven." Lizzy laughed.

"My Father and birth-mother tried a reconciliation. It didn't work, and father married Lady Catherine a year later, when Elenor was three months old. Mother handed us all over to father and his wife as soon as they got back from their honeymoon. We've barely seen her since."

"Oh, how awful, to be cut off from your mother! You poor dear boys!"

"Don't fret on our behalf Lady De Narvel. Our birth-mother cut herself off from us when she sent us away to school when we were five. If Father hadn't taken us in, we'd have been a deal sorrier than we appear now."

"The Duchess has been more mother to us than Lady Eleanor, especially to Elenor. Father took us out of school as soon as he had permanent custody of us all. As to when he'll adopt and legitimise us? That depends on our birth mother, she has refused to sign the paperwork since she gave us up."

This wasn't news to Lizzy or Charley; they'd both tried to convince Lady Eleanor Shipton that she should allow the adoption to go ahead, with no luck; though she didn't want her children she wasn't prepared to let

190

anyone else have them either.

"It's quite extraordinary; she is devoted to her legitimate children."

"It's Sir Jonas, Lady Eleanor's husband. He's a Traditionalist."

The Ambassador curled his lips. "You have my sympathy; my own former wife fell in with a group of Traditionalists and left me for a nunnery. They're poisonous."

"I couldn't possibly comment, and neither can the twins."

Lizzy elbowed Alex as he opened his mouth. He looked at her, puppy dog eyes asking what the assault was about. A raised eyebrow answered his question. Alex sighed, shrugged and nodded in agreement. He looked a Lawry, who grinned but nodded; Lizzy was right.

It never occurred to the three of them that their silent communication might be considered odd; they did it all the time at home. Ambassador Conort had never seen it though and stepped back slightly while Lady De Narvel merely nodded as if to confirm her own suspicions and smiled at the three. Charley, who'd seen them talk to each other for twelve years rolled her eyes at the differing responses, certain her grandmother would try to get evidence from her about the twins and Lizzy's supposed telepathy. She knew it was familiarity, not magic. In Belenos such a thing would be celebrated, but not in Albon.

"They say, Ambassador, that familiarity breeds contempt, but with these three all it did was make them more impossible. They scare so many people; we had a family of Fundamentalists at Court four or five years ago who were convinced that it was magic."

"Oh yes, I remember them, what were they called? They were from the western valleys, weren't they?"

"That's right, Lizzy, the, erm, the Forthgist or something like that?"

"Oh yes, we've been keeping an eye on them, or the Office have. They've been causing trouble in the valleys. You know how old fashioned they are over there."

"Really, and what happened? When they visited the Court?" Connort hadn't heard this story before.

"When they accused us of being possessed by devils, because we're atheists, Father had them thrown out of Court and banished to their estate for ten years."

"That may not have been the wisest move." Lady De Narvel smiled.

"Probably not, but Father had a few health problems at the time and he really didn't want to deal with their nonsense."

"The king is young to be unwell."

"Oh, it was nothing, just a lingering infection. I think he'd been overworking. He's fine now." If she didn't think about his occasional memory loss and his swollen knees.

"That's reassuring to hear."

Lizzy excused herself again and began circulating among the other guests, who were all Embassy staff and their spouses. She nodded, smiled and attempted to remember names and faces for next time.

Just before sunset Harry sidled over, having been

engaged in a deep conversation with some official or other, Lizzy couldn't for the life of her remember his name right now, and hugged her.

"Tired?"

"How'd you guess?"

"You've been staring out to sea for ten minutes. I suggest we send our lovely guests away and sail into the dock?"

"Have the captain organise it, will you? I don't think I can manage to be civil much more today."

"Nor I my dear, nor I. Well, except possibly with Forier."

"Who?"

"Oh Lizzy, weren't you listening when I introduced him earlier? No, I suppose you weren't. Justin Forier, the ambassador's secretary."

Lizzy looked 'round until she spotted the young man Harry had been speaking to. She looked back at Harry, "He's pretty, but does he possess a brain?"

"Oh yes, and a marvellous one at that. He's due home this winter."

"Really?"

"Indeed, I think he's hoping for a posting in the Isles next."

"Isn't Joshua in Calman in need of a secretary?"

"Joshua Sermin? I think so, or he will be soon. Will Mustard is due for retirement."

"Well, we'll have to see what we can do. Have you seen Sarah and Callia around?"

"I think they're in the state room interrogating people politely about Gos."

"Good, when you've told the captain we're

heading into the dock, tell Sarah and Callia I want a report from them. I have a feeling we don't have long before we need to head back to King's Ford."

"Something in the wind?"

"War."

Harry nodded and went to carry messages. Lizzy leant against the rail around the deck, watching the coast, "Please still be alive Gos, please."

"Talking to yourself again?"

"Why, dear cousin, of course, it's the only way to get a decent conversation, or so I've found."

"When are we putting ashore, I want to sleep in a real bed."

"Soon, I've sent Harry to the captain," Lizzy patted Alex's hand, "Do me a favour, round up everyone else so I can say thank you and throw our guests overboard?"

"Not literally I hope? This shirt cost far too much for it to be drenched." A young man, slightly shorter than Lizzy, with red hair cut in the manner of the Belenosians – short all over – was plucking at his green silk shirt. They hadn't been introduced, however the young man was being steered by Sarah.

"Ah, Lizzy, this is Gos's assistant, Felix Redfern."

"You suit your name sir."

"The whole family do, unfortunately, and we burn so easily. I'd have much preferred a place in Camar."

"I'm sure. Now, what have you to tell me Sarah?"

"Nothing much new, Mr Redfern has confirmed Calia's observations."

"When?"

194

"Two days ago, Gos, Lord Val I mean was still alive, that I could tell. Of course I couldn't get too close."

"Yes, you wouldn't want to spoil a shirt."

Redfern lost his smile.

"I've done my best Your Highness. We lost all track of Gos from the inn, only when Alex sent me the message three days ago was I able to find the villa and establish Gos's status."

"Fine, fine, I'm sure you've done your best." Lizzy turned to Sarah, "Did you get all the information you need?"

"Yes, we'll go in tomorrow night, while you and Charley are at the Court. It'll be dark moon, which'll help."

"And Redfern?"

"Oh, he's staying in the Embassy cells until we know what's what."

"I say, that's a bit rough."

"Be quiet Redfern. If you weren't involved you might just get a promotion out of this."

"I, oh, alright. I'll stay under lock and key while you go and rescue my friend."

"Stop whining or I'll have you locked up in the bilges while we wait for Lord Val to return." Sarah growled.

"Sarah." Lizzy warned as Redfern started to look stubborn, "There's no need for unpleasantness, is there? Ah look, Alex has got everyone's attention."

Sarah ushered Calia and Redfern down on to the main deck, taking her place behind Lizzy once again. She had been busy about her work for the Office, but was relieved to see that the young men had managed to keep Lizzy safe in her absence. She didn't think anyone would try anything in such a crowd and so close to the Imperial capital but she never could be too certain. She looked over the water to the still lurking Sumoasti barge as Lizzy thanked their guests for their welcome and told people to push off, politely.

Chapter 28

Lizzy collapsed in her bed, too exhausted to care about taking shoes and clothes off. She fell asleep fully dressed and slept into the next day. A knock at the door woke her around midday, their first in Belenos.

"Come on Lizzy, Grandmamma and I have already been dress shopping. I had to guess your sizes, but I think I did alright."

"I have court dresses; Caro made me some before we left."

"They'll be too heavy for the fête tomorrow or the ball the day after, but I suppose they'll do for tonight. I'll have the slaves heat the bath house for you."

"I, oh all right."

Lizzy slumped back on to her bed, accepting defeat. Lizzy was slightly uneasy about something, but she couldn't place it. Yes, she was worried about Gos and this evening's rescue attempt, and about meeting the Empress, but once she'd sorted those to one side in her mind she couldn't fix on what else was causing her uneasiness. She tried to forget about it and prepare for the day ahead.

The bath house was a novel experience. Slaves carrying clean robes and towels led the way to the bath house which adjoined the main house, a rectangular, two storey villa with an internal courtyard. The bath house was joined to the house by a corridor warmed by underfloor heating. This too was a novelty. Lizzy felt the heat rise through the soles of her slippers as she walked the hallway. She crinkled her toes in them and savoured the new sensation. A slave bowed and pushed open the door to the bath house, steam billowing out of the changing room into the hallway.

"You can leave now." Lizzy instructed the slaves as she sat down on a carved wooden bench in the changing room. The steam had settled; she could make her way through the complex alone. Beyond a red painted door, she could hear Charley talking to Sarah. She bent to take of her slippers and stood to remove her robe only to find a slave taking them from her hands.

"I said you were to leave. I can manage alone."

The slaves bowed and shuffled out as Lizzy continued to strip off her underwear. She poked her head through the door.

"Charley, where do I put my clothes?"

"On the shelf, the slaves will take the laundry away. Have they brought you clean towels and a robe?"

"Yes, they've left them here with me." Lizzy picked the clean items up and put them on a shelf next to her 'dirty' clothes.

"Bring a towel in with you."

"Right. Be there in a second." Lizzy took the largest towel from the pile; she wrapped it around herself and walked through the red door.

"There you are Lizzy. Dump your towel on your slave and get in."

The bath was a square, about ten yards by ten yards, with steps leading into the water and carved stones niches around the edge to act as seating. Sarah was swimming about in the water while Charley sat

198

back enjoying a face massage.

"I've dismissed my slaves. I don't feel comfortable around them."

"Darling, slavery is normal here. You'll get used to it."

"Charley you might be used to it but I never will be. I don't understand how you can accept the idea of people as property."

"Oh Lizzy, you're not working now, try to relax."

"I can't; something is wrong."

"Lots of things are wrong, right now; which particular wrong are you worrying about?"

"I don't know Sarah; I just have a feeling."

"Don't let Grandmamma hear you say that; she's already convinced you're a Seer."

"What nonsense, there's no such thing."

"Not at home maybe, but other nations believe in such things. Did you never study the religions of the Empire Lizzy?"

"No Sarah, uncle thought we'd be fine knowing what people in the Isles believed since we were more likely to be dealing with other Islanders."

"He should have done a better job of your education."

"You've been in charge of my education for six years."

"Yes, well, I didn't know he'd missed out something did I?"

They lapsed into silence, enjoying the warmth of the bath and the clean, damp air. After so long aboard a cramped ship with only sea water to wash in, it was a blessing to splash about in hot water with soap to wash with. Even Lizzy gave in eventually and accepted a facial massage.

"We should cool down now, or we'll be all red for the introduction."

"And I need to be leaving."

"Of course, take care Sarah."

"I will. Don't worry, we'll bring him back."

"I know."

Sarah walked up the steps out of the bath and accepted a towel. Lizzy and Charley followed her but when she turned left to return to the changing room, they turned right, into a cooler room, where they lay on cushioned beds while receiving a massage, and listening to musicians playing Belenosian water music. Lizzy drifted off to sleep.

A simultaneous pain in her head and stomach brought Lizzy to wakefulness as she screamed in agony. She sat bolt upright on the couch, knocking the bowl of massage oil on to the floor smashing it and sending the oil rolling across the floor. She sat stiff, panting as the pain receded then collapsed once more back down on to the padded bed.

"Lizzy! What's wrong? Stupid slave, you hurt my friend."

"No, no she didn't, it was, I don't know what it was."

"Do you need a doctor?" Without waiting for a reply Charley looked around and found the frightened slave quickly clearing the broken bowl and oil from the floor, "You go to my grandmother, tell her the princess is sick."

"Charley it's nothing, I'm sure. Maybe I'm just overheated?"

"Well, let's get cooled down. We'll hit the plunge bath then get dressed. The garden is usually cool in the late afternoon. You," She pointed at another slave, "go back to the changing room and get clean towels and our robes."

Charley helped Lizzy off her couch and into the cool room. Compared to the other two rooms it was freezing, although the water in the pool was only a few degrees lower.

"We have Ice brought from the far north every winter and keep it underground. Grandmama likes to drop a lump in the plunge pool every day during summer."

Charley climbed in quickly, dunked her head under the water and then climbed back out again.

"Your turn. You can't stay intoo long or your body doesn't like it."

"It can't be any colder than swimming in the sea at home."

"No, not really, but after being in the hot rooms it feels colder. Go on, our towels and robes are here."

Lizzy stepped in boldly but yelped as the water felt colder than she expected. Charley laughed. Lizzy stuck her tongue out at her and dived in, taking the last four steps in one go and ducking straight under. She burst above the surface a few seconds later and shook her head before climbing the steps out again.

"That was refreshing. I feel quite well now." There was some residual pain in her stomach but it seemed to be receding quickly. Her feeling of unease

201

seemed to be fading with it. Maybe she was becoming accustomed to slaves after all. She shook her head, no it couldn't possibly have been that. She still found the submissive shuffling of the silent slaves disturbing.

Chapter 29

Despite her reassurance that she now felt perfectly fine, Charley and her grandmother continued to fret around Lizzy.

"Are you sure? We can always send our apologies and go tomorrow night?"

"No, no Lady De Narvel, it wouldn't be good manners, and I'm quite alright."

The three women were waiting for their carriage to the palace for Lizzy's introduction to the Empress; Lizzy was dressed in the height of traditional Albonii fashion, and sweating copiously. She hoped the empress wouldn't notice.

"Lizzy, you've pulled your blouse all out of shape."

"Have I? I'm too hot."

"Next time you will be able to wear something more suitable, but my dear Princess, you must wear your own people's fashions this evening. The Empress is quite keen to learn of the manners of the less advanced nations."

"I see."

"Lizzy."

Lizzy turned to Charley, her grimace quickly replaced with a false, bright smile.

"Ah, here's the carriage." Lady De Narvel smiled at the younger women and seemed oblivious to the insult she'd given as she chattered away, sharing court gossip.

Lizzy climbed into the carriage, pushing back the soft, rippling silk curtains that hung from a light wooden frame. The vehicle seemed to provide little protection from the elements; the roof and walls were of the same silk as the curtain she'd just pushed through. The seats were of wood and covered in a plethora of cushions. She arranged her skirts awkwardly and found they took up an entire bench. Charley and her grandmother were forced to sit together on the opposite seat.

"These skirts are ridiculous; I can't imagine how inconvenient they must have been when mother was a girl at court."

"My mother told me they used to see if they could block the halls with their big hooped skirts."

"I've seen portraits of Grandmama in the Royal Gallery, she looked really bored. I'm glad we don't have to wear the big figure eights anymore; these hoop skirts are nuisance enough."

"Your Queen, I am told by my friend the Sumoasti ambassador, favours a return to formal court garments."

"That bitch would."

"Lizzy, I know you don't get on."

"She tried to kill me, several times."

"Yes, well, I suppose so, anyway, you really shouldn't insult the Queen."

"Charlotta is quite correct, if such comments were to get back to Tarjan."

"It wouldn't make much difference. When, if, she returns, father won't let her get away with any nonsense, not now, not with everything we know she's done."

"Like what?"

"Oh, you know, inciting treason, attempted murder, that sort of thing." Whatever else the bitch had done was a state secret until the Duke and her father said otherwise.

"I see, and nothing else?"

"Not that I know of." Lizzy was beginning to feel suspicious, Lady De Narvel was asking some very pointed questions. Was she working for Tarjan? Or the Empress? It would suit either of the two Courts to prise information from Lizzy. She'd ask Sarah as soon as her friends returned with Gos.

The coach bounced along the road and soon passed through the Night Gate into the palace grounds. The palace sat on a hill above the city, and overlooking the bay. The bouncing of the carriage over the cobbles jolted Lizzy from her worries as she looked up.

"Oh, how uncomfortable these cobbles are, I have no idea why the late-Emperor had them laid."

"For the same reason he had the summer palace built in the Lower Strigona style, he liked it."

"Strange man. But I suppose it does look rather elegant from a distance. But oh these cobbles!"

"Don't Belenosian carriages have springs?" Lizzy asked with a shark's smile, "But perhaps that's something only we less advanced Islanders would need?"

The carriage drew to a holt and the curtains were draw back by waiting slaves. Lizzy stood, swinging her skirts and climbed down from the carriage.

"Gosh, it's nice to be out of that silk tent, Charley. I have to say, this palace in quite impressive, definitely

205

in the Strigonan style." Lizzy smiled back at her friend as she too stepped down on to the cobbles, followed by Lady De Narvel, who had a curdled smile wrinkling her paste.

The older woman stepped around them and with a wave said, "Come along girls, we can't keep the Empress waiting you know."

Charley took Lizzy's arm as they followed her grandmother into the palace.

"What did you say that for?" Charley whispered hoarsely.

"Tit for tat."

"It wasn't nice. She is putting us all up."

"I'll go back to the ship then; it might be safer anyway."

"Really?"

"Yes, I don't think I should have come to Belenos."

"But we spent so long planning it."

"I know, but something isn't right and I don't feel good."

Lady De Narvel turned back to look at them, having heard the last few words.

"Are you quite well, Princess Elizabeth?"

"Yes, quite ma'am."

"Are you sure, you look quite pale, it must be nerves. Of course, it's nerves, everyone is nervous when they first meet the Empress."

"I assure you I am quite calm; please, don't let's be late to meet the Empress."

"Of course. This way."

A slave led them through a series of corridors that

turned unexpectedly every few yards. It was a maze of short corridors and outer halls, all filled with visiting aristocrats and neighbouring royals. Lizzy recognised a few faces, diplomats and visitors to her father's court in the past. Each bowed or curtsied before returning to their conversations. Eventually Lizzy realised that the further in they got the more important the people. In the first hall, she had seen merchants from Calman and the Essenmouth region of the Empire among wealthy citizens of the imperial capital, in the next lesser nobles of Belenos. Lady De Narvel nodded to a few friends and explained that she couldn't stop; she had to take her Alboni visitor to the Heart of the Palace. The nobles looked Lizzy over quickly before dismissing her.

In the next hall were high ranking nobles and diplomats; Lizzy saw Ambassador Conort among them and waved him over. Their two parties met at the entrance to the next corridor.

"Your Highness?" The ambassador asked with a bow.

"Accompany me Ambassador. I really could do with your experienced advice."

"It will be my great pleasure Your Highness."

Charley relinquished Lizzy's arm to the ambassador and joined her grandmother.

"How delightful to see you again Lady De Narvel, are you well?"

"Thank you, Ambassador, I am. And you?"

"Well enough. Excuse me one moment." He turned to his aide, "Do join us Forier, my dear fellow."

"Of course sir. Your Highness." The young man

bowed to Lizzy and joined them. They walked in amiable silence for a few moments before the younger man asked, "Is Sir Henry not joining us?"

"Not this evening, the boys went exploring down the coast earlier, they must have found something interesting or I'm sure they'd have returned to join us."

"Oh, I do hope they're safe; after young Gos Val disappeared I've been quite reluctant to let any of my people go out of the city."

"I'm sure they'll be quite safe sir, the Duke's sons are competent soldiers, as are Lord Henry and Sir Phil."

"Of course, of course. Is there any news about young Gos, Forier? I knew his parents, we went to school together, you know. His father and I were at the university as well." Conort seemed quite upset by the loss of his Assistant Ambassador.

"Not yet sir, but our investigations are getting closer." Forier looked at Lizzy, who nodded after a second.

"I'm sure now the Duke's sons are here it'll go faster. They are from the Office aren't they, Your Highness?"

"Did the Duke not communicate with you?"

"Oh, yes, yes, oh, I shouldn't have said anything."

"It's quite alright Ambassador." It wasn't but the old man seemed quite distressed by his lapse. If anyone was involved in espionage at the Embassy, it wasn't him. Forier was perhaps the Duke's real contact in the Embassy now that Gos had disappeared. Either him or Redfern.

As they walked the sounds of music floated down

each winding corridor, getting louder with each turn. Lizzy's brow wrinkled as the map of their movements that she built in her mind resolved itself.

"Lady De Narvel," she called quietly, "Is the palace built like a labyrinth?"

"Of course not, didn't you see in from the bay? It's a perfect square."

"I see." Lizzy mused to herself.

The music became louder as they made the final turn into the great hall at the centre, known as the Heart of the Palace. Lizzy stood rooted to the spot in amazement. The walls were panelled in mirrors thirty feet high that reflected the thousands of candles burning in the many chandeliers that hung overhead, while the ceiling was painted with a riotous scene from Belenosian mythology. While these were enough to stun, what dazed her was the scene before her eyes. On long low couches the scions of the Empires most powerful families lazed, consuming food and drinks from the burdened tables around them. At first she thought the revellers naked and blushed to see so much flesh on display, but realised that the material they wore was so fine as to be almost transparent.

"Gosh, I know it's warm but really?" Charley leaned back to whisper to Lizzy.

"I know. It's quite." She had no way to finish her sentence, still struck by the sight, "Ambassador, how did your wife react?"

"My former wife refused to come to the Court after our introduction. Myself I stay in the outer courts; my heart can't take such pressures."

"First time I've been this far in; can't say I

disapprove."

"Forier, any more inappropriate comments and I'll send you back to the outer courts."

"Sorry Ambassador, won't happen again."

"Well, now what?"

"Grandmama has to take us up to the Empress. Lizzy straighten yourself up."

"It was that carriage, it's too small and bumpy."

"Can I offer you my vehicle for your visit, Highness, I had it imported from home. It's the latest model. These Belenosians haven't taken up springs yet."

"I noticed. And I'd very much appreciate it, at least if I come here again. My spine does not like those cobbles."

Lady De Narvel had left them at the doorway and now scurried back to their little group.

"I've had a word with the First Minister, he's a cousin you know, and he's going to inform the Empress of your arrival. Charlotta and I will lead, if you gentlemen will follow behind. The Princess should walk through alone. Please try to be regal dear, I promised your father that this would go well."

"Oh dear, has he roped you in as well?"

"Into what dear Princess?"

"The great get-Lizzy-married venture?"

"No, that was the Duke. Your father is just concerned about you making a good impression."

"Thanks. Come on, let's get this over with and go back to your villa, I'm too hot."

"Oh but you must stay a while or the Empress will be insulted."

"She won't even notice."

"The Empress sees everything, dear."

A tall, ascetic looking man in a dark, pleated kilt hurried towards them, and bowed to Charley's grandmother.

"My Lady, if you would please follow me, the Empress will receive you now."

His eyes flicked to Lizzy but he did not acknowledge her. In Belenos, Lizzy recalled, unless a visitor to court had been recognised by the Empress none of the court officials would acknowledge the stranger. Lizzy found it a trifle impolite, but kept a pleasant smile on her face and her eyes blank and innocent. The man, Lizzy assumed one of the Empress's advisors led the way down the centre of the hall, diners on either side. Lizzy endeavoured to look straight ahead, but noticed one or two looking at their party with interest. When they recognised Lady De Narvel or Ambassador Conort they turned away in disinterest. As they got closer to the throne, one group of diners seemed to keep their eyes on the party. Lizzy quickly glanced at them and then glanced away. With the ambassador so far behind and Lady De Narvel so far in front she was alone and couldn't ask either to identify her watchers. The group was exclusively male and all had similar features. Their couch was closest to the throne and they seemed to be in conversation with the Empress until she sat up straight to welcome her visitors.

Lizzy's first glimpse of the Empress shocked her almost as much as the room in which she found herself. She was a girl, no more than fourteen or fifteen. But how? Lizzy had heard the offer of marriage had come from her adult son.

Lizzy almost walked into the back of her friend; the group had stopped while she was musing on this oddity. She stumbled backwards and felt a hand steady her. Lizzy looked round into a pair of warm brown eyes.

"Thank you."

"A pleasure Your Highness; it is a greater pleasure to meet you at last."

A shrill voice interrupted them before the young man could introduce himself.

"Cthinn-Erthy, take your seat." The child Empress had spoken.

So this was her suitor; Lizzy looked him over as he bowed and returned to his couch. Not bad. Long, strong legs, lovely hands, and such a sweet smile. She sighed, he was probably an awful bore; the prettiest ones always were in her experience.

"Great Empress, True Heart of the World, may I introduce you to my Granddaughter and heir, Charlotta De Narvel."

Lady De Narvel and Charley had prostrated themselves before the Empress, who merely nodded. The two women crawled backwards, allowing the Ambassador and his assistant to step in front of Lizzy. They bowed deeply but did not crawl.

"Ah, Ambassador Conort, it is a pleasure to see

212

you again. Any news of the lovely Lord Val?"

"As ever, Gracious Empress, I'm honoured to be in your presence. Unfortunately, we have no fresh news."

"How awful, I'm sure some word must come soon. And, so, this is Princess Elizabeth Alboni?"

Lizzy nodded slightly; no more or less than equals should.

"Indeed and you are the Empress of Belenos."

"I am. Please, join me." The girl indicated a seat beside her, "I'm sure we have much to discuss."

"It will be a pleasure." Lizzy smiled and mounted the three steps to join the young Empress at her table.

"Excellent, we weren't sure when to expect you, I know it's been a long voyage, your little island is so far away." The Empress smiled through her mask of make-up and picked at the meat on her plate. She waved to the slaves behind her who filled a plate for Lizzy, "Try the chicken, it's delightfully spiced."

Lizzy tried a small piece of what she hoped was the chicken and tasted it, before agreeing with the Empress.

"It is; have you never visited the Isles?"

"Oh no, I couldn't possibly leave the city for so long. Besides what is there in the Isles to interest me?"

"I suppose when the world will come to you, then you have no need to travel to see the rest of the world."

"Indeed. Have you travelled much?"

"Not really, my father has had so much need of me in the last six years there hasn't been time."

"It's so often the way; before my dear late

213

husband the Emperor returned to the Ancestors I had more time, but you know, youngest wives usually do. Now, with all the former senior wives in religious orders I'm left with the burden of ruling."

"Did not one of the Emperor's sons want to help with the burden?"

"Oh, yes, but they are so immature I couldn't possibly allow it."

Lizzy almost snorted, the chit wanted her to marry one of her stepsons but wouldn't trust them to hold a throne herself.

"You've met my son Cthinn-Erthy?"

"Briefly." Lizzy laughed quietly, "Though he didn't introduce himself."

"Later, or tomorrow I'll have him visit you. You're staying with Lady De Narvel?"

"I am."

"Excellent. He's a sensible young man, but too sweet tempered. I'm sure you'd rather not marry for politics, but I hear that your little island may soon need all the allies it can get. For one of our daughters we would be prepared to send two legions and one of our fleets."

"I shall think on it; I should ask my father though."

"We have communicated with your father; he has accepted if you are willing."

"I see; as I said, I shall think on it. It is a great honour."

"A pleasure my dear Princess Elizabeth. I hope soon that you will join me here as my daughter rather than an honoured guest."

"How truly kind of you, Empress. It would be a great honour, but you know, I couldn't make such a decision without knowing the man I may be spending my life with." Lizzy smiled though her heart raced. She had to get out of this somehow. Nice as he probably was, and as useful as two legions and a fleet would be, she didn't fancy marrying Cthinn-Erthy or spending even a few years in Belenos before she politely divorced him and ran home to King's Ford.

Lizzy sat in silence picking at her food until another visitor arrived and she was ushered away to join Lady De Narvel and the ambassador at a guest couch.

"Thank goodness for that. Can we leave now?"

"Lizzy."

"Yes Charley?"

"Who is that speaking with the Empress now?"

"Oh I don't know, a new envoy from somewhere."

"I know who it is, that's Lord Hakon Tarjan; you know, the new Lord Holmgard's son."

"How do you know that Justin?" Charley nudged him, "You can't have seen him before."

"I know how to do my job, they arrived late last night after you'd docked your ship. I hear he's come to offer his sister as a bride for one of the Empress's sons."

"So they're after the two legions and a fleet too?"

"What?"

"That's what she offered if I married Cthinn-Erthy."

"I wonder; my Lady, it's possible the Empress is

215

playing us off against each other. If you'll excuse me, I have to speak with some people." Justin stood, bowed in the direction of the Empress and to his party and left the room.

"What on earth was that about?"

"Nothing to worry about Lady De Narvel, nothing to worry about. Your Highness, while you were dining with the Empress, Forier reminded me to invite you to tea at the Embassy tomorrow, and all your companions of course. We will be picnicking in the gardens, about five after noon?"

"How delightful, I do love a fete!"

"Indeed, Lady De Narvel you must join us then."

"Why, Ambassador Conort how kind of you."

"I shall send my carriage in good time to collect you all."

"Excellent, and now I think we may leave the Heart, don't you girls?"

They stood, all but Lizzy bowing to the Empress, who wasn't taking any notice anyway, and left. They didn't find Justin Forier in either of the lesser halls. As they waited for carriages the ambassador muttered to himself.

"The boy must have gone off somewhere."

"He'll be back at the embassy eventually."

"That's what we thought about young Val and we haven't seen him since."

With that cheerful thought the carriages arrived and the party broke up.

Chapter 30

"Well, dears, that went well. The Empress never spends so long talking to visitors." Lady De Narvel patted Lizzy's thigh, the heavy skirt crinkling further under her hand.

"Business deals always take time."

"Don't be so cynical, it isn't attractive."

"I don't care to be attractive."

"Lizzy, are you quite well?"

"Just tired."

"I see."

The carriage turned into the grounds of the De Narvel villa at last. Lizzy sighed with relief. She needed to get out of this corset and discover the results of the rescue mission. Lady De Narvel's secretary was waiting for them as the three ladies entered the house. He handed a note to his mistress then bowed out. Lady De Narvel slowed to let the younger women past, and stopped in her tracks as she read the letter.

"Girls! Come back at once. Mello, go wake up Miss Charlotta and the Princess's maids. Have them pack. Quickly."

"Master FitzAlboni instructed us to pack our visitor's belongings when he brought the note my Lady. The wagon is ready as soon as the ladies are."

"Thank you Mello." Lady De Narvel reached out to grip his arm as she swayed. "Help me to a chair, please."

Mello silently assented as Lizzy and Charley returned, confused.

"What is the matter grandmother, why are our

bags packed?"

"Oh, dear, you'd better read the letter. Mello explain, please." Lady De Narvel passed the letter to her secretary, who passed it to Charley.

"My ladies, after you left for the palace, Sir Alex arrived in a dishevelled state looking for you. They found Lord Val already dead and the Sumoasti ambassador preparing to visit the Empress to make a counter offer of his sister. When the ambassador left they found a letter from Queen Jocinta to her cousin, confirming a plan to poison you in the Empress's court this evening."

"But he got their too late."

"So it would seem. Ma'am, your cousin wishes you to return to the ship and for you all to leave the empire immediately."

"Run away in the night, like we're afraid?"

"It'll save your life." Forier clattered into the entrance hall, panting and blowing. He found them in shock, staring at the crumpled note from Alex.

"Sir, you can't barge in like that." Mello tried to block the secretary's route.

"Move man."

"Mello, we know him, let him through. Justin Forier, what are you talking about?"

"Lady De Narvel, I apologise for barging in so late, but the Ambassador sends me with important news."

"More?"

"Yes Your Highness."

"When I left you I went to speak to a friend at the Sumoast Embassy in the city. He confirmed that the

Queen has been in communication with the Empress for months. He takes the copies of the letters for the Embassy records."

"Why? What can the Empress gain from all this?"

"With a foothold in the Islands then the Empire could control the trade routes to Camar."

"And we'd never give them that." Charley gasped.

"No, but Tarjan would if the Empire helped in Jocinta's war. Jocinta wants revenge, she isn't bothered by what happens to Albon so long as father suffers for choosing me over her."

"I believe so."

"Do you have the letters?"

Forier smiled crookedly, "Of course. My friend was easily persuaded to get them for me."

"I see; where are they now?"

"I've woken my scribes up; copies will be made by morning. Come to the Embassy tomorrow as planned and I'll give you them then."

"We should make it a breakfast picnic."

"Yes, I'll tell Conort and the staff as soon as I get back."

"Mello, provide Forier with an escort and a fresh horse. He does not leave your chosen man's sight until they present him to the Ambassador, do you understand?"

Mello looked at his mistress who nodded, "Yes, Your Highness. Who shall I send to accompany you?"

"I'm staying here."

"If Charley's staying, so am I."

"No you aren't Lizzy. I'm visiting Grandmamma, and half-Belenosian. If anything should happen to me the Empress is obliged to have an investigation. If anything happens to you it'll cause another war, and Albon cannot defeat the Empire. Go to the ship and our friends. We'll collect you in the morning in the Embassy coach."

Lizzy sighed, Charley could be quite annouyingly determined when she wanted. She stared at her before nodding in agreement.

"And you need to maintain some appearance of being here. Mallo, have Charlotta's bags removed from the wagon. I want another guard to escort the baggage and the Princess to her ship."

"My lady, if I may make a suggestion?"

Lady De Narvel nodded for Mello to continue, "I shall accompany the princess and our visitors' belongings to the ship and then proceed to the Embassy with Master Forier. This way I only need to split our household guards between here and the escort party."

"Of course, it'll make your journey longer though?"

"It will, but I'd prefer to keep a greater force here under Dolmon, should our enemies attempt an attack."

"Of course. See to it would you?"

The secretary left to arrange the escort and returned several minutes later. The ladies and Forier sat in silence, waiting for the word to leave. Slaves carried Charley's baggage back to her bedroom.

"I have sent the wagon ahead, it's slower and won't attract much notice at this hour. The early morning market carts are heading to the city and the docks."

"Well done man."

"Your Highness, can you ride?"

"Yes, but not in this."

"You will have to try; we have a horse waiting."

"Well then, we'd better be going hadn't we?"
Forier smiled.

Lizzy set her teeth and nodded, standing. She hugged Charley and thanked Lady De Narvel for her truncated hospitality.

"We'll see you in the morning, Lizzy, it's not the end of the world."

They rode out less than ten minutes later.

Chapter 31

The escort was met at the entrance to the private dock by Alex and Lawrence, who'd been waiting for an hour. Restlessly pacing the road outside the gate.

"At last, what took so damn long?" Lawrence gripped the bridle of Lizzy's horse as she slid down from the saddle, her thighs sort from riding without trousers.

"Justin turned up with more news." Lizzy panted out. They had ridden fast and as obliquely as they could, trying to throw of potential followers.

"Oh yes?" Alex asked. He looked Justin Forier over, remembering him from the reception when they'd arrived; Harry had been impressed but Alex wasn't so sure they could trust him.

"We saw the Sumoati ambassador at the palace talking to the empress."

"I went to speak to some friends at their embassy; I got some interesting letters that will add some urgency to getting the Princess away from here."

"Really, and do you have copies of them?"

"Indeed, I'm having the incriminating letters copied as we speak."

"What happened on you trip out yesterday?" Midnight had passed long since and Lizzy was beginning to fade as the sun started to rise.

"I'll tell you later."

"Whatever happened, I think you should tell the ambassador as well. We're having a breakfast picnic in five hours. Has your baggage arrived yet?"

"Yes, just before you, where's Charley?"

"Miss Charlotta will be residing with my mistress for some time. She insists she will be safe once you are out of the empire."

"And you let her, Lizzy? Why?"

"She's an adult, she can make her own decisions." Lizzy shrugged.

"But I thought you two were" Lawrence nudged his brother into silence.

"I must return to the Embassy and I'm sure Mello here is eager to discharge his duty and return to his mistress."

The slave-secretary nodded, looking around vigilantly.

"Be well." Lizzy saw them off, and followed her cousins back to their ship.

It's been less than two days, Lizzy thought as she collapsed on to her bunk, and here I am back again. There was a knock at the door.

"Come in." Lizzy cracked out in her exhaustion.

"It's me." Sarah poked the door open, "I brought some clean clothes from your baggage in the hold, and your journal and pen."

"Thanks. Dump them on the desk, take a seat before you fall down and for goodness sake, tell me what happened."

"In the morning; something's shouldn't be told in darkness."

"The sun is coming up."

"Don't push it Lizzy, I'm knackered. We'll talk when we've all had some sleep. Do you need help getting your dress off?"

"I'm just going to sleep fully dressed. I can't move."

"You'll ruin it if you do."

"Fine, I'll ruin a dress I hate anyway."

Sarah sighed, pulled herself to her feet and left. Lizzy closed her eyes again and tried to sleep.

Chapter 32

Morning, and Alex hammering on the door to her cabin, came all too soon. Lizzy cracked her eyes open, her head full of fluff and eyes like boulders weighing her head down.

"Not so loud."

"Sorry, are you dressed yet?" He poked his head cautiously around the door.

"I just woke up."

"Everyone's waiting."

"Send Sarah to help me dress, I need to get out of this corset."

"Why didn't you get out of it last night?"

"This morning you mean! I was too tired to move. I'm still too tired to move but you need to tell me what happened yesterday and we have an appointment at the embassy." Lizzy creaked and cracked as she rolled out of the bunk and stretched, a grimace on her face as the boning of her corsets found new places to poke her.

"I'll send Sarah." He shut the door and seconds later Sarah arrived. Lizzy was bent over, stretching her cramping back muscles and rolling her stockings down at the same time.

"Well, you've made more progress than last night, I suppose." Sarah was also tired and grumpy. This picnic, Lizzy decided, was going to be a joy if everyone was exhausted.

Half an hour later, washed and dressed, Lizzy joined the rest in their dining cabin for a quick cup of tea.

"Decided to join us at last?" Harry grumbled.

225

"Yeah, I thought I'd better. Where's Phil, and Callia?"

Sarah started to sniff as the twins looked away from her. Harry coughed, "Phil's in his cabin."

"And Callia?"

"She didn't make it back." Sarah said quietly. She'd lost a colleague and friend in Callia, and the Office had lost one of its best agents.

"Oh." Lizzy sat down heavily. "What happened?"

"There was a fight, when we went to get Gos, his body, I mean, he was already dead, they'd bashed his head in and stabbed him in the stomach then hung his body in the woods for the carrion birds." Alex spat. "Phil lost it when we tried to cut Gos down and Callia died defending him from the guards."

"Did you, did you manage to get their bodies?"

Lawrence nodded, "Just. They're in brandy, in the hold."

"And the information you got from the villa?"

"It's in my bags, I'll give it straight to father when we get back."

"I want to see it."

Alex looked exhausted as he shook his head, he'd been up all night reading the letters and they still haunted him.

"No, Lizzy you don't." Lawrence lifted his hand to stop her next comment, "I've only read a page or two and you don't want to see them, believe me."

"What now?" Harry asked quietly.

"We're going home."

Grief palpable in the air, the group fell into silence, tears still unshed.

"I'll send a message to father as soon as we get to the embassy." Lizzy gasped suddenly into the silence.

"The coach is waiting for us." Sarah mumbled.

"We'd better go then." Alex hauled himself up with a sigh, his whole body arguing against doing anything but going back to his bunk and sleeping. They had work to do though, and as tired as they all were, Alex knew that not completing their mission would be disastrous for their family and island.

The coach barrelled out of the dock gate and on to the main road into the imperial capital, bouncing its exhausted occupants around.

"I thought the embassy had imported a decent carriage?" Lizzy muttered.

"Best springs can't compensate for rubbish road building." Sarah muttered back. They were both sat back against the carriage walls, cushions under their necks as they tried to make themselves comfortable and nap for the short journey. It wasn't working.

Lizzy grunted and opened her aching eyes to look round at her reduced companions. There was only herself, Sarah, Harry and the twins now. Phil was in deep mourning for his brother, refusing to leave his cabin or eat.

"We're going to have to tell Charley."

"What? Oh, yeah, one of us will."

"And we need to send a message to father."

"I sent a message to the Office last night." Sarah

added.

"New information?"

"We'll do it later."

They were jolted fully awake as the coach came to a halt.

"We can't be there yet."

Lizzy looked out of the carriage window.

"We're not, it's an inspection patrol."

"We should get waved straight through."

"Well, game faces on just in case."

There was a knock on the carriage door and then it was opened.

"I say, you there, what is going on; don't you know this is an ambassadorial conveyance. Let us through." Lawrence drawled at the woman in kilt and tunic, a sword by her hip who glared around their carriage suspiciously.

"Papers please."

"Oh really." Alex drew out the e-a in the word and yawned. "Don't you recognise the crest?"

"Papers please." It seemed to be the only Albonese she had.

"Wretched jobsworths. Don't bother with her. Demand to speak with the commanding officer."

The woman scowled.

"Papers please."

"Run along and get your commanding officer, we're important members of the Alboni embassy and you're making us late for a meeting." Harry repeated exasperated. The twins could draw things out sometimes, but they didn't have the time. They planned to leave in the next few days and they needed to make arrangements with the Ambassador and their contacts. Sitting in a queue to get into Belenos City was wasting time.

The woman looked round the carriage at their pleasantly blank faces and turned on her heel. They heard shouting in the distance and soon a group of men on horses rode up. Lizzy gave a sigh of relief.

"My dear Prince Cthinn-Erthy, what a surprise to see you here." Lizzy stepped down from their carriage as she spoke. The man with warm brown eyes smiled down at her from his horse. He really did have very lovely legs and that kilt wasn't doing its job effectively. She almost swooned. Sarah, climbed down from the carriage and stood discretely behind her, as she always did.

"Princess Elizabeth. Is there a problem?"

"Yes, we have an important meeting at our Embassy in less than a quarter hour, and this person," Lizzy waved in the direction of the soldier who had demanded their papers and was stood watching the interaction, "Has importuned us. What is going on?"

"There was an attack on two villas last night, the Sumoast Embassy's summer villa and Lady De Narvel's property. You were not there?"

"No, we had forgotten some of our belongings on the ship and went there. It was so late I stayed on my ship. We're planning to return to the De Narvel villa today, after our appointment at the Embassy. In fact, we were meeting Lady De Narvel and Charley there."

"I am glad you weren't at the villa; it was rather badly damaged by a firebomb."

"Oh dear." Lizzy staggered backwards against

Sarah, "And my friends?"

"Are well; the fire brigade arrived just in time, but we didn't catch the attackers."

"Thank you so much. And do you have any idea as to who they may have been?"

"We can only think it is some group who wishes you harm. I would suggest you stay within the Embassy or on your ship for the rest of your visit."

"Thank you Your Highness, we probably will, but first we need to get to the embassy."

"Of course, I will escort your coach."

"It's very kind of you." Lizzy smiled up at the prince and climbed back into the carriage. Her flirtatious smile turned to a grin as the door shut behind Sarah.

The Prince was heard instructing his riders to move the carts in the queue out of the way to allow them through and soon they were moving again. The mounted escort rode alongside and in front of their carriage, the Prince by the door. Lizzy drew the curtain back and smiled at him again. The prince smiled back and sat up a little straighter in his saddle. He seemed like a lovely young man; unfortunately, Lizzy was serious in her refusal to marry. It didn't suit her to be bound to one person for so long. The Empire's Laws insisted couples must be married for five years and have at least one legitimate child before a divorce could take place, and Alboni Law only allowed for divorce in the case of adultery or abuse. Neither legal system suited her, she didn't want children, and Albon couldn't afford to pay any sort of recompense if they divorced because she committed adultery.

Within ten minutes they had passed through the crowded city streets and had arrived at the Embassy. Forier was waiting in the courtyard for them as the carriage and its unexpected guard arrived. He was pacing and holding some papers in his left hand as the carriage rolled to a stop and the twins jumped out. Lizzy was helped down and then Sarah, with Harry following up behind.

Chapter 33

"Won't you join us for our picnic, Prince Cthinn-Erthy?" Lizzy stood by his horse's neck, gently patting the animal's fur.

"As much as I would enjoy an hour spent in your company Princess Elizabeth, I must return to my duties. We must find the bandits attacking the villas."

"Of course, and thank you again for your assistance. I hope we'll see you again soon?"

"I'm sure we will meet again before long." He bowed over her hand from his saddle and left, leading his men out of the Embassy. Lizzy watched the gates close behind him and nodded to the guards. The gates were locked as she walked towards her friends.

"Now, where were we?"

"Damn woman, you need to stop flirting with him, it'll only cause trouble when we leave." Alex growled at his cousin.

"He doesn't know we know about the Sumoasti offer, therefore I'm playing along. That's what you told me to do."

"Yes, we did, but really, Lizzy, now is not the time."

"Yes, it is, it's the best time. We've got too many enemies and even a slight friend is better than none."

"Fine, fine, but it isn't going to end well."

"Look, can you three stop arguing for five minutes, I have news." Forier waved the pieces of paper at them in frustration. "I went to take the originals back to my contact at the Sumoasti embassy but I couldn't find him. He's not at his lodgings or at his desk."

"What did you do with the originals?"

"Put them in someone else's desk and walked out after delivering a dinner invitation for next week to their ambassador. I sent a few of my messengers out to the other embassies with invites as well. No doubt they'll all turn up and pretend to like each other for a few hours."

"If he's 'missing' will he talk?"

"Possibly, but it's too late. We know about their plans and they can't afford to admit to planning an assassination. Nor the Empress.""

"Even so, we shouldn't hang around long."

"Come in and we'll eat. If there's planning to do its best you're here. Charley and her grandmother arrived earlier. They're somewhat shaken up."

"We heard about the fire; any ideas?"

"Same as the rest of you I suppose, Tarjan."

"Probably, but we can't prove it, not now."

"No, we've definitely burnt our bridges on that front." Lizzy looked up at the embassy roof as a door slammed. She saw a set of six panels flapping in the windless sky. "You have a tower?"

"Yes, why?"

"How quickly can you get a message home?"

"It takes about three days for the message to get to King's Ford and a response to come back. Why?"

"I don't like being out of touch, not with the way things have been going."

"We're at the end of a long rope, but the rope is still there and it'll hold us."

"Good."

Sarah was also watching the flickering boards, "That's the Duke's sign. Something important must be coming through."

"How, we only sent him the message last night?"

"Must be something else, because that's the code for urgent." She pointed to the boards as all six turned from black to white and back to black again.

"Damn. Come on, we'll need that message as soon as possible. Conort is in his office with Lady and Miss De Narvel."

"We'd best join them then."

"Ah, here you are at last, we were getting worried." The ambassador lounged on one of the local style couches drinking iced lemonade and eating a bowl of fruit. The ladies, in their soft linen tunics shared a couch across from him and smiled tiredly as their friends arrived.

"What news? Where's Phil?" Charley lifted her hands to Lizzy, who took them and placed a kiss on her wrists, so glad to see her friend safe. Lizzy sat beside her and smiled sadly.

"We had casualties."

"Callia didn't make it back. And we didn't get to Gos in time." Sarah sighed.

Lizzy looked down into her lap. "We'd have been here earlier but they're stopping and searching everyone coming into the city."

"We heard about the fire." Alex bowed to Lady

De Narvel, "I hope neither of you were injured."

"My dear Sir FitzAlboni, it takes more than a ruffian with an oil soaked rag to harm me. The villa took some damage, but nothing we can't repair easily enough and we're going to the summer estate soon, so the work can be done then. I was just telling Lord Conort that I think we'll have to trespass on his hospitality a week at most and then we'll leave early for our summer visit."

"And I am sure it's no trespass, my dear lady; it's quite refreshing to have a woman of your education and elegance in residence. At least you'll wait until after the Islands Embassy dinner, and honour me by being hostess?"

"How very kind of you Lord Conort, but surely the Princess?" She indicated Lizzy with a tilt of her head.

"Oh no, Lady De Narvel, I couldn't possibly. The way things are, my presence would cause rather too much discussion. I believe we are going to be otherwise engaged by an invitation to the Imperial Theatre that night."

"Ah yes of course, your engagement to the prince must be forwarded somehow."

"Something like that." Harry laughed quietly as he took a seat on the couch beside Forier.

"Lizzy, come and sit here, there isn't enough room on that couch for all three of you." Sarah commanded quietly.

Lizzy rolled her eyes at Charley and went to sit with Sarah. The twins took the remaining couch. The six seats made a hexagon around an array of small hexagonal tables placed on a blue and turquoise hexagonal rug. Lizzy was beginning to suspect a pattern when she looked upwards. The ceiling was painted with interlocking geometric shapes in a variety of blues and greens.

"We should turn to business now I suppose, since we're all present."

"Yes, we should."

"I have the copies of the letter between the Sumoasti Embassy and the Empress."

"Harry take them for safe keeping. When we get back to the ship put them with the ones we found in the villa."

"Right oh. Hand it over Justin." Harry pointed to the packet of papers the man was still holding.

"Any time."

Conort rolled his eyes, "Save it for another time Forier, we don't have time for your ridiculous antics."

"Really, Lord Conort, flirting is harmless enough."

"But it's not really acceptable in Albon, Grandmamma. The Curates don't like that sort of thing." Charley giggled and looked at Lizzy who collapsed on to Sarah, laughing.

"Young people today have no respect for their elders' beliefs, Lady De Narvel, and they expect the world to be run for their enjoyment."

"Hardly, we'd just prefer not to be flogged for following our natures." Lizzy coughed herself into seriousness.

"Can we please return to the matter in hand?"

"I thought we had." Alex nudged Lawrence and

236

they both collapsed in laughter.

"Poor Forier is blushing; be nice now." Sarah said sharply.

Their laughter, a release of their tension and grief, however inappropriate, was silenced by a knock at the door.

"Your grace." A messenger in the Alboni colours panted as he hurried across the room, bowing to everyone indiscriminately, and carrying a copy of the message they'd seen arriving from the ground. "It's come from the Palace, just now."

"Thank you Stevens, keep this to yourself."

"Of course sir. Any return message?"

"Wait outside and we'll call you back in in a few moments." Lizzy waved the man away. Stevens looked at her curiously, then bowed out of the room. "Well, Conort, what does my uncle say?"

"It's quite brief. Come home. Immediate effect. War."

"Oh drat."

"My thoughts exactly."

"Really? Mine were, 'how unexpected'." Alex sighed, "They must have found some other evidence. Our intelligence wouldn't have arrived before this was sent."

"And it's urgent, whatever it is."

"Yes. Yes, it is. We must leave today."

"Bit precipitous aren't you Lizzy?"

"Stay awhile if you want Harry but the twins and I need to go home."

"No, no I shall not stay. I have a regiment to command if there's to be war. And probably Phil's too;

he's in no state to command a dog to sit let alone a thousand soldiers into battle."

"It might be what he needs, an outlet for all the anger." The Sumoasti had tortured Gos before they'd killed him, his body a bloody mess when they'd cut it down.

They were silenced for a few moments.

"We need to provision the ship if we're going to return immediately." Charley spoke in little more than a whisper.

"My dear child, you are staying here. I won't have you running back to a war zone."

"But I can't leave them."

"Yes you can Charley. Stay safe and come home after the war. You don't need to get involved."

"Lizzy?" Charley appealed to her friend after she saw the nods of agreement to Lawrence's suggestion.

"Well, I'd be happier knowing you were out of the war zone."

"And what about what I feel? You can't expect me to let you go back to a war, any of you, alone?"

"Yeah, we can. You have a place that's safe. We've only got Albon, all our families are there. Most of yours is here."

"He's right; you can have a future here. If the war is long or vicious you won't in the Isles."

"Grandmamma!"

"Well, do you really think I want my only grandchild to die before I do?"

"No, if course not, Grandmother."

"You two," Lizzy and Charley were indicated, "discussed this last night anyway, you agreed then and

238

you're outvoted now." Harry told her with a smile. "Be thankful you won't be in the middle of a battle."

"I am, but still it's hard."

"It is indeed. Ambassador Conort, I'd like permission to resign and return home to help in the war effort."

"Of course m'boy, of course. Have you anyone who can do your job?"

"Lord Gos's former aide? Felix Redfern."

"Hmm, isn't he in our cells at the moment?"

"I let him out this morning. I believe he's decided to go into mourning and won't leave his room."

"Stevens!" The messenger was shouted into the room. He poked his head around the door. "Oh, good, there you are. Run up and get Aide Redfern down here immediately and send an encrypted message back to the Duke. The ship leaves on the next high tide. And send in my steward."

Now a decision had been made, the Ambassador showed his metal. He enjoyed playing the lazy aristo, but had been trained by the Office just as the Duke had. He wasn't in fighting trim anymore, but he still knew when to act. And now was a time for action.

"Now, m'boy, go and pack the essentials, I'll have the rest sent with the next shipment of silks."

"They won't be far behind us then; the silk ships leave in a week."

"Fine, fine, I'm sure your books, clothes and whatnot can be packed by the servants in time. Go on, go on."

"I'll go with him, to make sure he doesn't bring anything that's unnecessary."

"Of course." The two men left as the Embassy steward arrived.

"You sent for me Ambassador?"

"Ah, yes, Steward. Have one of your most trusted men ride out to Her Highness's ship and inform the captain they'll be leaving by this evening's high tide. That should give us time to provision you." He smiled at the young people. "Eat up, do, you must be famished. Ah, yes what else? That's right. How many provision suppliers can you contact urgently?"

"Five or six, sir."

"Good, they're to fully provision the ship today, on our account."

"Father will send the money with the next fur shipment."

The Ambassador waved away Lizzy's assurance.

"They know we'll pay eventually, but it might help if we gave them something on account. How much do we have in the petty cash?"

The Steward rolled his eyes, it was hardly petty cash and they kept it in a safe under the building. "Twenty thousand sir."

"Promise them anything up to a thousand each if they can get everything aboard before mid-afternoon and as discretely as possible."

"Yes sir, of course."

"Off you go then."

The Steward left as Felix Redfern arrived, dressed in black and looking thoroughly haggard. He drooped on to the couch vacated by Harry and Forier, picking at the slices of orange they'd left untouched.

"You wanted to see my Ambassador?"

240

"Yes. How'd you like a promotion?"

"What?"

"A promotion. Forier is resigning early, he's got something going on in King's Ford, so I need a new Secretary. Lord Val trusted you implicitly, and Forier recommends you. I can't imagine a better reference. So do you want the job?"

Redfern was stunned. "I er, well, yes, I do. Thank you."

"Good, you start today, after you've had some sleep."

"I couldn't possibly, if Forier is leaving us so soon."

"I would advise you to take the chance to rest while you can, Redfern, the next few days are going to be busy." Lizzy nodded around the room.

"What's happened?"

"Nothing official yet, but I have to leave urgently and we don't want the news getting out until we're out of the Bay."

"Of course." Redfern nodded and left.

"As soon as Harry and Forier finish packing we'll leave for the ship. If anyone asks why we need so many provisions, we'll have to tell them we're hosting a party or something."

"The Prince did suggest you make the ship your residence. We could just tell people that?"

"One, or both would work well. I don't mean to be impolite Ambassador, and I'm grateful for everything you're doing to help, but I really want to get back to the ship."

"We can't sail until after sunset Lizzy, we have all

day, you'll only be pacing up and down the dock. People will know something's up."

"FitzAlboni's right, here you can fret and pace all you like and nobody will notice. In the docks, there will be watchers who'll report back to someone."

"You're right, I know, but it's frustrating having to wait."

"We can't sail if the ship isn't ready to go."

"I know. All right, we'll wait here, but only until midday."

"Agreed. It would look suspicious if you stayed longer, and you all need sleep."

Plans made, they settled into wait, picking at the food laid out for them and napping. Lady De Narvel went to speak with her own servants, arranging for most of her salvageable belongings to be sent north to her summer estate a month early. She left before midday with Charley to visit dress makers to replace their damaged clothes and a man-hunter to investigate the attack. It was expected of her that she would institute a search of her own in addition to the Imperial investigation; anything out of the ordinary would be noticed and commented upon. They needed to keep suspicions as far removed from the De Narvel house as possible.

Chapter 34

Lizzy hugged Charley before climbing out of the carriage and plastering a fake smile on her face.

"Come on, do, I want to get sailing; if we're going to be in Malan tomorrow morning to see the sun rise."

Lizzy laughed as her friends fell out of the carriage one by one, the moment they became actors barely recognisable to anyone who didn't know them. Certainly, the Empress's spies, masquerading as dock workers, didn't notice anything out of the ordinary.

The group wobbled and giggled as they boarded their ship then lay about on the foredeck enjoying drinks in the afternoon sun. On the main deck their captain ordered his men into action as a pale and drawn Phil joined them for the first time since they'd returned with Gos's body. He took a long sip of the wine Harry offered him and stared at the docks.

"Are we going home now?"

"Yes, yes we are."

"Good."

Chapter 35

Sailing away was not as straining to the nerves as sailing to Belenos; they had the winds with them most of the way and once they reached the Essen, the current too. On the first night a ship followed them to the island of Malan, about half way across the inland sea, but turned back once they stopped for the night. After that the journey was uneventful. They did not stop at any port and were in the Northern Ocean in seven days. They took on fresh water at Essenmouth and collected the messages waiting for them. Lizzy sent a single message, letting her father know where they were, before ordering the ship out to sea with the tide.

Three days later they were back in King's Ford.

Chapter 36

Prince Michael waited for the ship to dock, tapping his boot on the ground. Around him the docks bustled with the clamour of war preparations. Nothing had been declared but the Sumoast ambassador and his household had left unexpectedly only three days before and the city, if not the nation, knew it war was coming.

"Your Highness." A guardsman bowed in front of Michael.

"Yes," Michael fished around for the man's name, smiling when he remembered, "Johnson?"

"Her Highness's ship has docked, but they need to bring Lord Gos Val's body ashore before anyone can disembark."

"Oh dear, has Dowager Val been informed?"

"Couldn't say sir, but Lord Phil Val is acting as escort."

"Of course, of course; allow them through, and send an honour guard with them to the Palace."

"Yes sir."

The Guardsman smiled to himself at the young prince and trotted back along the Hythe to the newly-docked ship. The wrapped body of the deceased lord descended the gangplank, carried by half a dozen sailors. Sir, now Lord, Phil Val followed, his face drawn and hollow, and clothes wrinkled and stained. Guardsman Johnson bowed to the grieving man and ordered his troops to form up around the bier. They passed along the length of the Hythe, and into the city.

Lizzy and her remaining companions followed

slowly behind. Prince Michael saw his sister reach the Hythe in safety and rode to join her.

"Hello little brother. What've we missed?"

"Nothing much, we're going to war with Sumoast, that's all."

"I know. What did they find at the Rocks?"

"Lizzy, time and place?" Alex gently chided. The young prince smiled at his sister and cousin, while Lawrence rolled his eyes appreciatively.

"Come on Lizzy, that can wait until we get back to the Palace." Lawrence grumbled.

"Oh, your mother has gone back to their estate."

"Why?"

Michael shrugged, "A lot of ladies have gone to the country."

It was Lizzy's turn to roll her eyes now. "What do they expect to do there?"

"Recruit and knit bandages I think. There was something in the paper about it a few days ago."

"I see. Well, if that's all they can manage, I suppose it's better than nothing."

"And what do you plan to do Lizzy? Father won't let you fight."

"I haven't had any fun since he legitimised me. Any chance we can get him to change his mind on that?"

"Don't joke about that."

"Why?"

"..." Michael tried to find the words and failed, so he shut up.

"Leave him alone Lizzy, we have to get to the palace."

"And I should go to my Regiment, introduce them to my new ADC." Harry smiled at Justin and then his friends.

"Come to the Palace first, father will want to know everything we found out in Belenos." Lawrence suggested. "You need to get orders from Lord Marshal Sommerton."

"And you don't know where your regiment is." Alex added.

The wind started to pick up as they talked. Sarah looked to the sky, mused in the advancing clouds and their metaphorical aspects, and tapped Lizzy on the shoulder.

"I don't want to interrupt this family reunion, but it's going to bucket down soon and I'd like to be inside when it does."

"She's quite right sister; there's a carriage waiting and your baggage can follow us."

Grateful for the chance to stretch their legs after so long confined to a small ship, the party turned their steps towards dry land and the waiting coach. The rain hit just as they crossed the Hythe bridge. Huddling inside the guard towers as their documents were checked, Lizzy noted the change in the atmosphere. Nobody had bothered to check her documents on her previous, rare, visits out of the city by ship.

"What's this for?"

"Uncle thinks we might have an infestation."

Sarah snorted, "I knew I should have sent someone else to Belenos with you. I've been gone a month."

"It's in hand, Sarah. Colson is dealing with it."

"Oh dear. Lizzy, if you don't mind, I need the carriage to drop me at the Office first. I'll join you at the palace once I've got my subordinates straightened out."

"I knew it!" Lizzy turned on her, "I bloody knew you were more than you admitted to. How long has this been going on?"

The twins synchronised their eye roll, Harry and his amour laughed. Everyone had known who Sarah was in the Office structure, except, apparently, Lizzy.

"Yes, yes, Lizzy, we'll talk later." Sarah waved her away. "Come on, the rain's slowing down, and I have work to do, even if the rest of you don't."

Lizzy sighed and gave in; someone was going to suffer later, probably her uncle. They hurried to the carriage in the splattering rain. Lizzy stopped suddenly as she opened the door, looking up at the driver, the unfortunate but loyal Dawson.

"While we're going through the city we need to stop at the Press. And try not to let anyone steal me this time"

Her companions skidded on the wet cobbles, piling into her. Lizzy fell forward, Sarah and Lawrence almost on top of her.

"What's so pressing?" Alex laughed, he had avoided the collision but still felt the need for poor puns, while Lawrence groaned and shuffled backwards, regaining his balance. Sarah straightened up, smoothed her dress and scowled at everyone as she helped Lizzy to her feet and into the vehicle. As they pulled away from the Hythe and docks, Michael riding ahead with his Guardsmen, Lizzy answered the question.

"I need to let them know I'm back; there are things I have to do."

"She's going all cryptic on us again."

"That's what we get for not telling her about Sarah, isn't it?"

"Probably."

The twins carried one in this vein, getting sillier and sillier, until Justin threatened to kiss them both. Lawrence shut up while Alex became thoughtful.

"You really shouldn't have said that."

"Why not? It worked, didn't it?"

"We're not in the Empire now Justin. An accidental slip like that could get you into trouble."

"Oh nonsense, nobody thinks like that anymore."

"You've been away too long." Harry patted him on the knee.

"What, have things got worse?" Justin laughed.

"'Fraid so, mate, the Conservatives and their"

"Slightly barmier"

"friends – thanks for the qualification their bro – among the Fundamentalist are gaining ground for some unknown reason. They'll get worse if the queen comes back."

"People fear the war, that's all. We've avoided them for a few hundred years."

"That's not it Lizzy; the Fundamentalists were gaining followers before the prospect of war arose, the last three or four years at least."

"But I thought it had steadied out at thirteen percent?"

"Of the clergy. Didn't you read the census report I

gave you before we left?"

"Strangely enough Sarah, I didn't. I wonder why?"

"Oh do stop it the pair of you. Where is safe?"

"Anywhere with us, and in most of the city, just don't go into the more conservative chapels. Some people might laugh but most of them won't say a thing."

"It's hardly fair, is it?"

"No, it's not, but we're working on it." Harry patted Justin's shoulder, "We have friends."

"And it's not as bad as it could be. At least that woman isn't here."

"Why are you so certain thing's would be worse if she were?"

"I saw how things were going, before I went to Belenos."

"She was playing on already existing fears and ignorance."

"You plan to do something about the fear and ignorance?" Justin challenged Lizzy with his eyes.

"I'd be a hypocrite if I didn't." She smiled crookedly, a gleam of something dangerous dancing across her face.

The coach clanged to a halt; the coachman leaned down, "Press house Miss Lizzy."

Lizzy sighed, "Shan't be long."

Lizzy stepped down from the carriage and ducked

under the awning. The paper caller bowed quickly and returned to shouting the news from the relative dryness of the canopy. Lizzy pushed open the door, revelling in the bash-whomp of the presses as they hit the paper, and the shouts of the workers. One or two recognised her and nodded as she passed journalists scribbling on desks littered with paper and climbed the stairs to the editor's office.

"Lizzy! You're back at last." Peterson looked up from his latest proofs, "Any news?"

"Nothing you can print yet. I can't stay long, is there anything for me?"

"Some letters from the Ladies Guild and the Emancipationists."

"Great; now that I'm back, we can return to normal."

"Normal's the last thing the city is right now."

"Do tell."

"You said you didn't have long?"

"I don't, give me the short version."

"The High Curate has died."

"Another one?"

"Yeah, they drop like flies in that job, don't they?"

"They do indeed; who replaced him?"

"A fellow called Barnsmath, proper Fundie too. Might be trouble for us and our friends."

"Maybe, depends on how the other Curates react."

"They've already had a minor dispute, over chapel clothing. All women must cover their heads in chapel."

"I thought we'd dealt with that a decade ago?"

"We did, and now we have to deal with it again. I haven't been to a service myself, but I work seven days a week, so."

"So you hear the Holyday sermon in the square every week, and publish as much of it as can remember."

"You remember!"

"Of course. What have you been hearing?"

"Not good stuff. Apparently, this war is a punishment from the One that we shall surely lose unless we allow the bitch to return and stamp out licentious behaviour and," he was reading from his notes, "here it is, 'the King's continued approval of immorality and perversion'. I think you're the immorality, but I'm not sure who the perversion is."

"Probably me, and a few of my friends."

"Our friends."

Lizzy smiled.

"Oh, and they denounced any reform of the Moot as unholy. The One ordained, and all that nonsense."

"I see; more than one war to fight then?"

"Pick your battles Lizzy; now isn't the time for divisions, not when we have to defeat the Tarjani fleet."

"Just the Tarjanis. Not all Sumoast?"

"The northerners and western clans won't play nice, according to my sources."

"Interesting. And talking of sources, you want to tell me about your contacts in Belenos?"

"Oh, who did you run into?"

"Someone at the Embassy."

"I see; problem?"

"Not really, but I could do with a warning next time."

"Hopefully there won't be a next time." Peterson muttered under his breath. At Lizzy's raised eyebrow he spoke more loudly, "I mean, hopefully you won't need to go abroad for a few more years?"

"We'll see. I'd like to visit the rest of the islands at some point. And now I must be going, those messages please?"

"Of course." Peterson stood and retrieved the bundle of papers from a locked file against the wall. Each letter was addressed to Lizzy under her pseudonym of 'Maggie'. Lizzy briefly glanced at each envelope before placing them in her bag. Everyone had their own jobs, and now she had hers.

Chapter 37

"Anything good?" Alex looked over Lizzy's shoulder as she read her messages.

She shook her head, exhausted from the long day. After visiting the printer, their carriage had delivered Sarah to the Office then the rest of them to the Palace. After being welcomed home by the King, they had joined Phil in the chapel with his mother, and Gos's body, for the funeral. After waving Phil, Dowager Lady Val and the corpse off to their estate, the remaining travellers had to meet with the Duke and the King's Council to debrief and hand over the documents they'd acquired. Forier was introduced as an expert on the situation in Belenos. The Duke eyed the younger man sceptically then nodded his thanks when the news that the letters taken from the Sumoasti embassy had been liberated by him was imparted to the gathered admirals, marshals, spies and government officials. Finally, not long before midnight they'd got out of the meeting, with promises of more on the morrow. Harry departed after offering his new aide-de-camp accommodation at his town house and the three remaining travellers slouched out of the Council Chamber and headed to their suites in the palace.

"Lizzy, you just walked past your door."

"Huh, what?" Lizzy looked up from her letter, slightly dazed.

"Your room?"

"Oh yes." She laughed and back tracked, pushing open the door, "night you two."

"Night."

"Night."

Shutting her door on her cousins' backs she glared at her still-packed baggage and bent to pull off her boots and cloak, dumping them on a chest. Her trousers and shirt were next to find the floor as she traipsed through the parlour and into her public office and library. She shouldered the next door, into her bedroom, open with a crash as it banged back on to a bookshelf. Throwing the satchel of letters on to her desk before kicking off her underclothes, she threw herself on to her bed, naked as the day she was born.

"Oh what a lovely sight." Sarah stepped out of the private closet, where Lizzy's most valuable books and private notes were kept.

"Piss off Sarah, don't you have spies to organise?" Lizzy rolled over, wrapping the topmost blanket around herself.

"All organised; and your father hasn't relieved me of my duties as your Lady-in-Waiting yet."

"Then go to bed and I'll ask him tomorrow."

"No you won't; it wouldn't be safe now."

"War to fight, more important than babysitting me." Lizzy mumbled, too tired to form complete sentences.

"I'm sure it is, but, nevertheless, those are my orders."

Lizzy grunted and rolled around on her bed again to rearrange the blankets. Somehow (Sarah had witnessed this feat several times and had yet to work out how she did it) Lizzy was under the slightly rumpled sheets and blankets, and looked to be sleeping.

255

"LIZZY."

"Told you, go 'way."

"I'm going. Is there a Guard on your door?"

"Prolly no'."

Sarah sighed, shook her head and left,
unimpressed by the mess she passed. Someone would
get a thick ear in the morning for not unpacking the
Princess's travelling cases, and the Household Guards
weren't going to be in a much better situation either.

Morning, and the next round of war councils,
inevitably came. Lizzy was woken by the banging of
doors and servants hurrying to unpack her chests and
tidy the rooms. Sarah stood in the parlour, a vision of
ire.

"What's going on?"

"Sorry Your Highness, we didn't mean to wake
you, but Mistress Sarah is rather angry." A maid, of
indeterminate age and a harried expression gabbled as
she opened cupboard after draw after cupboard,
putting away clothes.

"I see. That box is laundry." Two more maids had
appeared, carrying a box clearly marked 'laundry'.
They looked down, looked at her incredulous face,
turned round and carried the box out of the room.

"Idiots, I told them to take it to the laundry."
Sarah stamped into the room, "Aren't you finished
yet?" She glared at the maid unpacking the clean
clothes.

"Yes, ma'am."

"Wait, those need to go to Mistress Caro, my
dressmaker. Take them to her, will you?"

The maid held up the Belenosian dresses she'd managed to acquire during her attenuated visit – thanks to Charley and her grandmother's shopping trip – to confirm which she meant.

"Yes, those ones. Take a message to her for me, will you, with the dresses?"

"Yes, Your Highness, of course."

"Tell her I'll be along when I can, there's so much to do here yet."

"Yes ma'am. Is there anything else?"

"Send someone up so I can order my breakfast."

"Yes ma'am."

"I've already ordered your breakfast; it'll be here in ten minutes. Hurry away girl, the princess is busy."

"The princess isn't awake yet."

The maid grinned at Lizzy's grumpy response and left, carrying the dresses, to visit Caro's establishment.

"Any particular reason you decided to wake me up so early?"

"You have to be at the Council Chamber in an hour, there's going to be a full War Council now that everyone's here. We've been waiting for our Ambassador in Calman to send a representative, and for the rest of the Umari to arrive."

"The rest, who are we expecting?"

"The Queen of Umar sent her eldest two with three regiments apiece."

"I see; I don't think I've met them. Aren't they cousins of Aunt Catherine?"

"They are; and they've arrived with a proposal."

"Oh dear, not another one."

"You might like these two better. And they have

257

lent us a small army."

"That's nice. Have they brought a large navy with them, because I suspect this war will be fought at sea?"

"Yes, twenty ships, fully armed with their new cannons."

"Is that all?"

"It's all they had spare; they can't risk Sumoast attacking Umar while their forces are defending Albon. Be grateful that they have, we'd be further in the shit than we are if they hadn't."

"How bad is it?"

"Bad enough."

Lizzy dropped back on to her bed. "Can we win?"

"Maybe. Look, we won't know until the Sumoasti declare their intent. We have evidence of their intentions, they'll either have to back down or declare war."

"They'll declare war; they can't do anything else but complain that our evidence is false and declare war, or they'll lose face, especially with the Belenosians."

"Don't be so pessimistic; for all we know, Tarjan will say that a group of conspirators is responsible, punish some random group of political rivals and pretend to be contrite."

"Such hope. Much likelihood."

"Well, I'm only the Spymaster, obviously, I don't know as much as my Princess."

"Yes, yes, alright. Point taken. So, what do your minions tell you?"

There was a knock at the door.

"You can find out when everyone else does, at the council meeting. Your breakfast is here. Put a robe on and get out of bed." Sarah extracted a dressing gown from the back of the bedroom door and threw it at Lizzy.

"Be there in a minute; go let them in."

Sarah curtsied and left as Lizzy dug herself out of her blanket nest to pull on the red silk and brocade garment. She found a pair on matching slippers under her bed and went to face breakfast.

"Lizzy! Are you decent?" Michael's voice called from her public office.

"Well I'm not naked at the minute, is that good enough?"

"It'll have to do. Ooh, this bacon is yummy."

"You leave that bacon alone, you rat!" Lizzy scampered out of her room to confront her bacon stealing brother, slipping slightly on the parquet flooring.

"There's plenty left. You coming to the meeting in that?"

"No, I was going to get dressed first, but now you mention it, it would make an interesting fashion statement."

"Lizzy!" Sarah snapped and pointing at one of the chairs, "Sit."

"I should really object to the way you talk to me."

"You should but you won't."

"No, probably not. Are you two eating as well?"

"I've eaten." Sarah sniffed, she'd had three or four hours sleep then returned to her office to work while Lizzy had been snoring.

"I have too, but I could eat a second breakfast."

"You always can. I swear you have hollow legs."

"That's John. I hope he stops growing soon, or he'll be taller than me."

"He's only fourteen, he's got a few more years yet."

"I don't want him to be taller than me; it'd look ridiculous if the Duke of Albon is taller than the King. The portraits would be unbalanced."

"I'm taller than you are. So with one of us on either side it'd be quite a balanced picture."

Michael rolled his eyes.

"So, what'd I miss?"

"Nothing much. You know about the raid on the Rocks?"

"Most of it, father and the commanders told me yesterday."

"Hmm, okay, we're having a load of trials of traitors next week. I'm going as the representative of the Crown." He grinned, it was his first major public engagement.

"Really?"

"Do you want it instead?" Michael looked disappointed.

"No, you can have it. It'll be good experience. I think I'm mostly being kept out of the way anyway."

"Why?"

Lizzy shrugged and concentrated on her food. Nobody had said anything but she felt they blamed her for the war in the first place. If she'd stayed away from court the queen would never have become so paranoid. And then she'd not have plotted so much and wouldn't have been exiled.

Michael listened to the silence and grinned at her, "Father said he'd rather fight a war than let mother back in the country."

"Really?" Lizzy laughed.

"Oh yes, he had his serious face on and everything. John's a bit upset about it to be honest, but all he remembers is a lady who used to give him sweets every time he saw her."

"And you? You're only three years older."

"I remember enough to know she barely tolerated father and only visited the nursery when it suited her."

"Careful brother, you're becoming a cynical as I am."

"I'm not cynical." He grumpily munched a sausage sandwich.

"Yeah you are. Sarah, how long will we be in Council today? There's something I need to see Caro about."

"Clothes can wait Lizzy. You have more important things to do that chat with your dressmaker."

"Who says it's about fashion?"

"Why else would you visit your dressmaker?"

"Because she's my friend?"

"She knows you're back in one piece, I'm sure she'll write and let your mother know without any help from you."

"Sarah."

"Alright, we'll probably be in meetings all day. Happy now?"

"No, but I'll manage."

Frustration burned in her stomach turning the breakfast to lead and grease. She needed to speak to Caro soon; she was her contact point for the Women's Suffrage League and the Campaign for Women's Marriage Rights. They couldn't come to the palace but Caro's house was a safe intermediary; she needed to set up a meeting with the leaders of both organisations and soon.

Chapter 38
Late Weedmonth A.E. 1336

War hadn't been declared but the long wait was nearly over. The Calmani ambassador, who had acted as a peace envoy between the opposing islands had given his final deadline for a resolution but both sides had remained resolute. Albon required reparations for the damage done by the Sumoasti pirates; Sumoast denied any responsibility for the piracy.

Lizzy, spent her first week home sending messengers to various landholders informing them of their responsibilities for the foreseeable future, and attending meetings with Sarah and the twins. She felt, temporarily at least, that she was back where she would have been had she not been adopted and legitimised, fighting the covert war that had already started; she still wasn't allowed anywhere near the 'front lines' but instead she acted as an informal Minister for Public Information, controlling what went into the paper and what didn't.

Eventually, a fortnight after returning home, Lizzy escaped the palace alone, on horseback, to visit Caro. It was a late summer evening, a chilling breeze off the sea making a light cloak necessary. Caro had moved premises since Lizzy had first endowed her with the funds to set up her own dress making establishment; she now worked from a large building on Royal Square (owned by Lizzy) where her creations were seen and bought by the most important ladies in the land. She had a stable yard 'round the back and a quiet parlour above the shop where favoured clients came to inspect works in progress, drink tea and gossip about fashion. Tonight, it would be the scene of a most unusual gathering.

The leaders of Albon's fledgling Women's Movement had been persuaded by personal messages from Lizzy to meet in the parlour above Caro's Couture Clothing; many were wary of being noticed, the new High Curate had denounced as heretical the movement to improve the 'One ordained position of the female sex' and threatened any woman with a long imprisonment if they were caught involved in the Movement. The Curacy had the power to try them in clerical courts for the crime of heresy, though it had been a century since anyone had (during the campaign for male householders' enfranchisement). Waiting nervously were the Working Women's Association chairwoman, Angie Burgess, and her deputy Lou White. Less nervous but still cautious, was the chairwoman of the Suffrage League, Breda Tailor and the chairwoman of the CWMR, Margie Cooper. Lizzy had watched them for a few seconds before entering the room, trying to fix in her mind the dynamics of the group. There was some tension between Angie Burgess and Breda Tailor; Lizzy watched as they avoided each other's eyes and the tension when they were forced to speak to each other by a lull in the general conversation.

"Ladies, how good of you to come, especially when we have such difficult days ahead."

"Is war definite then, Your Highness?"

"I'm afraid so Mistress Burgess."

"It's Miss actually."

"I do apologise; it's very wrong of me to assume."

"Most people do."

"But Lizzy isn't most people,"

"My dear Caro," Lizzy held out her hands to her oldest friend, "how wonderful to see you again. I'm sorry I haven't been before; it's been hectic at the palace." The two women hugged and then took their seats at the tea table.

"Now ladies, I asked you here because I think what you're all doing is important, and I'd like to support you."

"All of us?"

"Of course, why not?"

"Most of your kind don't take kindly to working women muscling in on this stuff."

"I can't imagine why; I'd have thought working class women would be the experts on their own lives?"

"That's what we said." Lou piped up. Her voice belied the lines on her face; she looked thirty but couldn't be more than eighteen.

"Who has said otherwise?"

"That'n there." Angie pointed to Breda, glaring angrily, "She said in one of their pamphlets that they thought only women of the same class as the men who can vote should be given the vote."

"I did not. I said that unless all men were given the vote, only middle class women should have the vote, to ensure parity. You clearly can't read."

"And you're a snob."

"Your Highness, I did not come here to be insulted by this ignorant baggage, I must leave."

"Ladies, ladies, please. This infighting is doing

none of us any good." Margie placated the two women.

"You're quite right, may I make a suggestion?"

"Ma'am?"

"Universal suffrage."

"I don't understand."

"I do; you think we should campaign for everyone to get the vote?"

"Yes. It hardly makes sense to give the vote to one set of adults and not another based purely on social class."

"But, everyone? Really? I can't imagine what will happen to the Moot if anyone can vote?" Breda seemed confused; Lizzy, a lady, wasn't supposed to side with the poor people, was only supposed to provide polite charity.

"It'll be more representative?"

"I think so."

"We'd never get the MM's to agree to that."

"Why not?"

"Because everyone knows they quite enjoy their boy's club."

"Hang on a minute, my husband's an MM; it's not a club at all."

"Margie, we both know that only Guildsmen and Burgesses get to vote and they always vote for their own."

"I'm not denying that Ma'am, but that's how it's always been done."

Lizzy couldn't deny the truth of that, the Guildhall had been the template for the Moot; she took another sip of tea and thought about her next comment while the other women discussed their differences of opinion, Caro acting as referee when necessary.

Suddenly, she coughed. The women looked at her.

"I think we need to make an agreement, a treaty of sorts, for the time being."

"I understand you."

"You do?"

"Of course; you wouldn't have got us all together if you didn't want something."

"Well, I thought it made more sense to talk to you directly. The war is going to happen, unfortunately, and whatever happens I want us," she pointed at the women representing the various factions, "to be in a strong position at the end of it. If the queen returns the Curates will have her backing to reverse all our gains. If they can find a gap to exploit they will. So we won't let them."

"You want us to amalgamate?"

"No, I want you to agree to disagree and work together. All of us want to improve the situation of women in this city and the country as a whole, is that not so?"

The women nodded tentatively, waiting to see where she would go with this, though Angie was smiling slightly.

"Well, then, we have taken the liberty of drawing up a declaration of shared goals for all of the associations. I'd like us all to agree to a set of common goals to work towards. Caro, you have the declaration?"

"Here." Caro pulled out a sheet of paper with an

initial announcement for them to read through.

"Whatever we decide, I'll have to put it to my members first." Angie tapped her lips.

"Of course. All of you should."

"Have you spoken to your party about this?"

"Yes, I've been able to speak to most of them since I returned from Belenos, we're in agreement."

"The Radicals are going to lead us all, are they?" Angie sneered, Lizzy's Radical Party were mostly upper class and upper middle class, they didn't have to worry about losing their jobs if they were discovered, in the main because they didn't need to work.

"My husband won't approve of me associating with the Radicals." Mistress Tailor tutted.

"He's a Moderate, isn't he?"

"Yes."

"I thought so, I think I met him once; did you go to the Guild of Tailors Annual Dinner three years ago?" Caro wrinkled her brow, wriggling out the memory; she'd the ought Breda's face was familiar.

"Why yes, we did. It was the last time, we're not in tailoring anymore."

"No, you sell cloth instead, I get some of my best cottons from your warehouse." Caro smiled at the woman, hoping the compliment would mollify her.

"Have you seen our Belenosian lace? It's new in and we probably won't be able to get much more if the war closes the trade routes."

"Let's hope it doesn't but you never know who the Sumoasti will attack."

"They wouldn't attack a Belenosian ship surely?"

"Well, they attacked Calmani ships going to

Umar to buy furs."

"Weren't they pirates though?"

"Under the orders of Lord Tarjan." Lizzy reminded them.

"Horrible man, trying to start a war just to get his niece back here where she's not wanted."

"Is that the general feeling, that the Queen is unwelcome in Albon?"

"Among my customers and the Campaign members? Yes. She's a Fundamentalist believer."

"That's true, and her politics are in line with the Fundamentalist Curates League. She has a new curate, or had, a while ago."

"Really? I thought we weren't allowing people to visit?"

"He got through by claiming to be going to Calman on a Mission, and then got a ship to Tarjan after six months."

"How?"

"Our ambassador in Calman thought the Curate was going on another Mission after trying Calman." Lizzy shrugged, "It happens."

"How careless, but that's neither here nor there. I will put this declaration to the WSL members at our next meeting."

"I'll talk to the girls, see what they think."

"Is there anything you disagree with, on first reading?"

Angie and Lou glanced at the declaration, muttering quietly to each other. Before turning back to Lizzy and passing the paper over to Margie who read through it herself.

"Well, we were wandering, what about the whores?"

"I beg your pardon?" Breda coloured up, "That's hardly appropriate."

"No, no it's fine, please, explain?"

"Well, we represent all working women, and whores do work for their living. This declaration is for 'respectable' women."

"As it should be, those with low morals don't deserve to be involved. They'll taint us all."

Angie rose from her seat, wagging an angry finger at the burgher's wife, calling her ignorant and callous, while Breda returned the insults in kind.

"Hang on a moment both of you, and do sit down, you'll spill your tea."

Feathers ruffled but slightly calmer the two women sat down.

"I see what you mean Angie," Margie muttered through a bit lip, "We should be working for all women, not just the ones whose jobs we approve of. I'm sure there must be hundreds of reasons women become prostitutes."

"It's mostly poverty; don't have much choice at times."

"Really, there must be some sort of choice."

"Freedom to starve is no freedom at all. You're right, it's a sort of choice."

"That's why the WWA wants a social pension for them as fall on hard times and a legal lower wage limit." Lou turned to Caro, "How much do you pay you shop girls?"

"Ten crowns a day."

"How many hours a day do they work?"

"Well, it depends, up to fourteen though."

"Not that fair a wage, is it?"

"It's better than most shop girls earn!"

"That doesn't make it right though, does it? A shop man earns twice that."

"So do most men, it's normal."

"That should change too."

"Quite right Lou." Angie looked round at the others, "We should add equal pay to the declaration."

"I agree; it's hardly fair for a man to be paid twice as much as a woman for the same work."

"And equal access to training and education, and the professions."

"That's already on the declaration."

"Not the professions, it isn't."

"Angie's right, if we're going for full equality and equity, we need to fight for equal access to all professions." Margie dug a pencil out of her purse and started adding notes to the declaration she was holding. "Anything else while were thinking about it?"

Lizzy stood, stretched and walked about the room as the women talked about amendments to the declaration and tried to work around their differences. She lost track of the conversation at some point, walking over to the window and leaning her head on the glass. Something wasn't right, something was missing.

"It feels like we're just tweaking things." Lizzy mumbled, looking out of the window at the now dark square. In the centre the raised dais held two men in the stocks for the night and the sounds of revellers rose from the taverns on the other side of the square.

"What was that Lizzy?"

"Oh, I'm just remembering something Sarah said." Lizzy turned her back on the scene and smiled at her friend.

"What's that?"

"If we get what we want, it'll only be surface change. The change needs to go deep down into the roots."

"I think what we're proposing is a great change, what more do we need to do?"

"I don't know, but it doesn't feel like enough."

"That's the problem with you radicals, never happy." Margie laughed, teasing gently.

"You want to turn the world inside out." Breda accused.

"No, I just want to make things right, for everyone."

"You're a strange princess, that's for certain. Does the king know you're here tonight?" Angie asked quietly.

"No, and he doesn't need to. He's trying to organise a war."

"War ain't organised, is it? My father was in the last one we had with Calman, fifty years ago, he said it was a bloody mess, no one knew what anyone else was doing."

"That war ended in a truce and a trade agreement though."

"It did. How will this one end?"

"Chuffed if I know, well for us and badly for Tarjan I hope."

"So do we all; now, unless there's anything else I need to get home to my husband and children, and I'm sure the rest of you must have work in the morning?"

The meeting broke up after Lizzy assured the four women that copies of the amended declaration would be available for them to collect from Caro before the end of the week.

Chapter 39

War was declared during the annual Fall of Leaf Festival, when, the harvest mostly gathered the farmers of Albon shut up shop for a week to eat, drink and relax after the hard work of the year. The Sumoasti ambassador, from his retreat in Calman sent a message warning the Albonese that unless they retracted their claims against the Sumoasti then Lord Holmgard had no choice but to declare war. King John sent an immediate message to Lord Holmgard in the Sumoasti capital, Tarjan, that given the evidence he would not and could not do so.

The first attacks came a day later.

An Albonese trading ship heading to Camar was taken by surprise by half a dozen Sumoasti war ships. All hands were lost. Jonsey immediately ordered every ship out into Alboni waters, guarding the trade routes and major ports.

"Will they attack?" Michael asked Alex as they watched the fleet sail away from the Hythe.

"Us? Probably not, this war will be fought at sea, I think."

"Why?"

"We get our wealth from trade, so do the Sumoasti, and all the islands. It's about controlling that trade, it always was. We have to starve each other into submission."

Michael nodded, taking in the information and connecting it up to other bits and pieces he'd heard over the years.

"Did mother marry father for trade?"

"Yes. Sorry kid, I know you don't want to hear it, but that's what royal marriages are. Even Dad and Catherine were introduced for political reasons. It just so happens they fancied the pants off each other."

"And that's not the case with my parents?" He didn't have any illusions on that score but having it confirmed by someone who was there was important.

"No." Alex looked down before turning to his young cousin, a fraternal urge to protect him taking over, "You're going to have to make the same choice one day, I just hope you get to choose."

"Won't I?"

Alex shrugged, "Maybe, if uncle has learnt anything from his own marriage."

Michael nodded and thought some more.

"Did Dad love Lizzy's mother?"

"I don't know; he's fond of her, but she married Sir Philip a few months after Lizzy arrived, so I think it was more a passing infatuation rather than love. He does love Lizzy something strong though."

"I think she resents us."

"Who, Lady Mary?"

"No, Lizzy."

"Nonsense. She loves you beyond reason."

"Does she?"

"Of course."

"But if Mother hadn't married Father, she'd have been able to stay in the city."

"True, but eventually Lady Mary and Sir Philip would have wanted to go back to East Marsh and play at farmers, and Lizzy would have had to go with them."

"But ten years?"

"That was your mother. It's her Lizzy resents, keeping her away from the king, you, us, for so long."

"And the city."

"Yes, and the city."

Michael turned away from watching the ships, now over the horizon, and they started back up the Hythe to the gate to collect their horses.

"She was out late again last night; has she got another lover?"

"Not that I know of. I think it's Party stuff; she's got something going on she's keeping from the rest of us. I think she needs a distraction from the war."

"The war just started."

"But she's been fighting it for two years already; everyone on the Council has."

"And you?"

"And me. It's exhausting."

"What should I do? I should help."

"Watch and learn. That's all you can do. Uncle won't let you go to sea. Come to the Council meetings with us?"

"That could be interesting, but it's to going to help the war effort."

"Help with the home front campaigns? Lizzy is organising some of them."

"Yes, I heard she's the new Minister for Information."

"Well, we had to make use of that wicked tongue somehow. Afternoon, Jossep, get our horses will you?"

The door into the gate house opened and

Lawrence stepped out. He was grinning and holding up that morning's paper.

"There you are; did they get off alright? I think we know where Lizzy's been disappearing to every other night."

"Give it here then." Alex grabbed for the paper, which Lawrence let fall.

Michael sighed at his cousins' behaviour and grabbed the paper before it hit the cobblestone path. He flipped it open and scanned the front page.

"Oh dear. Father isn't going to be happy."

"Lizzy's already had a bollocking for it."

"Het timing isn't exactly great."

"No, it's not."

"Actually," Michael looked at them, "it's kind of perfect."

"How?"

"Distraction. People need something to gossip about other than rationing and casualty rates don't they?"

"And what could possibly be more scandalous than a princess joining the Suffragists?"

"It's hardly news to us though."

"But how many people, outside our circle, know about her politics?"

The three young men looked at each other and shrugged. Clearly none of them had thought about that.

"She's pushing it though. Disestablishing the Curacy? Dad'll never let that one through."

"It depends on how much popular support the Movement gets."

277

"People won't like it; they may not like the Traditionalists and Fundamentalists, but most people don't have an objection to Moderate theology."

"Except where it hurts people."

"Well, the Moderates generally try not to. They're a bit wet."

"Michael! You're going to be secular head of the Curacy one day, the One's appointed representative in this world."

"How dull. I'm with Lizzy; let's leave them to their own devices, I'll have enough work to do." Michael laughed.

"Not for years yet, and you might change your mind by then."

"What else does it say?"

"I don't know about the paper, but I say let's get going before those clouds empty their load on us." Alex pointed up at the purple bruised grey clouds rolling in.

"I wouldn't want to be at sea in this." Lawrence muttered as the horses were brought to them and the wind picked up.

Michael rolled up the paper and forced it inside his coat before mounting his horse.

"That's because you get seasick in the bath." He grinned and spurred his horse along the Hythe and up on to the road back to the palace. The twins mounted and road after their cousin, determined to avenge the insult.

278

Chapter 40

The door banged open, squeaked and clattered closed. Caro looked up from pinning a hem up on a dress she was working on, the young customer fidgeting as she stood on a stool. The mouthful of pins clattered to the floor as her mouth gaped open and stood up to curtsey.

"Mistress Caro, how delightful to see you."

"Your Majesty!"

"Please, no formalities, I've known you far too long."

"Thank you Your Majesty."

"And who's this young lady?" King John bowed down slightly to the girl who was having her dress fitted. He smiled gently as the girl curtsied to him, wobbling slightly on the stool.

"Jinny Fullen, your majesty, I'm getting a new dress for my seventh birthday party next week. Doesn't it look good?"

"Well Miss Fullen, I can't imagine a prettier dress. When are you seven?"

"Next Lastday, all my friends are coming to my house. We're having tea cakes and jelly, and ice cream, and sandwiches."

"Will there be a cake?"

"Yes." Miss Fullen nodded vigorously, "Mummy's having it made by the bakers across the street. She's there now giving them instructions."

"They are very good bakers. I like their cream cakes."

"Me too."

"It's a pleasure to meet you Miss Fallon, but I really must speak with Mistress Roberts."

"Oh." The girl's face fell.

"We'll be back down in five minutes, try not to move." Caro smiled at her little customer, "If you'll follow me this way Sir, I'm sure you prefer some privacy."

"Thank you Mistress Roberts."

"Now, Mistress Roberts, it's come to my notice that my daughter is spending an awful lot of her evenings here with you and some rather questionable women."

"Hardly 'questionable'; it's the Women's Movement Committee meetings."

"Yes, my nephews brought me the paper with their Declaration in it. I haven't said anything to her about it though."

"Why ever not?"

"We're busy worrying about the war, and she's concentrating on this."

"Really, it's hardly taking up much time, your Majesty."

"Every evening."

"Only for a couple of weeks. We're just trying to get the groundwork in place then the AWM will be able to manage without Lizzy."

"Why do you need her in the first place? She does have work to do at the palace you know."

"She doesn't really though, does she? All she does is write a couple of notes for the paper every week.

She's bored and this is a little project to fill her time; the WWA, WSL and the CWMR wouldn't talk to each other if Lizzy hadn't written to them and got them together."

"To what purpose?"

"Things need to change for most of the population in this country. Nobody but burghers in King's Ford have a say in how the country is run." Caro smiled.

"It's hardly the time to think about that sort of thing surely; we have a war to fight."

"And?"

"And we should be concentrating on that instead of this silly stuff."

Caro became indignant.

"Well, I don't think that equal representation of the populace is 'silly' and neither does Lizzy."

"It's not a particularly good time for her to get distracted."

"She's quite capable of being Minister of Information and helping to organise the AWM at the same time."

"I'm sure she is, but I need her to concentrate on the war effort."

"And what is the point of the war?"

"To stop the depredations of the Sumoasti pirates."

"We did that when the fleet raided the Rocks; why are we at war now?"

"Because Lord Holmgard refuses to compensate us for the damage caused by the pirates. There was going to be something eventually that started a war;

281

we've been dancing around each other for a century."

"I'm not going to tell Lizzy she should top helping organise the Movement."

"Caro, don't be so stubborn."

"I'm not; I'm telling you how things are." Downstairs the bell tinkled. "And now I have to serve my customers. It's a pleasure to see you in my establishment, but I really do have to be getting on."

Chapter 41

Winter's Start A.E. 1336

Lizzy sat at her desk, smiling at the paper in front of her; the latest MoI announcement had been published and she was pleased with the editorial Peterson had written beneath it. The war hadn't had much of an impact on the country, so far; there had been a few less ships from Belenos, but not enough for shortages to start biting. Her latest press release had only been to remind people that a licence was necessary to hold any large meeting; she had already had complaints from the Curates about the announcement restricting their prayer gatherings.

"What are you grinning about?"

Lizzy held her copy of the paper out to Alex.

"I see; how did Peterson know about the complaints?"

"I told him."

"Really?"

"Of course; how else do you thing he's getting news?"

"Lizzy you aren't supposed to give state secrets to the press."

"Hardly a secret; it would have come up sooner or later. The High Curate has been known to write to the paper."

"So now they'll have sympathisers who will accuse us of deliberately penalising believers." Alex settled on the sofa to read the paper himself.

"Oh please, as though that's anything new. They don't need an excuse to accuse of us that." Lizzy stood and stretched her tired shoulders.

"The party doesn't need the extra trouble; the AWM declaration caused enough last month." Alex leaned forward, snatching a glass of wine from the table as he put down the paper, looking back at Lizzy to continue the conversation.

"Really, it was hardly anything, a few letters from disgruntled Conservatives to the paper." Lizzy picked notebook up from the side table, pulling a pencil from behind her ear. She had a rally to plan; the whining of a few Conservatives and Traditionalists were flies buzzing about her head, and as easily sent away.

"There were Questions in the Moot, Lizzy and complaints in the Council Chamber."

"Ah, that's just form, the same thing happened when Father decided to finance primary schools for lower class children." Flipping the notebook open, Lizzy took a seat opposite Alex, chewing on her pencil. She couldn't decide who to ask to be their key-note speaker.

"That's because they want to control access to education."

"And how is state funded education different from the Movement's aims, since they both work towards our overall aim?" Lizzy's voice rose as her ire became more obvious; she put now the book and looked at her cousin with a disarming directness.

"It isn't, but taking such a big step is terrifying to the Traditionalists."

"They need terrifying. They're so, so," Lizzy thrashed around for the right word, "complacent."

"Complacent?"

"They think that once Jocinta returns their little

world will go back to the way it was before. They want to stop any progress we make before it gets too far."

"If the people get a taste for democracy then they might object to the queen and her pet crows taking it away from them."

"We can only hope. You think my timing was wrong?"

"Yes, Lizzy, it could have been better timed." Alex sighed and rested his head on the sofa back, staring at the ceiling.

"What would you have preferred?"

"You could have waited until our first victory?"

"We don't know when that'll be, the fleets haven't engaged each other since the war was declared."

"It's only been six weeks."

"And soon it'll be too rough at sea for the fleets, which'll delay any conclusion until the start of next summer."

"Yes, and it'll drag on for a year at least."

"Or it won't; there's discussion of a midwinter attack on the Sumoasti fleet."

"That might work actually."

"Well, try to keep it to yourself, won't you?"

"Oh, must I really?" Lizzy mock-pouted and laughed.

"Do try. Are you coming riding this afternoon?"

"No, I want to work on the plans for the midwinter conference."

"It'll be bigger than last year's rally."

"It should be; we've had several applications for membership from the AWM members recently. Every time I go to a meeting one or two ask for information."

"That's good; are you going to any meetings this week?"

"I'm going to a WWA meeting next Fifthday and a CWMR meeting on Lastday."

"Be careful, we've had a tip that some of the Curacy's more militant seminarians are going to start disrupting meetings."

"I'll let the ladies know."

"Do you want Lawry and me to come with you?"

"It could cause more trouble if you do."

"Well, we'll be nearby if you need us."

"Do you even know where we're meeting?"

"Yes, of course we do."

"I should have realised that." Lizzy grinned. She crossed her legs, rested her notebook on her knee and started making notes.

"Are you going to be working on that all day?" Alex stood up nodding at the notebook.

"Yeah, sorry, go have fun with the rest of them."

"The Umaris will be disappointed." Alex laughed.

Lizzy looked up from her notes briefly, "It won't kill them."

"The alliance would be useful."

"We've had this conversation Alex, I'm not marrying. You marry one of them if the alliance is so important."

"You know their mother wouldn't let them marry a bastard."

"Then why should they want to marry me?"

Alex rolled his eyes, "You're uncles oldest child, and legitimate."

"Only technically."

"Technically is good enough. Now if only Lady Eleanor would agree to father and Catherine's request, I could marry one of the Umaris."

"They are both very pretty, aren't they?"

"So you do fancy them?"

Lizzy blushed slightly, "They're not totally objectionable, slightly too pushy though."

"Mother says that's normal for the Umari."

"Aunt Catherine should know, I suppose."

"They're having some sort of festival at our house next month, Elenor is all excitement at the moment." Alex smiled fondly at his sister's enthusiasm.

There was a knock on the door, before a group of men and women burst in.

"Well, are you two coming or not?" Lawrence grinned.

"No, I'm busy, Alex is though."

"Such a shame Your Highness; we had hoped to see you ride today." The Umari prince, Donach, smiled.

"Yes, Lizabeth, you must come ride with us!"

"Sorry Danna, I really can't, I have to get some work done on the conference plans."

"Conference?"

"Party rally at midwinter." Lizzy smiled at Danna.

Danna nodded, understanding, "Do you go to the WWA meeting tomorrow night? We ride together then?"

"Er, yes, I didn't realise you were interested?" Lizzy smiled at the young woman, catching her eye.

"Ah, I am, very much." Danna nodded, holding her gaze.

"Come on, we'll miss the off if you keep on chatting." Lawrence laughed and turned to leave.

The group hurried out, some more disappointed than others.

Chapter 42
Fore-Midwinter A.E. 1336

"Lizzy, would you put that pen down." King John nudged her in the ribs, "We've got visitors today."

"What?" Lizzy jumped in her seat.

"It's dinner time." Michael laughed.

Lizzy grumbled and capped her pen, sliding it behind her ear. She closed her notebook and pushed it to one side. Taking up her cutlery to replace her pen, Lizzy started on her food. Chewing thoughtfully, she looked round at her family and their guests. She knew everyone, of course, but the Calmani ambassador, Carl Bordan, was a rare visitor. He'd just returned from a visit to his home island; rumour (and Sarah) had it that the Calmani were planning to join the war effort in the new year.

"What were we talking about?" Lizzy looked up from her plate eventually.

"You weren't talking at all." Her father laughed, "But we were discussing the recent message from Tarjan."

"What do they want?"

"Permission to visit and negotiate in the New Year."

"We going to agree?"

"Possibly; see how the next few weeks go." Her father winked at her. A planned naval raid on Tarjan itself was not far off. Lizzy had heard about the plan weeks before, but hadn't been involved in it. The Information Office had insisted that the number of people involved be kept to an absolute minimum; any leak would compromise their whole strategy for the war, and their IO agents in Sumoast. For Lizzy that meant frustration at not knowing everything, and a new Lady-in-Waiting, as Sarah was far too busy organising a war.

"You will not have any trouble from the Sumoasti fleet until the spring surely? The seas are getting rough." The Ambassador had only just made it back to Albon before most of the sea lanes had been closed by foul weather.

"We must be prepared Ambassador, for whatever happens. We will see how the winter goes and then maybe we'll talk."

"By spring our enemies may not want to talk." Danna commented, "If we wait too long they'll try to take advantage."

"A decision will be made before the New Year, I'm sure." Lizzy smiled at the Umari princess.

"Many decisions will be made by then, I hope." Danna tilted her head and stared across the table at Lizzy.

"Some of them already have been."

"Flirt later, eat now." Michael grinned and returned to his food.

"I'm worried about that boy; he hasn't got his priorities right." Duke Michael laughed at his nephew's affronted grunt.

"His priorities are fine for now. He's not even seventeen yet."

"Ha! At seventeen I already had two mistresses."

"And look how well that turned out." Alex gestured to himself and his brother.

"Now, boys, your father couldn't help having poor taste as a young man."

"Quite right auntie," Johnny told Catherine, who sat between him and Elenor, much to the young people's mutual disappointment, "If only their mother would see sense."

The family laughed, which wasn't quite the effect he was going for. Their visitors looked bemused, not comprehending the private joke.

Ambassador Bordan leaned into the Prince Donach, "Should we ask?" He spoke behind his hand.

"Probably not." Donach grinned at the question. The Alboni made things so unnecessarily complicated in his opinion. Were he or Danna to marry Lizzy, he thought, then the marriage would only be for the benefit of Alboni sensibilities. In Umar, she could be married, or the primary lover, to both, but not so among the conservative Alboni. They even frowned on people taking lovers; he found it most backwards. Katerina – the Duchess – had adapted well to their strange ways, he thought, but he wouldn't be constrained by their mores if he married Princess Elizabeth.

Donach smiled at the thought, though he knew it was an unlikely outcome; Lizzy showed no interest in marriage. While he was unsurprised by her need to be independent – independent women were hardly unusual in Umar -, he had thought the social traditions of Albon would have forced her to at least consider it. He speculated to himself that Katerina might have been responsible for Lizzy's unconventional views on the matter. He would have to discuss it later with

Danna. Perhaps if they represented to her the fact that her independence was welcomed in Umar, she might be persuaded to form the alliance?

Donach caught himself staring at Lizzy as she laughed with her family. When she looked up, he smiled, looked away towards Danna and then back. She wasn't looking at him anymore. She'd leaned into talk to her father, and laughed quietly with him. Donach coloured, imagining her laughing at his obsession. Not that he was all that obsessed, whatever Danna said. Alex FitzAlbon caught his attention as Donach began to stew in his thoughts.

"Prince Donach, how do you like Albon?"

"It certainly has its attractions; the war goes well?"

"My war or yours?" Alex laughed.

"Both?"

"Quiet, isn't it?"

"Indeed, when will it get loud again?"

"Hopefully it won't, but you never know."

"The Sumoasti request?" Donach was never more pleased to turn his mind to war, "I think they'll try to play for time."

"That's alright then, because so are we." Lord Jonsey joined the conversation, "My men need a rest and the ships need their bottoms scraping."

"You were at sea all summer, Commander?"

"Yes, with your Commanders Laitano and Armanno. Good women them. I could do with a ship full of them."

"They are our best Marine commanders."

"I noticed they know their way around a ship.

292

You been to sea much?"

"Yes, but not to battle."

"You'll come with us on the rai, in the spring?" Jonsey corrected himself quickly, the raid on Tarjan was still a secret.

"I'd love to, if the war lasts that long."

"You think Tarjan will give in by then?"

"I hope so. The war is costing us all dear in trade."

"How right Bordan, how right." Lord Sommerton added.

"My brother-in-law has a whole fleet of warehouses, he sells cloth, furs and such. Keeps complaining that it's interfering with his trade." Jonsey nodded along.

The five men chatted about the effect of the war on the trades of the islands while the next two courses were served. Lizzy had been watching them with a crooked smile and turned back to her notebook. They talked in circles around the thing that worried them most: how to end the war. It hadn't been a long war so far, but it had the potential to draw out into stalemate. A stalemate would be ruinous for all of the Islands; the Belenosi might form a trading alliance with some of the Camari Nations if the war went on too long. It hadn't happened yet because the Camari only trusted the Umari, their distant cousins who had migrated to the most isolated of the Islands a thousand years before. She tapped her pen on the page thinking, brain slowed by a large meal and little sleep. The raid had to succeed, but then what? And what if the raid should fail?

Chapter 43
Midwinter's Eve A.E. 1336

Lizzy paced the Council Chamber with her father and uncle, waiting for news from the twins. They, and the Umaris, had sailed ten days before, the fastest ships in the fleet following a day later. If things went to plan the raid on the Sumoasti fleet in Tarjan's harbour would be well under way. Sailing at night unlit to avoid being seen, the fleet should have joined forces with a small Umari fleet two days before. She knew the plan, sending fire ships, towed by the war ships to Tarjan, into the harbour and ambushing any ships that escaped the flames, was simple, and had worked before, but they'd been unable to communicate since the ships sailed north of Calman.

The Council Chamber became steadily fuller as people gave into their anxiety and joined Lizzy and the king. The Secretaries of the Fleet and Regiments joined them, bowing quickly before continuing their quiet conversation. Sarah arrived carrying a sheaf of messages that she kept to herself, reading through them repeatedly. Catherine, Elenor, and the princes joined them from the Ducal Residency. Various Ministers arrived after a Moot meeting and took seats, waiting for news with their anxious leaders. Lizzy listened to the buzz of whispered conversations as people became too nervous to speak aloud, afraid to shatter the atmosphere. Lizzy took her seat, quietly tapping on the table until her father reached over and steadied her hands.

"We'll hear soon. They'll be fine."

"I know." She pulled her hand away and folded her arms across her chest where she continued tapping her fingers against her chest.

Eventually, after midnight, as Elenor was dropping off to sleep and three ministers had started a quiet argument about some obscure point of law, the came a knock. Lizzy jumped in her seat and raced to be the first to answer it. She was beaten by the Chamberlain, who opened the door slightly, took the message and handed it straight to the king.

Chapter 44

"Well?" Duke Michael asked his brother impatiently.

"They didn't succeed in attacking the fleet in Tarjan." King John told the assembled and attentive audience.

"Shit. What happened?"

"Don't swear Elenor, it's not ladylike. What happened John?"

"They met the Sumoasti fleet at sea. They didn't get a chance to attack the city. The fire-ships worked but they had to back off and take survivors out of the sea when the fire got too wild. Lord Tarjsn is among the prisoners. It looks like they were on the way to attack us while we were celebrating New Year."

"So, we won?"

"How many casualties did we take?"

"Are they returning?"

"Is there any word from Sumoast?"

"Ladies, gentlemen, please, it's only a dispatch. We'll have to wait for a more detailed report. Now, I suggest we all relax and get as much sleep as possible. Lizzy, have a Message ready for the morning paper?"

"I'll do what I can, can I have the dispatch?"

"Of course, of course."

Chapter 45
New Year A.E. 1337

News of the battle spread rapidly through King's Ford and the surrounding countryside; new dispatches were eagerly read as they arrived and were published. The list of important prisoners arrived three days after the battle, and a week later the ships themselves returned, some putting into northern ports for repairs, others limping onwards to the south coast to repair and restock. Court and public opinion decided that the attack had been a qualified victory only. Lizzy, writing as 'Maggie' for the Daily, expressed the disappointment that the enemy's fleet hadn't been completely destroyed that many people in the city felt. As Minister for Information, Lizzy distributed the daily press releases, attempting to counter the disappointment with news of negotiations.

The negotiations started off badly; Lord Tarjan refused to speak to anyone until he had heard from his father. He had no instructions for such a negotiation, as he'd expected to attack and defeat the Alboni, not be surprised at sea and captured. He wouldn't even speak Alboni, or communicate with anyone at Court.

Lizzy and her cousins walked out of the pleasant yet secure tower room in which Lord Tarjan was residing at the Goal after another failed attempt at negotiation. Sarah trailed behind, flicking through her notes.

"Why don't we just leave him in there alone for a few months?"

"Because we need to get the negotiations

started?"

"I suppose so. Sarah, did you get anything out of him?"

"Nope, he wouldn't answer my questions, he doesn't like professional women apparently."

"I suppose he thinks it's beneath him to talk to you?"

"To all of us. He keeps referring to you as the Bastard. He'll only talk to your fathers, and only then once he has instructions from Tarjan."

"His father or the city?"

"Both, he needs their tribal assembly's permission to act too."

"Oh, of course." Alex had forgotten the complexities of Sumoasti government. He mused that it must be difficult to get things done when there were three High Lords and three Tribal Assemblies to consult and agree on an action. As he got older, Alex had decided, the spy business was getting too active, he was considering joining the ambassadorial corps and spying in comfort, rather than spending his nights climbing around other nations' embassies and the private residences of suspected traitors. He'd have to consider these things if he wanted to persuade the King and his father that he was a reasonable choice for an ambassadorial position somewhere. Umar would be a pleasant place to start, since he already had friends there, if they survived their injuries.

"How are our Umari?" Lawrence asked with a smirk towards Alex. Donach and Danna had both been injured badly in the violence, a fact not known until the morning light shone on the ships after the battle.

They'd been among the first back to King's Ford. For two weeks, since they'd returned, they'd lain in fever dreams in their quarters.

Lawrence must have been reading his mind, Alex grimaced, before speaking, "The Physicks think Donach will recover full use of his arm, if he breaks the fever. Danna." He shrugged, "Danna might not make it, even if she does wake up. The stomach wound isn't healing at all."

"Damn. What will their mother say if her heirs die here from fighting our wars?"

"The queen will demand blood money and might even declare war." Lizzy had already considered the matter, with Catherine's help.

"We can't afford another war." Sarah muttered behind them.

"Then they had better survive, hadn't they?" Lizzy growled, "Are the Physicks allowing visitors?"

"Only one at a time, why?"

"I haven't seen them since they were brought to the palace. I might go when we get back home."

"That will be nice for them."

"They're delirious, they won't even know I'm there."

"I'm sure they'll respond to your mellifluous voice." Lawrence smirked.

"Yes, because my crow screech can rouse even the dead."

"Only when you sing. Come on, the carriage will be waiting." The main door was in sight, heavily guarded and locked against the raging snowstorm they'd forgotten about while they spent the afternoon trying to prise information from their prisoner.

"Are you going to join us Sarah, or return to your office here? That snow is getting heavy."

Sarah nodded, "Yes, I suppose it is. I'll stay here, rather than try to get back from the palace later. Take it easy going through the city. It'll be worse on the Royal Road, with no protection from buildings."

The Gaol and Office were closely connected, wings on either side of the main entrance, that mirrored each other. The joint front entrance was much more salubrious than the entrance used by prisoners and their visitors.

"Dawson knows what he's doing, though I can't think of a time when we've ever had this much snow."

"We haven't, not for a couple of hundred years at least." The group looked at Alex quizzically. He shrugged and answered their silent question, "I looked it up last night."

"You need better hobbies." Sarah laughed, "Or maybe I should find more work for you, if you've got enough time to delve through two centuries of weather reports."

"It was really easy actually; the Astronomer Royal kept weather records as well as observations. It was quite interesting. Did you know, in the year of the Crow Rebellion, the summer was unusually long, hot and dry. It probably contributed to the Rebellion, when you think about it."

"Thanks for the history lesson Alex, can we go home now?" They'd reached the door, and even in her heavy, fur-lined cloak, Lizzy shivered. The guards hovered by the fireplace, trying to watch the door and keep warm at the same time. Someone always had to be by the door so they were taking turns switching places. Lizzy watched the shuffled dance of frozen guardsmen, pitying them.

"Of course, after you, dear cousin. Dawson has arrived I see."

"He looks frozen."

Sarah smiled and waved before pushing through the discrete brown door that lead into the Office complex. An unwary visitor might assume it to be the door to a cleaning cupboard or cloakroom. The Office did not advertise.

Lizzy braced herself for the buffeting cold, pulled her hood up and pushed open the door. The wind had risen, and become sharper since they'd arrived, dragging her breath from her lungs and filling her hood with snow as it was pushed from her face.

"Get in Miss Lizzy." Dawson called down to her and watched as a guard wrenched the carriage door open for the three royals. Hunkering down against the wind and snow, Dawson pulled away from the shelter of the Gaol and out on to the empty city streets as soon as his passengers were aboard. He took it slowly, despite his nagging desire to get the back to the palace as soon as possible. Something wasn't right about this weather; Dawson wasn't a superstitious man, but he spent a lot of time with horses and his horses were not happy about something. The Curates would be incensed if anyone mentioned the possibility that something unnatural was happening; only the One could influence the weather and only the Curacy knew how to placate the wrath of their god. The High Curate had already announced that the weather, unusually harsh, was merely a natural phenomenon, and not signs of divine displeasure. Dawson didn't like to question the pronouncements of the High Curate, but he knew magic when his horses felt it.

The horses must have felt to impulse to return to their warm stables as well; despite Dawson's determination to keep a slow and steady pace they pulled away, travelling faster as they reached the Royal Road and the gates to the palace grounds. The churned road had frozen into a lumpy quagmire, the coach bouncing painfully over the once perfect and picturesque grassy lane. There was a rap on the roof before Alex shoved his head out of the roof window.

"What's the hurry Dawson, we're hitting the roof in here?"

Gripping the reins tightly Dawson turned to answer,

"Sorry Master Alex, it's the horses, something's spooked them. It's the weather, there's something not right about it." He shouted to be heard above the wind's roar.

"They know that do they?"

"They know everything. You should listen to your horses and dogs; they know things we don't."

"What's in the wind?"

"Someone is trying to hurt Albon, weaken us, maybe harm you."

"I see. Get us to the Palace in one piece and you can have a raise."

"Thanks Master Alex, I'll do what I can." Dawson turned back to his horses as Alex popped back into the carriage and the window clanged shut behind him.

"Alright, my dears, let's get back home quick and safe." The horses tossed their snow matted tails, looked back, before dashing forward, moving smoothly over the snow. They found the gentlest path for the carriage, aware of their human's delicacy. They no more liked the snow than they did the spirits whirling in the air, but snow they could cope with. The only way to defeat the spirits was to outrun them, back to the herd and the shelter of the stables.

In the carriage Lizzy and the twins had no idea that a conversation was taking place between their driver and his horses, only registering a slight increase in comfort. Alex repeated his conversation with Dawson to his incredulous cousin and brother.

"It's ridiculous superstition! The horses are frightened by the snow and wind, there's nothing attacking us."

"Mother wouldn't agree with you; the Umari believe spirits inhabit the world just like we do." Lawrence looked thoughtfully out of his window while his cousin sighed and brother nodded.

"Yes, yes, I know, I do remember our lessons Lawrence; you can't seriously believe that rot though?"

Lawrence and Alex looked at each other; sometimes Lizzy thought they spoke to each other in the silence, but dismissed it. They merely understood each other so well because they were close. The twins nodded to each other before Alex spoke for them both, "Some of it. Mother taught Elenor and John a few things."

"And they told us. I caught Elenor muttering a charm against the spirits in the wind this morning."

"Well, the wind hasn't settled down so it can't have worked."

Lawrence looked over at Alex, not wanting to explain that the wind had dropped for a few seconds as they'd left the house to ride to the palace from their father's house. It hadn't lasted long, just long enough for them to get out of the gates and on to the Royal Road. Lizzy wouldn't hear it even if they told her. She was too convinced of her belief that there was only the material world to hear their evidence. Once she got an idea in her head, everything else was pushed out. They'd seen it with her politics; once she'd been as complacently liberal as most of the court, but since Sarah's 'education' she'd been a leading figure among the Radicals, seeming to burn with a passion to change their country.

"I suppose you could say that." Alex conceded at last.

"Of course it didn't, stop being daft. It's only a winter storm."

They sat in silence until the quality of the vibrations echoing up through the wheels changed and they stopped in the stable yard behind the palace. Dawson rapped on the roof and they climbed out, out of sorts with each other and the world around them. The horses shied away from them as they stalked across the yard. Dawson muttered, shook his head and directed to horses to their stable, where a team of ostlers waited to help unharness the carriage and get the horses settled. They all felt the bristling danger in the air, and opted to stay the night with their animals rather than risk the walk back to their cottages in the servants' village.

"Your Highness, Masters, Prince Donach has woken; he calls for you all urgently." A servant, loitering by the door, awaiting their return, took their cloaks as he gave them the message.

"Of course, we'll go to him now. Have someone inform the king we have returned."

"Yes Your Highness." The man bowed and hurried away to the servants' quarters to send a message using the newly installed air tubes to the royal chambers, where the king's servants would pass it to the king. The whole system saved a lot of rushing about but some of the servants didn't understand the new technology and were convinced it was devilment.

"Lizabeth, thank you for coming." Donach was propped up on a mound of pillows, pale and drawn, dark circles around his dark eyes.

"Well, we could hardly have stayed away," Lizzy took a seat beside him as the twins grinned to see their friend awake.

"I should say not; we were on our way up when the servant told us you were awake."

"And we're glad you are; we were getting worried about you."

"I am touched, my friends, but you must help me get to Danna. The Healer won't let me out of my bed."

306

"You've only just woken up."

"If I don't go to her and bring her back, she won't wake up at all."

His three visitors looked at each other for a few agonisingly long seconds then nodded.

"What do you need us to do?"

"Distract the Healer and help me into Danna's room. I'll do the rest."

"Do what, precisely? Our Physicks have done everything they can."

"I need to call her back. Her souls wanders in the wind, I need to anchor it back in her body."

Lizzy looked at him in confusion then nodded. If it was what he wanted to do, then she'd help. It was pointless, but Lizzy wouldn't be the one to tell him that; Donach obviously needed to cling to the hope that his sister would live so that he could recover, himself.

"Where's the Physick now?"

"In the other room, preparing some potion to draw the poison from Danna's wounds. It won't work if we can't call her back to her body though."

"I'll go talk to the Physick if you two get Donach to Danna?"

The twins nodded in agreement. It was probably best if Lizzy wasn't in the room while Donach called his sister back. Their step-mother had done something similar when they were younger, calling back the soul of a servant who'd fallen repairing a barn roof and knocked themselves senseless. When Lizzy disappeared through the door to the apothecary they stripped back the covers on the bed. Donach swung his legs around as the twins sat on either side ready to brace him and stand. In this way, they got their friend out of bed and slowly across the room to a further door that led into Danna's sick room. Donach stretched his toes and legs, feeling the muscles ache with unexpected movement. The wooden floor was smooth and cool under his feet, as his nightshirt flapped around his knees.

"Don, you really need a wash."

"I need a bath. Do you think Lizzy could persuade the Healer to let me get one?"

"She could try, if you asked her nicely enough. Alex, get the door."

Lawrence braced himself as Alex let go and unlatched the door, pulling it open. A gust of hot, putrid air, overlain with the scent of incense spilled out. Donach coughed and lifted his hand to his mouth as Alex covered his own mouth and nose with his sleeve. Lawrence, supporting Donach could only breath shallowly and hope they could do something soon. It didn't smell like Danna had much time left in the world.

The twins led Donach to the bed to sit beside his sister. He took one of the still, withered hands that lay on the blanket and closed his eyes. Lawrence and Alex stepped back, and looked around the room. The Physick had left his pots of medicaments in a row on the table under the window. Alex sauntered over to read them; some were like the concoctions his Mother made to help when the family were sick, but most were recent inventions. There was a mercury compound and sulphur powder, and ground up elder bark. No clean water though, or an unsullied cloth. He sighed at the stupidity of some people and left to find a pitcher of water and a bowl he could heat it up in.

Lawrence watched his brother go and nearly followed; they'd find the water and pan quicker with two of them, but Don needed one of them to stay and help, so he turned from the door and returned to his friend.

Donach had been silent, searching through his sister's blood and bone for the infection, burning it away with his Will, re-knitting sliced and infected flesh. Sweat dripped into his face, his body shook as the strength drained from him into his sister's dying body. Danna didn't move. He searched for her soul, chasing any trace in her body but found nothing. He looked around the room with his Inner-Eyes, seeing only the Twin-Lights of Lawrence, muted without his twin to share energy with. The room held no spirit life; he looked out of the window. Outside his Inner-Eyes say the swirl of ice blue spirits, whipped into anger by some unknown creature, and among them, hugging close to the window, buffeted and jostled by the wild spirits, was Danna, a brilliant red soul now pale and ragged about the edges. He had to let her in and tried to rise from the bed.

Alex returned and set the water to boil. Donach gasped and collapsed on to his sister. Lawrence rushed to his side, waving a piece of paper over his face.

"Donach Umari, come back this instant."

"Window." Donach hissed between cracked lips, "Let her in."

Lawrence raised one eyebrow as a tapping came

at the window. He looked towards it but saw no stray leaf.

"Open the window, she won't last much longer out there."

Lawrence nodded and rushed past his brother, knelt still at the fireplace, to open the window.

"You'll have to hold back whatever else tries to get in Don."

"I will, just so long as Danna gets in."

"Okay, on the count of three."

Donach nodded as Lawrence reached for the latch. Weakly, Donach counted down and prepared for the confrontation. He closed his eyes and opened his Inner-Eyes; with a final nod to Lawrence the window opened and the storm spirits came swirling in. Or tried to. Donach pushed back against them as he pulled at his sister's soul, searching out the bright red flame and pulling it towards him. He collapsed against her prone body again as the final wrench of her soul from the grips of the storm spirits overwhelmed him.

Lawrence grabbed a pot of salt that Alex had brought back on a whim to use as an antiseptic, and poured it along the window ledge.

"You can't come in here. This place is ours."

Catherine hadn't taught the twins much, they'd been too old and cynical by the time she'd come into their lives, but this he knew: salt borders could not be breeched by a spirit. He stood at the window, a green flame in the sight Donach's Inner-Eyes even as he lay apparently unconscious, negotiating Danna's soul back into her body.

Alex looked up and smiled at his brother's back,

his own green Twin-Light flaring at the sight. Donach sighed at the sight; his friends had such power, if they learnt to use it. The Duchess knew, he was sure, but these were thoughts for other times, times when they could be discussed with Danna. He sewed her soul back into her body, leading it to heart, brain, stomach and genitals, anchoring it in place with threads of his own soul, feeding it from his meagre resources, until her soul-heart beat again and her body-heart beat was strong

"Clean her wounds with that." Donach gasped out before fainting dead away.

The twins rolled him on to the other side of the bed and pushed back the covers. Danna was naked from the waist up, a pair of silk draws covering her lower half while bandages wrapped her belly and chest. Some of the smog that had greeted them when they entered the sick room had dissipated with the opening of the door and window but an odour of decay reeked from the bandages.

"We need to get these off her. What were they thinking, leaving filthy bandages on so long?"

"Mother will have fits when we tell her."

"Do you think we should?"

"It would hardly have help us if Danna died because our Physicks are useless."

"True. Get the scissors, we may as well cut these bandages off. And the rest of that salt."

"Sulphur powder?"

"Maybe, let's see what we see."

Lawrence brought the salt to his brother and watched as Alex carefully cut the bandages away. The smell got worse once they were removed. He looked over them quickly, assessing the colour of the puss and trying to remember what Catherine had said, before carrying the bandages to the fire to burn them.

"Hmm, Alex, this isn't good, there's some sort of infection eating holes in her skin."

"We need to clean it, pack the holes and redress the wounds. Did you see any honey on the table?"

"No, I'll go get some."

"Send a tube down to the kitchen and tell them to hurry."

The two men went about the task of cleaning the great gash across Danna's stomach in silence, knowing only that they had an important part to play in her recovery even now that Donach had returned her soul to her body. They cleaned wounds with boiled salt water, lanced and drained infections, cleared out the root and packed the holes with honey soaked cloth, washing the skin around her wounds with more salt water before re-bandaging them with new bandages. They washed as much of her upper body as they could and checked the sheets were clean. They were soaked with sweat, so another tube was sent to the servant to bring clean bedding. The servants arrived at the same time as the Physick, who, trailed by an anxious Lizzy had heard the rattle of doors opening as the servants arrived.

"What is this?" He screeched at the twins who had invaded his domain.

"We're doing your job for you. Lizzy help Don up. You two, don't just stand there gawping, change Princess Danna's sheets, these are filthy."

"But not as bad as the bandages we took off her. Those reeked with pus so badly we had to burn them. Are you trying to kill our allies, Physick?"

The wrath of the twins as they faced to arrogant Physick made the man pale and step back into the waiting arms of Commander Laitano, who had come to visit the sick and heard the exchange.

"Yes, Physick, why do you leave my Lady in filth?"

"It's not my job to change the bandages, look to the servants."

"We shall." Alex turned to the two women making up the bed afresh, "Who is responsible for changing bandages and bedding in the infirmary?"

"We are Master FitzAlbon."

"And why haven't you been changing our guests bandages and bedding?"

Both women paled and looked at the Physick across the room. They looked at Commander Laitano who's expressive eyes and strong grip informed them that they would be safe should the Physick have been involved.

"Physick Moore, he told us not to, 'cause he wanted the pus for an experiment."

"And now it's been burnt how am I supposed to continue my work?" Physick Moore snapped at them, wincing as Laitano gripped him harder.

"Commander, take this man to the cells. In the morning have him transferred to the Goal; I'm sure the Office would like to talk to him about these experiments that, had Donach not asked for our assistance, would have resulted in Lady Danna's death."

"It will be a pleasure. Before we go, how is Lord Donach?"

"Worn out from his efforts, but he'll survive." Lizzy assured her.

Donach had started to come too as she had helped move him to the table, sitting him down. Still weak but conscious, the young Umari smiled at Lizzy and pushed himself closer as he giggled quietly. A blush rose in her cheeks and the Twin-Light in her heart flared purple. He looked at her with his Inner-Eyes, surprised. Lizzy didn't have a twin, as far as he knew, why did she bare a Twin-Light in her soul? He shook his head, assuming his Sight was off, but still the Twin-Light remained a smaller flame in her soul-heart. In her heart, he saw a tight ball of pure white light – the Source of the Fire she carried; he knew what that meant even if the Twin-Light puzzled him. Sometime soon Lizzy would burst with the Fire she carried. No one else, not even Katerina seemed to have seen this, though Laitano had said something about Lizzy having the Sight. He checked her brain and saw the Inner-Eyes pulsing but tightly bound. It had never occurred to him to look at her like this, and now he had he knew why his mother was desperate for this alliance. Such a strong Fire would shine like a beacon in the night to his mother's Sight, even bound as strongly as it was. These Alboni didn't know what treasures lived among them. The FitzAlboni were powerful, their Fires burning steadily, but something about Lizzy put even the twins in the shade. He put the ideas aside to look at later, and fell asleep on her shoulder, exhausted from the extended use of his magic, and from his recovery; he had only returned to himself twelve hours before.

During Donach's discoveries the conversation had continued and a new Physick brought to the Palace to care for both, with strict instructions from Alex to watch them both closely, and change both dressings and bedding daily. A further tube was sent, a message to Catherine to ask for her attendance in the morning to advise on the patients' care. A message came back almost immediately to say she was on her way with Elenor, who needed to see Healing in action, as part of her education.

Alex and Lawrence carried Donach back to his own bed as soon as the servants had changed the bedding. His arm had gone numb and he couldn't move his fingers. When Catherine and Elenor arrived at the infirmary they went straight to his bed.

"See my dear, the bandage is too tight. We must remove it. Do you have your scissors?"

Elenor yawned as she nodded, it was well past midnight, and opened the leather case she carried. At fourteen she was quite mature, and Catherine trusted her with the medical bag. She took out a long, thin pair of extremely sharp scissors and proceeded to cut the bandage from hand to shoulder. Once free Catherine took her patient's hand and started to rotate it, feeding energy into his numb limb as she did so. Once a small amount of life had returned she let Elenor take over.

"First we must have skin to skin contact, to break through the outer shell, like this." Catherine tapped Elenor's forehead, waking her Sight enough to see the process with her Inner-Eyes as well as her body-eyes.

315

Elenor saw the shell around Donach's body breech as she took his hand and felt their individual shells fuse temporarily.

"Now, feed some of your Fire up into your hand. No, not so much." Catherine touched Elenor and blocked some of the Fire she was feeding out of the Source in her heart, sending it back. "Now gently, gently, that's it."

Elenor Saw her Fire, a pale green the colour of new leaves, slide into Donach's hand and along his arm until it reached the wound that had disabled him in the first place. She saw his own Fire, stitching the wounds edges together.

"Add some of your Fire to his." Catherine's voice was far off, distant as her own when she answered, "Yes Mother."

The green Fire swirled among Donach's more practised work, adding crude strength to the fine strands of crimson Fire.

"To his shoulder, then release the Fire to do its work alone."

Elenor, sent the Fire up to Donach's healthy shoulder and tried to release the Fire as she had been taught, breaking the link between her magic and her Source.

"It won't!"

"What's happening?"

"Every time I cut it the stands rejoin."

"Alright, I'll show you what to do."

Elenor became aware of another Fire mingling with her own and the flesh they healed. She watched as Catherine cut the threads she had attached to

316

Donach's flesh.

"You see, quickly, and draw the end back into your Source as you do it." The ideas came across more clearly than the words, showing Elenor the way.

Elenor saw, understanding at last, and as Catherine withdrew from the contact, she started to cut and withdraw the Fire into her Source. Once the Fire was in place, in her Source and in Donach's wounded arm, she returned her concentration to the join in their shells.

"Take your hand away, slowly, watch it, be certain the shells are back in place. We don't want to leave an opening for something to cause you or him harm."

"Yes Mother."

All through this Lizzy and the twins had watched in silence; a faint muttering from the ladies was all they saw as first Catherine and then Elenor closed their eyes and started to manipulate Donach's damaged hand and arm. Lizzy felt an itch in her gut but dismissed it as hunger; they'd been here for hours, and at the Goal for hours before that without eating. It was amazing to her what a bit of massage could do to restore the use of an arm, returning blood circulation and some movement to the limb. Aunt Catherine was certainly talented and had obviously taught her skills to Elenor.

The twins looked on, awed. They couldn't See clearly what was happening, but, as with their assistance to Donach earlier, they could feel something happening. It surprised them how talented their little sister was; she must have been having lessons for years. They barely saw their sister now, and hadn't spent much time with her in the last five years; her life, Alex realised, was as much a mystery to them as their activities must be to her.

Chapter 46

Lizzy watched as the triumphal procession made its way to the Hythe from the palace where the king and duke had offered grateful thanks and rich gifts to the leaders of the Umari forces, and a cash bonus to the regiments they had brought with them. Their brightly painted ships waited out in the bay to take them home to Umar and a fleet of small Alboni ships bobbed in the waves between the ships and the Hythe. Fluttering banners dressed the Hythe, hung over the seaward walls, and matching the flags hung from the masts of all the ships and boats tied up and out in the bay. A band played sea chanties to the waiting crowds held back from the Hythe by the Hythe Gate. The Hythe itself was lined with seaman and marines in dress uniform, while the royal fleet lined up to the south, preparing to fire a salute to their Umari comrades.

"What a sight." Prince Michael sighed.

"It's a rare one. I'm sure I've seen only one Alboni triumph in all my years here." Catherine told her nephew, "It's been such a long time."

John misheard the comment. He looked at his aunt and said, "Don't be silly auntie, it can't have been that long, you're not old."

"You sweet boy Johnny. I'm getting quite ancient."

The children laughed. Lizzy sighed, it almost felt like they had something resembling a normal family life now. With luck, the feeling would continue.

319

Lizzy Alboni returns in *Fire Betrayed.*

If you enjoyed this book, please leave a review. Thanks.

Visit rosemariecawkwell.wordpress.com for details of future releases in the *FIRE series*

About the Author

Rosemarie Cawkwell lives with her two dogs, Ezzie and Gyfa, a large collection of books and a couple of dragons in a small town on the banks of the River Humber, and dreams of other worlds and other times. A writer for decades, she has finally got around to publishing a book, with the encouragement of family and friends.

Hidden Fire is the first in a four-book series following the adventures of Lizzy Alboni. Rosemarie also writes historical fiction and crime, and has plans to publish several novels in the next few years. She is studying for her MA in Creative Writing and fits novelising around blogging and studying, reading books and writing reviews. She also likes to sew.
Photograph © Nicky Cousins
NK Photography 2017